THE

OCTOPUS

DECEPTION

Daniel Estulin

Published by:
Trine Day LLC
PO Box 577
Walterville, OR 97489
1-800-556-2012
www.TrineDay.com
publisher@TrineDay.net

Library of Congress Control Number: 9781937584238

Estulin, Daniel
The Octopus Deception–1st ed.
p. cm.
Includes index and references.
Epud (ISBN-13) 978-1-937584-24-5
Mobi (ISBN-13) 978-1-937584-25-2
Print (ISBN-13) 978-1-937584-23-8
1. Casolaro, Simone (Fictitious character) -- Fiction. 2. Asbury, Michael
(Fictitious character) -- Fiction. 3. Fitzgerald, Curtis (Fictitious character)
-- Fiction. 4. United States. -- Central Intelligence Agency -- Fiction.. I.
Estulin, Daniel. II. Title

FIRST EDITION
10 9 8 7 6 5 4 3 2

Printed in the USA
Distribution to the Trade by:
Independent Publishers Group (IPG)
814 North Franklin Street
Chicago, Illinois 60610
312.337.0747
www.ipgbook.com

ABC Radio News. This is Carl Jameson. The World Bank has dropped a bombshell on investment markets across the globe today, warning that, despite the recovery hype Washington and Wall Street desperately want us to believe, this great economic crisis is only growing worse.

The World Bank's words are simple and straightforward: "The global recession has deepened to levels unfathomable only six months ago." According to the World Bank, the Gross Domestic Product for the highest income developed countries will SHRINK 14.2% this year – and global trade will plunge by a devastating 39.7%.

In the World Bank's own words, "Unemployment is at its worst point since the Great Depression, and the total number of people living below the poverty line is set to increase to almost three billion from current estimates of seven hundred million."

Meanwhile, in the U.S., the newly re-elected President is being urged by leading voices in Congress to temporarily suspend the Constitution as a result of increasing unrest across the country.

PROLOGUE

Night faded slowly, holding its ground. It had rained last night. The snow had started just as the clock struck midnight, as if on cue, and continued steadily and vertically ever since. The dense flakes, like ornamental lace on a veil, curtained the view of the surrounding countryside. The slow dawn of winter picked its way furtively across a copper sky, shimmering on a thin layer of snow that held stubbornly to the asphalt, caressing it gently with fading reflections. The shadows of frosted trees lay on the snow like blue plumes.

Shawnee, Oklahoma, a not unremarkable town of about 30,000, thirty miles east of Oklahoma City, is the seat of Pottawatomie County. These are Native American tribal names, in keeping with our forefathers' policy of stealing the land and preserving the colorful name. Like most small but, bustling towns, Shawnee has a vital center, with outlying areas of decay. On a once-popular commercial strip, buildings now lie barren and empty, but a few gas stations, bars, convenience stores, and dilapidated motels maintain a precarious hand-to-mouth existence. Near the edge of the city limits is the Merry Kone Motel, a two-story, 28-room ghost from the 1950s, with neon-lit space-age columns framing a wood-paneled lobby.

The rooms are drab brown, timeworn; a slight mildew smell emanated from the carpets. Even industrial-strength cleaner could not entirely blot out the odor of decay.

In room 206 a thirty-something unemployed journalist had passed a fitful night. He was six feet tall, slender neck, with thick, curly hair layered at the back, his eyes an unclouded blue, with slightly protruding ears.

Danny Casolaro's dreams grew in vividness and color even as sleep itself began to ebb. "A few more minutes," he thought to himself. He turned over and tucked his right hand under him, listening to the soothing sounds of bubbling water somewhere in the distance. A beautiful tangerine light had filled the glassed spheres of a huge sand clock. A velvety-orange façade with a small door and a white sign opened, calling him to enter. He squinted to see the name on the brass plate. Nothing. Suddenly, he felt a growing lightness imbue his body. Restlessness dissipated and a wave of utter relaxation suffused him. Another image: 1974. He jumped a puddle ... running through a field, alone, beneath the magnificent clouds. Not alone. With Simone. She is holding his hand, the wind playing havoc with her flowing hair. Ouch! He stubbed his toe!

The hypodermic needle inserted just beneath the big toenail of his left foot blended quickly into his dream. "Come on, we're going over," Simone cried, as the two of them flew up, jumping, floating together over the rainbow. "Danny, Danny!" Danny took one more soaring leap – into paradise.

***

The phone rang only once before Henry L. Stilton, Associate Director of the Central Intelligence Agency, looked at the display, picked it up and cradled it in his large hand.

"It's done," the voice whispered, repeating the words he had spoken several dozen times over the years.

"Good," replied the CIA man. Stilton was tall, gangly and immaculately dressed. His craggy face was marked with a cleft chin and bushy eyebrows. Stilton stood in the center of the room, where the only source of light was the cold rays of the moon streaking down from the night sky. "Did you—?"

"I have it." The killer squeezed the handle of an oversized, well-worn suitcase.

"Bring it. The rest of the money will be transferred to you in the morning."

"Merci."

Stilton hung up, then immediately called the Boss.

CHAPTER 1

Simone Casolaro entered the lecture hall with great élan. Ninety-five pairs of eyes watched her attentively. Ms. Casolaro's Renaissance Literature class at Cornell University in Ithaca, New York, was the most popular academic option on campus, and this was day one of Winter term.

She stomped snow from her galoshes and kicked them off, revealing a pair of Roman-style sandals. Then she removed her full-length wool coat, showing off a fine Egyptian cotton dress with a low bosom and high hemline. Appreciative male murmurs rippled through the room as she eyed her troops for a few pregnant moments. Then, abruptly, she began.

"You will buy Dante's *Divine Comedy* today and start reading it at once. Read every word. Don't skip the "boring bits." There are no boring bits in Dante. Turn off the television, put your computer to sleep, take the iPod out of your ear. No twittering, texting, tooting, hooting or whatever new App you're addicted to. Dante is to be smelled, savored, tasted, chewed, and digested, like a juicy Italian sausage."

The hall erupted in laughter. Simone was an exceptional performer, with a unique flamboyant style. She felt a passion for her subject and had a knack for the provocative. More important, however, she animated her students' imaginations, a gift they would carry, and many of them treasure, for the rest of their lives.

"A hundred years ago," she began, "Flaubert in a letter to his mistress made the following observation: 'What a scholar one might be if one knew well enough some half a dozen books.'" She swept the room with her gaze. "Dante's *Divine Comedy* is one of those worthy to be included in any short list. Dante's allegory, however, is highly complex, and we shall examine other levels of meaning, such as the historical, moral, literal, and the anagogical. The development of the art of description throughout the centuries should be treated in terms of vision, of that prodigious eye of individual genius." She paused for effect, rising to the balls of her feet. "What we call genius is an evanescent quality, gradually yielding a complex spectrum for all to see. In reading and thinking and dreaming, you should notice and absorb the details. Let's leave generalizations, well-worn clichés, popular trends and social commentary at the door."

She strode to the blackboard, quickly drawing an outline of Dante's face. "Any real work of art is the creation of a new psychic world. A great writer is always a great enchanter, and Dante is a supreme example."

A skinny girl in the front row raised her hand. "Professor Casolaro, I was told in my last year's class that we can learn a lot about people and their culture from reading historical novels. By reading Dante, will we learn about Renaissance Italy?"

Simone looked at the girl and smiled. She made an expansive movement with her hand. "Can we truly rely on Jane Austen's picture of England during the Industrial Revolution when all she really knew was a clergyman's parlor? Those who seek facts about provincial Russia won't find them in Gogol, who spent most of his life abroad. The truth is that great works of art are, in a way, fairy tales and this trimester we will focus on one of the supreme fairy tales of all time."

The stage door on her right was pulled slightly ajar and a man's head emerged. "I am sorry to disturb you, Professor Casolaro, but could I have a word, please?"

She looked at the clock. "I can see you in half an hour."

The man gave her a heavy look. "I'm afraid it can't wait."

Simone felt a chill. "All right, give me two minutes."

He nodded his head and closed the door.

She turned back to the auditorium. "Although the two great events which made the fifteenth century a turning-point in human history – the invention of printing and the discovery of the New World – were still two centuries in the future, Dante's era was unique, essentially a period of great men; of free thought and free speech; of brilliant and daring action. Now, you'll have to excuse me for a moment. Please feel free to twitter and text away, but remember that what should interest us most is not Dante the political activist but rather Dante the great

Renaissance artist, his powerful poetic imagination and his peculiar vision of the world he created."

Simone exited the hall and confronted the visitor. "What is so important?"

"Ms. Casolaro," the man's voice was calm but strangely flat. "My name is Detective Lyndon Torekull." Simone swallowed hard, a sudden surge of panic jabbing her in the gut.

"What, what is it, Detective? Obviously something has happened?"

"Ms. Casolaro, I am sorry to inform you… we found your brother's body this morning in a motel in Shawnee, Oklahoma. He appears to have committed suicide."

As the blood drained from her head, Simone felt a series of conflicting impacts reverberate through her. Shock, disbelief, grief and, worst of all, guilt. She managed to turn away from Torekull, and re-entered the classroom. Her students looked up curiously from their ubiquitous electronic devices.

"Class… class dismissed. I have to… go home. You, I mean. Go." As she left the room in a trance, for a brief moment, her eyes locked on an incongruous shimmer of light gliding up Dante's left cheek on her chalkboard drawing. Somehow she found herself back in the hall.

"Ms. Casolaro, from what we understand, you are Danny's only living relative. I'm sorry, but I must ask you to look at this photograph, if you can?

She sucked in a long breath. "Yes. All right."

Detective Torekull reached into his pocket and held out a 5 by 7 color photo.

"Is this your brother?"

Simone forced herself to look. A spasm of horror struck her forehead like a hatchet. She spun away and shielded her eyes with her hand. Her whole body shuddered and she thought she might pass out. Then, the word hit her. Suicide. Never.

She sucked in a long breath, and looked again. It was Danny, and, oh God, yes, he was dead. No, it wasn't Danny. It was just a picture of Danny. But he was still… dead. Lying in a bathtub of blood. Both wrists were slashed, with a bottle of Jack Daniels, a dirty inch left in the bottom, clutched in one arm.

"This photo was taken five hours ago," the detective said. "Inside his motel room."

"He wasn't a heavy drinker. He was a devoted journalist. He said he was onto a great story. Not suicidal."

Two weeks ago, at his apartment in New York, they'd spent a couple of days together. He had told her that he was going to Shawnee. Why Shawnee? Where?

"It's the end of the quest. I'm bringing back the head of the Octopus. This is as serious as it gets. The story of a lifetime." Simone had never seen Danny so focused. The tremble in his voice scared her. "They are all corrupt. It goes to the highest level. I have a couple of contacts there, but they have no way of unmasking the corruption without compromising dozens of assets in parallel operations.

"Be careful," Simone had yelled after him. She could hear the echo of Danny's feet running, no, jumping down the stairs, two steps at a time.

"Don't worry, he will be fine, he always is," she had told herself.

Now, as her mind reeled, the image of an Octopus, its looming eyes staring implacably, hung like a gallows moon above her grief.

*****

Danny was an investigative journalist, three years her junior, politically incorrect, idealistic and incorruptible. In the course of a five-year investigation into what Danny called "a cabal of twenty-plus people who control most of the world's wealth," he had made enough enemies to last him several lifetimes. Last year, the Memphis County sheriff's department, supposedly looking for drugs, had ransacked his car. He'd spent three weeks in the hospital the previous summer after he was hit with a crowbar by a "burglar," who was never found and stole nothing; only his handiwork remained – a five-inch scar on the back of Danny's neck.

Simone held the color printout with both hands, as if her brother's life might be saved if she held on hard enough. Could this be some kind of a cruel mistake? Could this naked corpse just be someone resembling Danny? For a moment, she thought she was going to vomit.

As Simone stared at her brother's lifeless body, her initial revulsion and shock gave way to a sudden rush of anger. "Who would do this to him?"

"Ms. Casolaro," Detective Torekull spoke, "our preliminary reports suggest that he did this to himself. I am very sorry."

She returned the photo to the detective. "Dear God, why?" she murmured.

The words kept echoing in her head. "*Ms. Casolaro, we found your brother's body this morning in a motel in Shawnee, Oklahoma … In a motel in Shawnee, Oklahoma … Shawnee, Oklahoma.*" She clasped her hands again, instinctively, holding them tight.

"He is all I have… I have been waiting for him to come home for ice cream," she whispered.

Torekull awkwardly cleared his throat. "Ms. Casolaro, did Danny tell you why he was going to Shawnee?"

"I don't know. I mean, I don't remember." Her faced twitched. Torekull frowned. She tried to blink away the tears. "No, not really. Something about high-level corruption."

Torekull checked his watch. "We found a handwritten note in your brother's hotel room." He reached again into his coat pocket and pulled out a faxed copy of what the police had found back in Shawnee. Simone stared at a two-line printed text.

"Simone, I'm sorry. I didn't mean this to happen. I just couldn't take it anymore. I love you. Danny"

"Who did this to him?" she demanded, looking at him with wounded eyes. "Danny didn't kill himself. This doesn't even look like his handwriting."

Torekull studied her. Simone's body was angled and tense, her eyes wide. He shifted his body onto his right leg, and then spoke, choosing his words carefully. "Ms. Casolaro, we traced his last phone call to Langley." He paused. "The headquarters of the CIA."

"You obviously have all the answers, Detective. Why don't you simply call that person and ask them yourself?"

He tried another approach. "Ms. Casolaro, if your brother was murdered, as you insist, you will need our help."

Simone barely heard him.

"Thank you, detective. I will keep it in mind."

"We will need a signed statement. Would you mind coming to the station?"

"Of course."

Chapter 2

There were three trucks in the convoy, California plates, indistinguishable from any other truck rumbling through the area on any given day. The man sitting on a flat rock could taste it, feel it. It was at his fingertips. Absolute power. Power to end the madness. National sovereignty. Democracy. What nonsense.

Slowly, the Boss shifted his gaze as the lead vehicle stopped a few feet away. Power and wealth were simply tools to direct the crowd, the billions of raw minds swayed by elementary needs. The coming financial meltdown would destroy wealth and dehumanize the population, turn them into even more of a herd of frightened sheep than they were already. Then, true order could be established. He raised himself off the rock, and, for just a moment, remained standing under the hushed lindens.

World integration must be the ultimate goal of any progressive culture, and where the governments had failed, the industrialists would succeed.

"Greed is good, but control is greater," he said out loud as he stepped into the headlights and walked over to the first rig's driver-side window.

"He is meeting one of our men in Shawnee, tonight."

"You must be pleased, Boss."

"One day this young man would have died. Cancer. A heart attack. Leukemia. Parkinson's. Who knows? We're simply placing a rush order on that inevitable eventuality."

A high-pitched staccato ring interrupted their conversation. "Yes?"

"It's over," replied Stilton.

"Good," the Boss replied, casting a sidelong glance to his left. He slit his eyes as unseen memories came back to him.

"I guess, this means he took the codes to his grave."

"Indeed, he did."

"Might we be celebrating too soon? Surely, the government has options available to it?" asked the associate director of the Central Intelligence Agency.

"Our government's proposal to save the world is like taking cyanide for bad breath," replied the Boss man. "Call Lovett and keep me informed." He hung up and slid into the back seat. "Let's go."

"Yes, Boss."

CHAPTER 3

The Pinto Basin lies in California's Joshua Tree National Park, surrounded by the Hexie, Pinto, Eagle and Cottonwood mountain ranges. Running northwest to southeast through the center of the park, the Basin's north and west borders comprise the transition zone where the Sonoran and Mojave deserts meet. This arid region of southeastern California occupies more than 50,000 acres, and is world-renowned for its scented, steep-sided, bold outcrops rising abruptly from the desert floor, called monzogranite, that geologists believe to be more than 100 million years old.

All roads are marked on the Joshua Tree National Park map, which is distributed free at all visitor stations – all roads, that is, but one.

A casual traveler would not give this unnamed and unmarked road, nestled deep within the park, a second thought. Anyone who did, would be deterred by the sign reading KEEP OUT – U.S. DEPARTMENT OF DEFENSE FACILITY. If someone were to inquire as to the exact nature of the operation, they would be politely told that the area is part of RDTAE, (Research, Development, Testing and Evaluation), tasked with the performance of military equipment under desert conditions.

The sector is officially part of the Chemehuevi Indian federal reservation. Unofficially, the U.S. government rents it from the Indians and uses it for clandestine experiments. The heavily guarded, double-fenced compound, twelve kilometers inside the transition zone, is called Chiriaco Summit.

State of the Art audio and video security systems blanket the facility. Armed surveillance drones hover high overhead. All staff members are thoroughly vetted. To enter or leave the U-shaped installation, the employee swipes his chip card and presses his thumb against a biometric scanner, which checks the sixty indices of resemblance. Once the thumbprint is confirmed, access is granted to the next level of control.

There is no keyhole or card reader at the second level of control. Instead, there is the virtually infallible retinal scanner. No technology currently exists that allows the forgery of a human retina, and the retina of a deceased person decays too fast to pass the scanner.

Once inside the building, a person can access only his or her office space by keying in a server-generated, unique set of custom, high quality, cryptographic-strength password strings: sixty-four digit number/letter combinations, which for additional security are changed weekly.

Every one of the passwords from a cryptographically strong pseudo-random number generator guarantees that no similar strings will ever be produced again. Also, because the number will only allow itself to be displayed over a snoop-proof and proxy-proof high-security SSL connection, this custom generated number is, theoretically, hacker proof.

Finally, security protocols stipulate that employees are never to be identified by names, but by a three-digit code.

One such employee was staffer No. 177, whose human name was Paulo Caroni, For over eleven years he had occupied a brightly lit, second floor corner office of the main building. He was forty-seven years old, about 5'9," 215 lbs, a pasty-faced, stoop-shouldered and soft-bellied man, with thinning brown curly hair parted in the middle. He had a permanent nervous tic, bit his nails and wore non-descript American-made grey suits over a starched white shirt and a badly knotted polyester tie. He came to work each day between eight thirty-eight and eight forty-three. He spent the next five minutes organizing his desk: writing instruments on the right side, paper on the left, waste basket out of sight under the desk, staple gun in a silverware tray on a burgundy leather mat along with a pair of office scissors and a letter opener. His more personal items he kept in an office cabinet under the window, which overlooked the main courtyard. Between 8:49 and 8:57 he worked the *New York Times* crossword puzzle, which he always finished, seldom pausing between clues for longer than a few seconds. At 8:58, staffer No. 177 would go to the bathroom and wash his hands. At 9:00 A.M. on the dot, he would turn on his computer, put on his reading glasses and activate his secure e-mail.

One day, staffer No. 177 did not show up for work between 8:38 and 8:43. The crossword puzzle remained unmolested.

9 A.M. came and went. His absence was noted by none of his fellow employees, but had a profound effect on the people in charge at Pinto Basin. Within a few minutes, the warning flags went up. At 11:22, security guards arrived in Caroni's office, piled the silverware tray, pencils and pens and paper into the waste basket, emptied his drawers and his cabinet of personal belongings, locked his office and left.

About a week after his disappearance, the woman who worked in the office next door remarked, "Has anyone seen old 177 lately?"

* * *

Seven months later, and 3,000 miles away, a man named Reid popped the last succulent morsel of black bread and mountain cranberry sauce into his mouth, washed it down with Louis Rederer's Cristal Champagne, took his place behind a hand-made oval mahogany table, and logged on to his laptop. He was the keeper of an account number. *The* account number. More than the money itself, what turned Reid on was the unseemly number of zeros following a three-digit number. Ah, the beauty of wealth, the knowledge of potency... his eyes locked on the screen.

0.000000000. Zero. Zero by zero, plus zero, multiplied by a zero. Reid was suddenly seized with borborygmic convulsions as his stomach flip-flopped like a landed tuna.

He pressed his eyelids shut, counted to five, and opened them. The numbers hadn't changed.

He stood and stared out the window for a moment, as if hoping for a helicopter rescue team. Turning back to the screen, he rubbed his eyes, shook his head, and punched the return key several times for no practical reason, barely suppressing a primal urge to shake the monitor like a coke machine. Finally, Reid decided to turn the computer off and start again.

"This can't be, this can't be, this can't be...," he murmured through clenched teeth. Trancelike, he re-booted and logged back in. Password accepted. He entered the code.

Zero.

Reid swiped the flop-sweat off his forehead wiped his hands on his pants, and grasped at straws.

Maybe it's the wrong account number. You are CEO of Citybank. You control thousands of account numbers. He reached into the top drawer and pulled out a thick, brown leather notebook. He turned to page 47, beads of sweat pouring down the back of his neck, and re-entered the numbers. The code was correct.

Stay calm. There is a logical explanation for this. I must stay calm. Perhaps a temporary computer glitch? He would wash his face, change his clothes, have another drink and start again.

Unsteadily, he opened the door and walked out onto the balcony, staring at the collage of colors from his gorgeous penthouse overlooking the Hudson River on the west side of Manhattan. It was a cold night in February with misty rain swirling in the winter wind. As his body shivered, Reid's mind was transported 10,000 miles away, to Teresa, a landlocked valley surrounded by the Sierra Madre, the longest mountain range in the Philippines. Sixty years ago…

Only a few privileged insiders knew that Teresa formed a part of the greatest unknown robbery in the history of mankind, a mind-boggling treasure, first looted from southeast Asia and then hidden by the retreating Japanese Imperial Army in the final days of WWII – 1.3 million metric tons of gold.

The equivalent of 6.4 quadrillion dollars – ten times greater than the world's official gold reserves as estimated by the World Bank. A preposterous figure?

The gold in question existed outside official channels, a secret protected by a handful working for the United States government lucky enough to know the truth.

6.4 quadrillion dollars, hidden in the deepest and darkest of holes, in the jungles of the Sierra Madre.

Gold, Reid knew, like diamonds, is a lot more common in nature than people have been led to believe. If the truth were known, it would destroy the world economy, because most nations still use the gold standard as back-up for their national currencies.

A part of the Philippine gold, the equivalent of a few hundred trillion dollars, was quietly shipped to Marseille aboard the nuclear-powered aircraft carrier "President Eisenhower," then to banks in Switzerland by secret convoy.

The rest…stashed, and held behind kryptonite locks since the beginning of the 1960s, under the guardianship of 54 senior Trustees, in Teresa and in the mountains of Irian Joya of Indonesia, an area reachable only after several days trekking through a dense jungle. The Trustees worked independently, unknown to each other, but coordinated through a set of controllers who, in turn, were blind-controlled by their superiors. And behind them, at the apex of the pyramid sat the Octopus.

Reid swallowed hard. The government used the gold hidden in Switzerland as a monetary guarantee for an off-the-books government-run collateral trading program with unlimited drawing rights against the gold deposits. The money, a tad over two hundred and twenty trillion dollars, was deposited in thirty accounts at Citybank. His bank. He winced. The government was not the only entity with access to this money.

Through parallel accounts, the Octopus was able to tap into the government's money as well, using it to corner world markets through mergers and acquisitions, using misleading fronts as surrogates and manipulating prices. Reid's thoughts were like stones dropped one by one into a placid pool, rippling outward, overlapping, swamping each other. The government (splash) the Octopus (splash), interlocked interests, with diametrically opposite objectives. Now, someone had stolen all the money, and the world was in danger of a financial disintegration.

I wonder if they will kill me.

His phone erupted in the unmistakeable special ringtone, as if to say, "Damn right we will." Gingerly, Reid picked it up.

There was a moment's silence;,our earliest convenience at the usual place." There was a click. The line went dead.

Reid was being called on the carpet, the Octopus wanted answers … answers he didn´t have. The caller was extremely polite, but there was something inexpressibly savage about his voice.

CHAPTER 4

A man wearing military fatigues, with hands like axe heads, knocked politely on the pole of a tent not far from where the prisoners were herded, one-by-one, into a giant three-sided mud-walled field that had once, before the drought, been a lush apple orchard. Inside were eight large tents, each with its sides rolled up, ringed by three coils of concertina wire.

His name was Curtis Fitzgerald, 41-year-old Army Ranger and member of the U.S. 10th Special Forces Group. He was dubbed the Celtic Warrior, a man of many projects, and his body was obviously one of them. Curtis was a "high side" specialist. High side was intelligence jargon for lead investigator with top-level clearance, and after nearly two decades of service, Curtis still loved his job.

"Come in, Ranger," replied Captain Warner. Warner's pockets were stuffed with pens and male junk. Huge sweat-stains reached from his armpits across his gut.

"A revision of responsibilities. You are on." Inside, an assemblage of analysts and counterintelligence agents barely stirred.

This hell on Earth was Bagram, a former Soviet air base, located some 300 miles due north of Afghanistan's capital city of Kabul. A five-star unimpeachable cause, guaranteed to improve the lifestyle of that bedraggled bunch of foul smelling, goat farmers, was how his superiors had put it. During the Soviet occupation in the 1980s, it was always the most secure enclave in the country, never really in jeopardy of being overrun until the very end. Now, it was the premier U.S. detention facility for the most hardened Al Qaeda prisoners and sympathizers.

"They say this place used to be beautiful," uttered Warner with the side-of-mouth slur that told the world just what he thought of it.

"Yes, that's what they say," Curtis muttered as he and the Captain walked out of the tent.

"Thirty years of war took care of that. You know what I miss most, Ranger," he breathed in a husky voice, "My wife's honey-scented furniture polish. That's home." They walked in silence for about fifteen yards.

"Do you remember that famous panel in the Sistine Chapel, where God is leaning over, almost – but not quite – touching Adam's fingertip?" asked Curtis.

"Uh-hum." Warner pulled out a cigarette.

"Sometimes I wonder if Adam and God are actually pointing at each other, blaming each other for the mess they're about to make of Creation." Curtis gave God the same respect he had for a loaded gun, and the hand that held it.

"God is the only safe thing to be," he said matter-of-factly.

Warner drew on his cigarette. "Don't know about that, but I have been told you are very good at your job. That'll do 'til Jehova comes along." To Curtis' surprise, a glow of unlikely warmth lit Warner's grizzled face.

As they approached the gate, a prisoner was being searched. Something fell with a dull thud into the dirt. Someone shouted, "Bomb!" There was a blinding flash of light and a deafening concussion, followed by howls of pain, and then, after a few moments of dead silence, sobs and moans. Behind him, Warner lay motionless, eyes wide open; his last cigarette clenched between his teeth.

I am alive!

Suddenly, hot, searing pain spread through his right side, blood saturating what remained of his shirt.

Curtis closed his eyes briefly and then opened them again, as arduous a task as anything he had ever done. Blood was trickling out of his mouth, along with his hope of survival.

I am dying.

CHAPTER 5

A t an exclusive financial institution in London, three men – a Caucasian with an Australian accent, a Jordanian and his Palestinian bodyguard – stood around a table placed in the middle of a small, private room with frosted windows. The door opened and a diminutive bank official followed by two burly security guards carried in two wooden trunks and laid them in front of them. Each trunk bore padlocks. As the second trunk was carried in, the bank manager said, as if for the record, "We don't know what's in these trunks and we do not want to know."

Suddenly, Michael Asbury heard a faint noise, followed by two short beeps, indicating the arrival of a text message. He reached into his pocket, and then changed his mind.

"May I?" Without touching the cardboard, Michael looked at one of the texts.

"This collection is a treasure trove of ancient documents, Hassan. The texts speak of the mysterious sacred tree attended by strangely attired priests, all of them carrying a water bucket in one hand and a pinecone in the other."

The Jordanian looked at the scholar and shrugged his shoulders.

"Hassan, these images were never discussed on clay tablets on which the ancient writings were inscribed. Now, by the looks of it, we have found the historical missing link." Michael's eyes were sparkling with excitement.

"I don't know what you are talking about," replied the big Jordanian.

"I am talking about the Tree of Life," replied Michael Asbury, clearly excited, "the backbone of the mysterious Jewish practice known as the Kabbalah. In the interest of science, I think we should, at least, let some scholars know about their existence. Otherwise, these documents might simply disappear back into the deepest recesses of the bank, joining the many other priceless, historical documents known to be locked away in vaults and safety-deposit boxes."

The Jordanian stroked his thick moustache, deep in thought. "I will make a telephone call on your behalf, Michael." He took out a heavy, older model cellular telephone and with his fat index finger began pressing the buttons. Michael looked at the telephone's display. +9624.

He is calling Jerash. Jerash, an ancient town located less than an hour north of Amman, the capital of Jordan, was one of the best-preserved Roman towns in the world. From the conversation in Arabic that ensued Michael gathered that Hassan was passing his request to someone on the other end of the line. Suddenly, Hassan switched to English. "Michael Asbury is one of the most important religious historians in the world and the leading expert on codexes and Coptic texts." Michael could hear the man's even, unhurried voice coming through from Jerash. Hassan listened attentively to his specific instructions. "I understand," Hassan said in English before hanging up. "Michael, my boss, who is representing an influential client, wants you to take a good selection of photographs that you could show to prospective buyers."

"Absolutely!" replied Michael. " What about—?"

The Jordanian shook his head and looked at Michael. "You can't talk about this collection to anyone else, yes?"

Michael heard another faint but insistent noise, followed by two short beeps. He frowned. "I am sorry; someone is trying to reach me." He reached into his breast pocket and opened his cell. "You have two new messages," the screen said. "Simone?" That's odd. He scrolled down and read the text message.

The look of bewilderment and shock on Michael's face alerted the Jordanian that something was wrong, very wrong.

"Michael? You look upset."

"Will you excuse me, please," he stammered. "I need to make a call. I will have to fly to New York first thing in the morning." He looked at the Jordanian. "I shouldn't be long." He glanced at his watch. 9:23. The Jordanian pressed a button on the wall, summoning the bank's manager.

After exiting the building, Michael dialed the operator, who put him through to British Airways. Five minutes later he had booked a seven-thirty morning flight to JFK airport in New York.

Off into the distance, the silhouette of London lay in front of him. Simone Casolaro. Something rippled through him and he sensed an emotion, molten and dangerous, brimming, bubbling, and trying to get out. He saw her clearly now, the last time they were together, her white neck glistening through her long dark hair. He cocked his head. Was it love, loyalty or admiration? Simone was unique among his circle of friends. She was a woman of many callings who had chosen one of them at random but could just as well have been a painter, a marvelous stage performer or a juggler. A natural beauty, with an enchanting slant to her widely spaced eyes and that rare lip line into which the geometry of a knowing smile seemed to be implicitly inscribed.

Her brother was dead and she needed help. "And then...?" he thought. Another recollection flashed inopportunely past. The thought hovered in his mind like morning fog and then dissipated just as quickly. He simply could not entertain it now. That would have to wait.

CHAPTER 6

"**I** really find it quite remarkable, that something like this could happen on J.R.'s watch," snorted Henry L. Stilton, sitting immediately to the left of John Reid, Citybank's Chief Executive Officer. "At this stage, we can't even begin to fathom the consequences." Stilton was in his early sixties, having survived three presidential administrations. He flicked an ash off his Cohiba Siglo IV Cuban cigar and defiantly looked around the U-shaped mahogany conference table, as if daring one of the other men to contradict him.

Besides Stilton and Reid, two other people were seated in the carefully soundproofed space, privacy guaranteed by bug-proof Faraday shielding and wide frequency RF intercepts.

"Henry, I hope you are not implying lack of oversight or deficiency in our security measures." John Reid had a deep, honeyed baritone accentuated by years of chain smoking and drinking. "Bud" to his close friends, he was a seventy-five year-old Reagan conservative, which made him the oldest man in the room. It was said in the hallways of power that it was easier to see a President of the United States than to see Bud Reid. Today was clearly different.

"Well, I don't know, J.R., what would you call it? You are leaking like a sieve. No need to take it personally. I am only stating the bare facts," added Stilton.

"This is a once-in-a-lifetime predicament which, I am sorry to say, I wish I had never been a part of," said a fifty-three year old vice-chairman of Goldman Sachs. His name was James F. Taylor. "F" stood for Francis, his mother's maiden name. Taylor removed his double-breasted camel hair topcoat and hung it neatly on the backrest. He spoke softly, listening to the sound of his own voice, controlling every syllable as it slipped off his tongue. He was no one's privileged nephew. Nor did he study at Yale. He was a college dropout with unmatched intellect and financial prowess. Everyone at the table knew that he knew what he was talking about.

Reid wrinkled his nose, then blinked a few times. "The system is airtight," he insisted.

"Is it?" interrupted a balding, stocky man from Texas. "Then where is the money?" Officially, he was a senior analyst for the State Department. Unofficially, the man was a senior member from the Political Stabilization Unit, a branch of the U.S. intelligence known as Consular Operations. His name was Robert Lovett. Described as a "Cold War architect," he had been an executive at the old Wall Street Bank of Brown Brothers Harriman.

"It is airtight, believe me!" Reid pounded the table with his fist.

"You keep saying that ad nauseam, J.R., but the evidence directly contradicts you." Lovett added.

"Give me some time and I will get it back, I swear, I will get it back."

"You had better," replied Taylor. "Otherwise we are looking at an immediate, chain-reaction collapse of the world economy."

"I will—"

"Fuck the world economy." Stilton interrupted him, cocking one gleaming boot over the arm of his chair, and pursing his lips. "That money, J.R., is the decisive control mechanism for the financial interests of the Octopus."

"Once we find out how the perpetrators were able to override our multiple security systems we will have a clear sightline into their camp." Reid swallowed. "They gambled and it paid off. In any case, money is not the determinant of wealth. Our power is."

Taylor slid his hands into his pockets and shrugged. "Don't kid yourself. You have one week to find the money, J.R. One week."

CHAPTER 7

It was already late when Simone walked out of the police precinct, heading slowly towards the nearest train station. Emerging from a tunnel, to her right she heard the low rumble of an approaching train. The cold wind forced a few passengers waiting on the platform to huddle closer together.

Do you imagine that Hell is an invention of Catholic theology?

The memory startled Simone. She looked to her right. An attractive couple stood some fifteen feet away, their coats twitching in the wind. The train slowed, braking as it wound its way down a steep incline, and stopped, letting out a bellicose sigh of relief. As if in a trance, she got on board.

Simone made her way up the aisle. She stumbled against the door of the next car as the brakes of the train gripped a tight turn in the track. "May I?" she asked an elderly woman in a white-checkered dress, pointing to a book that lay on an empty seat.

"Yes, of course," she replied, putting the book on her lap. Simone sat down and absent-mindedly glanced around her.

Who would do it to him? Shawnee. Danny's lifeless body slouched in a bathtub, his wrists cut.

"It looks like suicide, Ms. Casolaro. Do you have any idea why Danny would want to go to Shawnee? Do you know what it was that he was investigating?" Torekull's voice rang hollow, his starched shirt-front bulging like a whitish hump. Simone turned her pale face to the window. Fragments of phrases broke the silence in short bursts, as if from far away, and then close by.

"Simone, if something should ever happen to me, I want you to do something for me."

"Danny, what are you talking about?"

"Will you do it for me?"

"Do what? Why are you being so mysterious and evasive?" She paused. "You are scaring me."

"I have stored away some of my private papers in an anonymous safe-ty-deposit box. You know, just in case… " He paused, biting his lip.

"In case? In case what?" She repeated louder and more forcefully.

"What I said. In case something should happen to me." He flashed a sympathetic but restrained smile at her.

"What are you saying?"

"Listen, Simone, it's just an insurance policy, nothing more."

"Well, how do I find it?"

"When the time comes, you will know."

She had never seen Danny frightened, but on that day he was.

She leaned forward. The train had stopped, for how long Simone didn't know, when she heard her cell phone chime. She must have dozed off. She fished it out of her handbag and activated the voice message. It was from Michael. He was in the boarding area at Heathrow and would be landing at JFK at midday. Could she pick him up?

Simone checked her watch. Thirty-four minutes past midnight, but London was five hours ahead.

As she came up the steps of her apartment building, a man with a poodle sitting on a nearby bench, olive-skinned and greying at the temples, got up, reached into his pocket and pressed a button on his hidden camera. He strolled away and took up an observation post across a diagonal path. He had earphones on and bobbed his head as if to a rock 'n roll beat, but the audio transmission he was monitoring had nothing to do with music.

Pressing a button on the transmitter, he said, "Eureka One." He kept his voice quiet and conversational.

"Report," the metallic voice crackled through the ear buds.

"Subject in sight and alone," the man said.

As she struggled to hold back tears, Simone reached for her keys and opened the door. Danny's apartment was off limits, at least un-til the police concluded their investigation. She had too much on her mind to notice an elderly homeless couple meandering down the street. Neither did she notice a nondescript, middle-aged female with a full mane of dirty blonde hair beneath her wide-brimmed hat and a raincoat walk out of the elevator as Simone boarded it. The woman opened her purse, removed a compact and checked her makeup, angling the small mirror first to the left, then to the right. Satisfied, she replaced the compact, closed her purse and let herself out of the building, turned left at the nearest corner, crossed the street and got into a waiting limousine.

"Yes." The man seated in the backseat responded to her smile. "Merci, Milena."

Chapter 8

The Committee on Prevention of Torture is the body of independent experts responsible for drafting reports to the High Commissioner. The CPT's observations and recommendations are confidential. One such report, marked "Secret" and "For Your Eyes Only" was hand-delivered in early January to the United Nations Office of the High Commissioner for Human Rights (OHCHR), located in Geneva, Switzerland with its headquarters in the historic Palais Wilson building by Lake Leman.

The U.N. High Commissioner was former Supreme Court Justice of Canada, Louise Arbour, best known in the corporate mainstream media as a chief prosecutor for tribunals on the genocide in Rwanda and human rights abuses in Yugoslavia in the 1990s.

"Sorry to interrupt," said a voice as the door to her office swung open. "May I?"

"Good morning. Yes, please come in." The High Commissioner leaned back in her chair, smiling to herself and enjoying the early morning view of the lake.

Frej Fenniche was the Senior Human Rights Officer and the man responsible for HCM, highly confidential material. In his hands he held a dark-blue envelope. "Louise, I think you had better look at this. Now, if possible." He paused, unsure how to proceed.

Louise Arbour sat up, facing him. The smile instantly disappeared from her face. She broke the security seal, put on her reading glasses, and quickly scanned the report. "Potential security breach for the last remaining witness to Operation Golden Lily – Security measures activated – Witness moved to Rome – Interpol takes charge of witness protection.

"XD-Top Priority Red Tab," she said to herself. Utmost importance. Interpol had special sheet files bearing different-colored tabs. Red tabs got first priority. These meant that an investigation was in progress against "High Value Targets" – individuals whose immediate arrest was sought by Interpol. In this report, however, the target wasn't named.

She read the last paragraph out loud:

"Conflicting signals have come in, suggesting that there is a serious breach of security. Additional measures may be required."

"Frej, nothing must happen to that man, do you understand?" She leaned back in her chair, thinking. "Who else knows about the witness being moved to Rome?"

"Just us, the United States government and Interpol." Frej Fenniche was a tall, slender man with aquiline features and meticulously groomed and fashionably cut blond hair. His English was refined under his Swiss intonation.

As a former Supreme Court Justice at The Hague and chief prosecutor for tribunals into human rights abuses in Yugoslavia, Arbour was well acquainted with the international intelligence establishment. She was meticulous in her investigations, and the often incomprehensible alphabet-soup of interlocking relationships within the U.S., Canadian and international agencies had always annoyed and frustrated her. It annoyed her because it reminded her how much of the intelligence establishment had no real oversight. It was a perennial problem. Each division of the military – the Army, Navy, Air Force and the Marine Corps – had its internal intelligence units: the "secret overlords of American might," as one journalist had put it. It ranged from the harmlessly mad to the murderously absurd, from insanely dangerous to the ridiculously inept.

The United States Department of Justice lavished its resources on Interpol-U.S. National Central Bureau, which in turn was competing for funds with the FBI, also under the watchful eye of the Drug Enforcement Administration. The Treasury Department had its own vast infrastructure with the Bureau of Alcohol, Tobacco and Firearms, while the Defense Department spent its resources on the Defense Intelligence Agency. The White House's National Security Council retained a separate staff of key intelligence analysts; additionally, the Office of Naval Intelligence worked closely with the FBI and Canada's Criminal Intelligence, which in itself was integrated through nearly three-hundred-and-eighty law enforcement agencies across Canada and the United States, whose collective purpose was to facilitate the timely production and exchange of criminal intelligence.

The lines of dissent and unaccountability boggled the mind, and each represented the potential for security breach and catastrophic failure. It was one thing not to know who was doing what to whom in the darkest, deepest and most desperate corners of the Middle East and Africa; it was quite another when the security breach threatened to undermine the Commission's most important operation in the area of Crimes Against Humanity.

"Frej, the fact that sixteen out of seventeen witnesses willing to come forward after more than sixty years of deafening silence have all died recently is a statistical improbability. A near impossibility." Her eyes flashed with anger. "Every one of the key witnesses came with a twelve-digit security code. Their identities were never revealed, isn't that right?"

Frej nodded gravely and silently.

"For security purposes that information on the witnesses is compartmentalized and kept separate from the security files, isn't that right?" She wasn't so much asking as telling.

Frej bowed his head.

"Either the Interpol boys are extremely incompetent or we have a mole, be it here or within the upper echelon of the United States government, in which case every operation in progress has been compromised."

"Louise, if our organization has been compromised, I can assure you, it must be on a very high level."

The High Commissioner gazed expectantly at her Senior Human Rights Officer.

"The major computer systems at Interpol aren't integrated internally because of platform incompatibilities with the contributing systems." Frej went through over two-dozen security categories and their related systems like a waiter going through the daily specials.

"The CIA and CSIC use Prosecutor's Management Infomation System software which comes with OCLC Numbered Code 5882076. The U.S. Justice Department and Treasury use Omtool technology."

Louise loved efficiency and, in her book, Frej Fenniche was as close to bureaucratic perfection as anyone had ever come.

"The point is, computer systems suffer from several limitations: they are subject to an intractably large state space for more complex scenarios, and they cannot take into account the influence of various parameters such as reliability growth of individual components, dependencies among components, etcetera, in a single model."

"Meaning?"

"Meaning," repeated Frej, "that somehow the system itself has been compromised through an override that negated all the security features."

"So, Frej, what does your gut tell you?"

"Interpol is receiving non-specific, but, nevertheless, persistent signals indicating some sort of off-the-books activity involving an unknown entity."

Louise knitted her brow and shook her head.

"Louise."

She looked up at Frej.

"What led this very old man to come forward after all these years?"

"A quirk of fate, Frej," she replied. "Shimada was a part of an undercover secret operation of the Imperial Japanese Army, known as Golden Lily."

She pushed a manila envelope across the table.

Frej picked it up and quickly scanned it. Tasked with the methodical plunder of Southeast Asia between 1936 and 1942, Golden Lily was led by the Emperor's younger brother. He turned the page. The sheer quantity and value of plunder gathered was mind numbing. "How many people died in order to satisfy the whims of the emperor?" he asked, shifting uneasily. "They should thank him for coming forward, and then hang him," he said, raising his voice in his quaint, old-fashioned English.

Louise shook her head. "The U.S. interrogators who questioned Akira Shimada after the war asked him why he did it. He told them it was the order of the emperor, and the emperor was a God."

"A violent man who never stopped trying to justify his crimes. Didn't the Americans know this?" he asked.

"Only too well, as I recently found out. Having duly noted his answer, Army interrogators, under direct Joint Chiefs of Staff order, classified the report Double Top Secret. Prosecutors at the Tokyo War Crimes trials were warned off. A curtain of secrecy was lowered."

"Not unlike the Iron Curtain, and certainly more durable and longer lasting," interrupted Frej.

"For over sixty-five years the activities of Golden Lily remained the most enduring secret of World War Two. For over sixty-five years, the U.S., the British and Japanese governments routinely denied these events took place. Until suddenly, fate intervened."

"Fate?" asked Frej with a doubtfully arched eyebrow. He reached for a diminutive bronze cowbell on the Commissioner's table, cupped it and jangled it gently for emphasis.

She nodded.

"Kanda district, on the outskirts of Tokyo, is a Mecca of second-hand bookshops, comparable to London's Charing Cross Road and frequented by university students in search of bargain basement prices."

Louise Arbour leaned across the table, and with her hand outstretched asked Frej to pass her the oddly evocative object.

"In 1984, a student browsing through a box of old, discarded papers belonging to a former military officer first discovered the appalling secret of Golden Lily. The documents revealed detailed reports on every town razed and every person buried alive by the advancing troops from the inception in 1936 through to its excruciating conclusion in 1942."

"Was Shimada's name in the report?"

"No. It was another twelve years, before a two-column article appeared in one of Japan's national papers. Even though it was published on page 16, it immediately became front-page news across the entire globe." She stubbed her cigarette out. "According to the article, Shimada has tried to bring himself to tell the story for over half a century."

Frej again picked up the manila folder. "A frail widower living near Osaka in Japan who worked with the Emperor's Golden Lily from 1936 until 1942. How did the world become aware of Akira Shimada?"

"He got in touch with the journalist who had written the article on the subject." She paused, again and then nodded stonily. "When did the Committee on Prevention of Torture announce the breakthrough in their investigation of Second World War crimes against humanity involving Japanese concentration camps?"

"Less than four months ago. "

She lit another cigarette, in a small fate-defying gesture.

Although all were obviously elderly, sixteen out of seventeen Japanese witnesses prepared to testify to the UN High Commission for Human Rights as to the nature of scorched-earth strategy used by the advancing Japanese Imperial troops, had died within a short period of time.

The sun had risen to the midpoint of the surrounding trees, streaming through the windows and passing away like colors on a drying palette. Louise stood up. Cigarette smoke spiraled above the table. The U.N. High Commissioner looked like she had her hooks in something. Lost ... no, rather found, in thought, Frej concluded.

"Someone out there is fast-tracking this thing to its premeditated and horrifyingly unfathomable conclusion. This someone might be one of our people." She felt a cold wave of anxiety in her stomach.

"I am going to Rome, Frej."

Chapter 9

Novodevichy, Moscow – three years earlier.

The centuries-old cemetery, "New Maidens Convent" in English, is the most venerated cemetery in Moscow. Founded by Vasily III in 1524, to commemorate the recapture of Smolensk from the Lithuanians in 1514, it is the resting place for some of Russia's most venerated writers and poets. Chekhov was one of the first to be buried there, in 1904. Gogol's remains were re-interred from Danilov Monastery not long after. Gogol's tomb is symbolically linked with that of another famous writer, Bulgakov, author of *The Master and Margarita*.

One of the cemetery's ironies is that victims of the Soviet regime – rejected, jailed, exiled and condemned by the State to work in special prison camps for researchers and scientists – are buried next to the State executioners. Thus, the cemetery houses Grigory Nikulin and Mikhail Medvedev, members of the Soviet Secret police who took part in the murder of the last Russian Tsar Nicholas II and his family in Yekaterinburg.

Many other prominent Russians are buried in the Novodevichy – Decembrists Matvei Muravyov and Sergei Trubetskoi; composers Sergei Prokofyev and Dmitry Shostakovich; singer and actor Fyodor Chaliapin, the greatest Russian basso ever to appear in Western opera houses.

Like all things Russian, the cemetery is vast – well over 150 acres – and poorly organized. The places of burial of famous Russians, indicated on the map with red numbers, often do not correspond to the places where they are actually buried.

Michael Asbury sighed as he approached a white marble bust of a woman enclosed in glass. He looked dejectedly at the map. "Abandon hope, all ye who enter here," he mumbled to himself.

A slenderly built woman with long, silky black eyelashes and a ready-made smile standing several meters away turned to him. "Dante," she said, giving the most radiant smile Michael had ever seen.

"Nice to meet you, Dante." He extended his hand. "I am Michael Asbury. I'm a Religious historian."

She laughed and shook his hand. "Simone Casolaro. I teach Italian Renaissance literature.

They stood silent for a moment. "It's quite confusing, isn't it?" "What is?" asked Michael.

"The map, I mean. It's quite confusing." She smiled and looked at him quizzically, studying his features.

Michael sensed in her demeanor a natural curiosity for everything in life, and smiled back.

"You are an American?"

"Yes, and you are British?"

"No, I'm Australian. But I live in London." He paused. " Well, if you consider three days a month to be actually living there."

They both laughed.

"Two strangers, standing in front of the grave of Stalin's ex-wife. You know," Simone went on, pointing to the white Italian marble bust in front of her. "This is one of the most haunting memorials in the cemetery. Nadezhda Alliluyeva was Stalin's second wife." She stood silently for a second or two, contemplating something. "Nadezhda means 'hope' in Russian."

Michael ran his hand along the base of the finely chiseled monument.

"Nadezhda Alliluyeva's death is still veiled in mystery. Some say she killed herself. Others, that she was murdered on her husband's orders. The legend says that Stalin would come at night and sit here, weeping for his beloved Nadezhda." She smiled again.

"I guess our lives are shaped as much by those who leave us as they are by those who stay," she said pensively.

For the next three hours they meandered through the nooks and alleys of Novodevichy, up and down sodden turf, cobbled walkways, smoothly paved asphalt and pillared walkways of limestone and slate. She told him about her love of Italian literature and Russian culture, about her brother Danny, her parents, their trips to some of the most exotic destinations the world over. He told her about his quest for the long-lost Gospel of Judas Iscariot.

At odd moments of silence, there were tentative rushes of warmth, and something else, too.

They kept walking and talking and looking at each other, the looks becoming warmer and longer. The something else was growing too, getting stronger.

They came to a semi-enclosed arcade, a round dome over a huge portico. It was a miniature columbarium, erected to house cinerary urns. Simone consulted her map.

"Anna Pavlova, indisputably one of the great ballerinas of the twentieth century, is buried here. Her ashes have been brought back almost seventy years after her death." She gazed at Michael.

"In 1931 she contracted pleurisy. Doctors could have saved her life with an operation, but it would have damaged her ribs and left her unable to perform, so Pavlova chose to die rather than give up dancing. As she lay on her death-bed, she is said to have opened her eyes, raised her hand and uttered these last words: 'Get my swan costume ready.' A few days later, at show time at the theatre where she was to have performed *The Dying Swan*, the house lights dimmed, the curtain rose, and while the orchestra played Saint-Saëns' familiar score, a spotlight moved around the empty stage as if searching for the great Pavlova."

They stood motionless, contemplating that moment. The light was fading rapidly. Simone shivered, only partly because of the cold. She stood beside him, looking down, and then, suddenly, raised both her hands, cupping his face. Michael stood still, transfixed. She leaned forward, brushing her lips against his. Her gaze was steady and unafraid, fixed on him. He reached for her waist and pulled her into him. The air around them filled with the excitement of discovery. They kissed and embraced with the intensity of two people who somehow knew that all of this was temporary.

* * *

"Ladies and gentlemen, we are on the final approach to John F. Kennedy International airport…" A metallic voice jolted Michael into the here and now, dispersing his memories like dandelion seeds.

He was thousands of kilometers across the world and three years removed. He gently gathered up the broken pieces of recollection. Novodevichy ... three years crumbled between his fingers.

He looked out the window. New York City, the Big Apple, lay beneath him, its immensity best appreciated from the air. He never thought of New York as just another city, but rather as a separate entity, a self-contained country in itself, a living and breathing organism unlike any other he, one of the world's most prolific travellers, had ever seen.

His thoughts returned to Simone. How long had it been? His mind raced back to their last night together. Last June. London. She was on her way to a symposium in Florence. He needed to be in Cairo the following day. God, that was eight months ago. He felt a pang. Could it be so long? Michael blinked hard, and thought back once again.

* * *

"Simone?" he remembered it as both a question and a futile attempt to postpone the inevitable. "What if we ..." He stopped, not sure how to continue.

She had sat motionless on the couch. "Michael," she had said, gazing at him, her eyes imploring. There was pain in her eyes and something like real love, too. She stood up and gently put her head on his shoulder. "If we try to create a normal relationship, we will destroy the most beautiful of romances." She stared into his eyes. " We are not normal people. What we have between us is a dream, a fantasy, if you wish."

"Simone," he had repeated, thickly.

"Michael, it can't get better than this."

"It can get different."

"Different is not necessarily better, just different." Simone said with conviction.

"Simone—"

"Please, please hear me out. The weekends we are together, we get to be who we really are." She paused. "If we try and fail it might ache in places you didn't know you had inside you."

"Just your quarterly sex partner. This is way past complicated."

* * *

From sheer exhaustion, they had dropped the subject and said their sad goodbyes. Had it all been lost in that moment of lethargy? Michael smiled ruefully and struggled to hold back tears.

Real life. Of course, she was right. It could never be real in a real-life sort of way. They both needed space. He let go.

The plane effortlessly touched down on the tarmac and began its final approach to the terminal.

When he emerged from the tunnel, there she was. His mouth felt dry. The next thing he knew, they had enveloped each other. The cheek he intended to kiss was supplanted by the passion of her mouth. Guilt and tenderness mixed with an aching desire washed over him. For a brief moment, the world stood still. Then he remembered why she had called him.

"Michael, I need you. They killed my brother."

CHAPTER 10

Caroni sat on top of a desk in his apartment on Via de Coronari, his head forward, his brows knitted together, studying a map of Rome. The quickest way to the train station would be through Via di Cuattro Fontane, take a left on Via de Tritone, past Via del Corso, circumvent Piazza Colonna and zigzag his way through. He frowned and checked his watch. Five to eleven. Stay out of sight. He had twenty minutes to reach the train station, five to buy a ticket and fifteen to make sure he wasn't followed. He threw a wary glance at the clock behind him, adjusting his Ruger .44 sidearm.

He had spent most of the previous day fast asleep, and a long, rambling, dreary dream had repeated, in a kind of pointless parody, his strenuous last evening with Danny Casolaro, and that ominous morning when he received the news of Casolaro's murder with incomprehensible calmness. Casolaro's drone of complaints, his suspicions of sordid betrayals that obsessed him.

Caroni stepped outside, strained his eyes against the sun, scanning left, right and center. All clear. He turned left, then right on the next side street, and headed towards the piazza and large crowds. People. Safety.

Then, it came, a narrow chasm of silence, broken by an abrupt, seemingly casual collision, but the eyes that stared at him were not startled; they were the cold eyes of a seasoned killer. Caroni lurched forward, then spun to his left just as the man attempted to clamp his hand down on Caroni's shoulder, missing his grip by a split-second. Zig-zagging left, then right, Caroni pulled his knife, its corrugated blade an extension of the hand that gripped it. Where is he? Where? An arm shot forward, surging in toward his ribcage. At the last moment, Caroni swung his right forearm up and blocked. The man's wrist glanced off his ear. The impact was deafening. As he reeled away, his eyes swept desperately for the assailant. Nothing. God damn it!

Who wanted him dead?

Was it the Boss? The Agency? Octopus? All of the above?

Something stirred to his left. He caught it at the last instant, turning instinctively to his right, but it was too late. The heavy punch landed on his right triceps, sending electric shock waves up and down his arm. His blade shot out of his hand. As he tried to pull his Ruger, something brushed against his throat, a cold, slicing period. Rivulets of sweat popped out and drenched his forehead.

His legs buckled under him as he crashed to the sidewalk with a dull thud. He looked across the piazza.

Blood was gushing from his mouth. Still, he wanted to know. Who the hell are they? And then he knew nothing.

CHAPTER 11

Fitzgerald felt a sharp twinge of pain. There were muffled voices somewhere above him. Where am I? He could hear squeaky footsteps. Rubber soled shoes. A whitish figure flitted across his vision like a spirit. Something plastic fell to the floor.

"Can you hear me?" A female voice asked quietly.

Army Ranger Curtis Fitzgerald nodded.

"You are hurt, but you will be all right."

"Where am I?" Curtis could hear his voice; it was weak, but he could hear it.

"You are safe and out of danger."

The voice floated in the air. Curtis tried forcing his eyelids open. God, that hurt. A shape came slowly into focus, a blurry form in a white coat. "Who are you?" he asked.

"A friend," said the voice, softly.

"Friend? Who are you?"

"I am a nurse, your nurse."

The door opened, and then was near-silently shut. Fresh set of footsteps. Someone had entered the room.

"He is awake, Madame."

Finally, his eyes focused. He was in a large, white room, sunlight streaming through half-open Venetian blinds.

Curtis squinted and with great effort made his head move ever so slightly to his right. Another woman was saying something to him, slowly, methodically. She had straight auburn hair parted in the middle, arched eyebrows, middle-aged but still beautiful, in an Earth-mother kind of way, with high cheekbones, hazel eyes.

"Where am I?" he asked again.

"You are safe and you are with friends. That's all that matters." She looked at Curtis and smiled. She was dressed in a blindingly white shirt and black pants.

Curtis looked straight ahead, desperately trying to remember something.

"How badly am I hurt?"

"Shrapnel in the midriff and neck and two wounds in the thigh. The wound to the stomach was deep and possibly fatal. It required two operations, but the neck wound was the real miracle. The metal missed the carotid artery by two centimeters. You're a lucky man."

"Relatively speaking. How long have I been here?" Curtis blinked, orienting himself. She glanced at the nurse, who looked at her watch, and then smiled back.

"Ten days, one hour and twenty six minutes."

"What is your name?" the doctor asked him.

"What?"

"I asked you what your name was." Curtis closed his eyes for a moment. "Curtis, Curtis Fitzgerald."

The doctor and the nurse looked at each other. "Nurse, could you please leave us for a moment."

"Yes, ma'am." She walked out and quietly shut the door behind her. "Curtis, do you remember what happened?"

"Bagram."

"Yes, Bagram. W hat can you tell me about what happened?"

"Who are you?" he asked.

"I am the medical officer in charge," she said.

CHAPTER 12

The limousine, a burgundy-colored soundproofed Rolls-Royce Corniche, pulled up in front of the Roosevelt Hotel at Forty-fifth Street, just off Park Avenue. Named in honor of President Theodore Roosevelt, with its copper-edged cornices and its upscale galleries and boutiques, the hotel was a throwback to a bygone era, a grand old lady in the epicenter of the Big Apple.

A tall, well-built, elegantly dressed man sporting a healthy tan walked unhurriedly across the faded red carpet through the foyer, an enormous room with a 45-foot ceiling encrusted with gold leaf, and past the curved marble staircase. Its appearance had hardly changed since it opened in 1924. A single chandelier dropped on a long cord from the center illuminating the room with its two-hundred fluted bulbs.

As he exited the building, the rear door of the Rolls opened. The man got inside, settling back on the leather seat. Another man was already seated in the back. He looked to be in his mid sixties, his age betrayed only by the face lined with a lifetime of secrets he would never reveal. His ash-blond hair was carefully cut and parted on one side, accentuating his high cheekbones and strong features. The man leaned forward and pressed a button. An opaque partition raised quietly, sealing off the back.

"Pierre, thank you for coming on such short notice." The elder man spoke with a perceptible trace of Midwestern accent. The Frenchman nodded silently. "You look remarkably well rested for someone who has just flown in from Paris. Would you like anything to drink?"

"Cognac, please," he replied in impeccable English, turning his head slightly in the direction of the ashen-haired gentleman, who pressed another button. A drinks compartment slid out from the partition. He removed a bottle of cognac and poured two glasses. "I think you will enjoy this," he told the Frenchman. "Richard Hennessy."

Pierre nodded approvingly.

His host smiled. "Nothing but the best for the best."

The Frenchman gave a wry smile, a Gallic shrug and sipped the fine liquor, then without any sense of hurry looked over at his host.

The older man cleared his throat and said after a pause, "We require the service of your unique set of skills."

The Frenchman nodded as he was passed a manila folder.

"Our police sources tell us that the dead man's apartment has been thoroughly searched, but that nothing of substance was found. I would like you to have another look. The address is enclosed. I can't stress enough just how vital this information is to the organization's plans."

"I admire the man's persistence. He had connected the dots, in a way, which would have made our members most uncomfortable." He looked at the Frenchman. "But, for him, enlightenment came at the ultimate price."

"I have no pretensions to enlightenment."

As Pierre opened the limousine door, the outside noise screeched and honked and squealed its way into the lush interior. The sun had abandoned the day to slate-grey clouds and a stiff quartering wind.

The door shut and the limousine set off gently into the rush-hour traffic. The Frenchman stepped off the curb, crossed the street and entered Tudor City Park, a getaway of lush greenery nestled amongst New York City's skyscrapers.

CHAPTER 13

Six miles northwest, in the Bronx, an attractive couple walked through the entrance of the seldom visited but nevertheless gorgeous gem of a park; the Pearly Gates playground, located on Tratman Street and St. Peter's Avenue. One of the smallest and least known of New York City parks, covering an area of less than two acres and surrounded by pin oaks, the Pearly Gates was designed to emphasize the integration of green space in urban living areas. The name was intended to evoke a little bit of heaven in the midst of the crowded city.

"Simone," Michael's voice was gentle, his look languid. He wore a plaid green and grey-checkered jacket missing the second button from the bottom. He held her hand in his. "Can you think of anything else Danny told you that might give us a clue as to who might have wanted to…?"

"I told you. I only know he was investigating corruption at the highest levels of the United States government."

"All right, so high level people were involved. People whose very existence would be threatened if the corruption were to be exposed." He stopped momentarily, working something out in his head.

"Yet, when the police searched his house, detectives did not find any evidence of it. No notebooks, no tape recordings and no documents."

Out of the corner of his eye, he glanced over at Simone. He had a feeling she must have thought of the same thing. For the briefest of moments, she squeezed his hand in hers, and then steadied herself, leaning on his arm.

"So, maybe whoever killed Danny got to his place first and stole the evidence before the police got there," he added.

"I don't think so, Michael. Danny was paranoid about that. He wouldn't have left anything lying around in his apartment."

"You said the sheer amount of physical evidence your brother collected over a five-year period would not have fit in a large suitcase or even in a large trunk. Did he bring some of it with him to Shawnee?"

She shook her head. "I don't know."

"Then, where is it? Even if he didn't want you involved, he must have had an insurance policy, someone else to pick up the pieces and run with it."

Simone pressed her left hand to her forehead and shut her eyes. "He said I would know when the time came, but—"

Michael stopped and held her in his arms. "Sweetheart, might it be remotely possible that Danny … well, that he really killed himself?"

She stiffened and pulled away.

"No, Michael! You didn't know him. He was understandably paranoid, not suicidal. Five years of grueling, thankless work. He had almost put everything together. The final piece was in Shawnee. Suicide would be the last thing on his mind."

"All right. I get it." He looked deep into her eyes. "I will stay with you until we find out, Simone."

She stepped back into him. "Thank you, that means everything."

"Someone knew Danny was meeting his source at Shawnee. What we don't know is what your brother had that set off the alarm bells." Michael put his hand on her forearm. "Aside from you, who else would Danny trust with this investigation?"

"He didn't have many friends. No matter how hard I pressed him on it, he wouldn't tell me any details."

"What about codes, aliases? Did he use codes to get in touch with people? Did others use them when they needed to find Danny?"

"What kind of codes?"

"I don't know, like, this is a message for Red Fox from Hound Dog."

"Red Fox? Hound Dog?" They both laughed, glad for a lighter moment.

"What if the assassin was the contact himself," Michael asked suddenly.

Simone leaned forward, folding her slender arms in front of her. "About three months ago, Danny was run off the road by a hit-and-run driver. Then, a few nights later, there were things he said in his sleep."

"Like what?"

"He kept repeating the word 'promise'. The next day, I asked him what he meant by it. All the blood drained from Danny's face. 'Oh, it's just subconscious gobble-de-gook, Sis. Nothing important.' But it was something, Michael. He was ashen."

She sat silently for a brief moment, gathering her thoughts and got up from the bench.

"He finally told me it was some sort of computer program that tied into a group of powerful people going back to the Second World War. He called them the Octopus. He also said that with Octopus controlling Promise, no data, no matter how secure, could be trusted in its electronic format."

"Splendid," Michael grunted under his breath. "That really simplifies things."

Simone turned to him, "There is nothing more. That's all he would say. I tried searching for Promise on the computer, but it turned up nothing."

"And?"

"And nothing. But it does exist, Michael. Danny was so frightened when I asked him about it. Not for his life, but for mine."

Michael gave her a long, level look.

"Let's suppose that this Octopus is a high-powered 'legitimate' organization rather than a group of criminals working together. They would need an army of minions to execute their orders."

"And if Danny had the goods on them, then yes, they would do anything to stop him," she added angrily.

"It gets worse."

"Worse? What could be worse, Michael?"

"Now that Danny is dead, whoever they are, they may be coming after you, because they can't be sure how much you know. Especially if they're still looking for your brother's evidence. As long as you are around, you are a threat to their very survival."

"But I don't know anything."

"You know it exists. And as long as they think you might know something more, you are in danger," he added gravely. Simone sat there, transfixed, staring in stony silence at her friend and lover.

"Danny told me the police are compromised. Not all, but many of them. I thought it was paranoia, but now don't I know."

Time passed while they each re-gathered their thoughts. "Michael, I'm glad you came," she finally whispered.

"Tell me about Danny. What was he like when he wasn't fighting international corruption?"

"He had a terrible sweet tooth. His favorite drink was chocolate milk. His favorite toothpaste was gummy bear Flinstone."

"What about his favorite movie character?"

"R2D2."

"No! Really? The squeaky little robot dude?"

"Danny said he was like Buddha on wheels."

"Ha!" Michael's genuine hoot of laughter startled several sparrows out of a nearby linden tree.

"After our parents died, we lived for a while in Egypt. I raised him, you know."

"I know."

"Then one day there was a fire and we lost everything. Our photo albums, dad's things, my mom's wedding band. I was devastated, but Danny took it in stride."

"He wasn't upset?"

"No, not really. You know what he said? 'These are just things. We still have each other.'"

Her dim smile changed all at once into an odd quiver and she leaned her head against his shoulder, staring up at him sideways.

"He's gone, Michael. He's really gone," she said, in a ghostly, incredulous voice.

Michael sat motionless. The deep lines on his forehead spoke volumes. He and Simone were caught in a deadly game of smoke and mirrors. The truth was out there, but the further they burrowed into this maze of deception and the more they learned about Octopus, the greater the chances of getting killed. Simone, he was sure, would never give up her search for Danny's killers, even if it meant her own death.

"Listen," he finally said. "It's just a matter of time before they figure it out. "They killed your brother and they won't hesitate to do the same to us."

"Are you suggesting we give up and disappear?" Simone said.

"No. We need help. Professional help."

"And where do we get it? Who could we trust?"

"I have a friend. Well, more of a guardian angel. Though I don't think he has wings." He laughed.

Simone stared at him. "Oh, this must be some story. Tell me all."

"Five years ago, I was part of a scientific expedition to the province of Ghazni in Afghanistan. It was a desperate effort to try and save the last two Buddhist statues left undamaged, dating from the second century BC. These were priceless monuments from pre-Islamic days, when the country served as a vital part of the Silk Road. After the Taliban's campaign to erase the history of any religion but theirs, they were nearly all that was left of the ancient world.

We were a little more than twelve miles away, but it was pitch dark and the road was dangerous, so we stopped for the night in an abandoned three-story warehouse on the outskirts of Khushali Torikhel that had served as regional headquarters for one of the UN local food agencies. What we didn't know was that the site had just been abandoned by the Taliban as they retreated north towards Pakistan.

American troops had this particular group in their sights for killing two U.S. servicemen during a routine road check. That night, when they detected human activity in the warehouse, headquarters called in an air strike. A drone."

"Wow! That's the worst case of bad timing I ever heard," Simone interjected.

"No shit. It came a few minutes past two in the morning. Leveled the place. One Italian archaeologist got off with two broken legs. I got pinned under a slab of concrete. Others, well, they weren't so lucky."

"How many of you were there?" she asked, holding her breath.

"Eleven. Three scientists, five archaeologists, me and two other experts on ancient cultures."

"And your friend?"

"Curtis. Curtis Fitzgerald. They sent him in with a small group of commandos."

"Thank God."

"Hardly. It was a case of 'friendly fire,' and we were potentially a very embarrassing bunch of dead and wounded scientists. Once they realized we weren't Taliban, they called headquarters, who told them to walk away and leave us to die."

"How do you know that?"

"I could hear their voices from a distance."

"Could it be that they just didn't find you under the rubble they were searching?"

"They would have, if they had looked hard enough."

"And this man Curtis?"

"He stayed behind, risking his life. The order was to evacuate," Michael said. "I would have been dead had it not been for him."

He took out his well-worn cell phone, typed in a name, pressed a button and waited.

CHAPTER 14

Curtis got up slowly, testing his legs. Mobility was coming back to him. The pain was subsiding, the wounds healing, and the stitches had been removed. Bandages still covered his midriff, but he was healing; he could feel his strength starting to return. The ruddy sunlight of mid-afternoon threaded itself through the lowered Venetian blinds glistening and shimmering on the wall of his sterile hospital room, and though it was not yet spring, the weather was warm.

He raised the blinds and stared aimlessly out the window at the city below, lost in thought. Below him, people walked, strolled, talked and laughed. They suspected nothing. It had been two and a half weeks, enough time to heal the wounds; not nearly enough to shut out the tormenting demons that still clawed at him inside.

He leaned his head back and took a deep breath. In his mind's eye he saw the grenade hit the ground, the flash, soldiers slumped on the ground, riddled with shrapnel. The sound of his cell phone broke Curtis's nightmare reverie. He blinked; who would want to call him? He flipped it open and stared at the display. It was a familiar number, although he couldn't quite place it.

"Hello?" His voice sounded more like a reproach than an invitation to speak.

Michael didn't immediately recognize the voice, but was overcome with warmth all the same.

"Guess who this is!"

There was a long pause. "I don't know."

"Hey, buddy, I know it's been a long time, but seriously, I'm not trying to borrow money!" He laughed heartily.

Silence.

"Who is this, for Christ's sake?"

"It's Michael. Remember me?"

"Michael! Oh, Christ, I'm sorry. Where the hell are you?"

"New York City."

"What, the Nubians are still after you?" The image of a gas station in the middle of an oasis on the wrong side of the Egyptian border near Abu Simbal.

"Where are you, Curtis?"

"Rome."

"Rome? Last I heard you were in Afghanistan. What are you doing in Rome?"

"It's a long story. What the hell are you doing in New York? Did they find remnants of the Old Testament under the UN building?"

Michael was silent for a moment. Then he told Curtis in detail about everything that had happened over the past several weeks, about Danny and Shawnee, about a group called Octopus and something called Promise.

In Rome, Curtis grimly listened to his friend's account. "Michael, get to the nearest pay phone and call me back right away." He hung up.

Less than five minutes later, Michael found a pay phone and called Curtis back.

"What do you know, Curtis?" Michael asked. He could hear his friend's heavy breathing over the line and his own heart was pounding in his chest.

"Did either one of you try googling the terms Octopus and Promise?"

"Simone did. When Danny was being non-responsive about his work."

"Where did she do it from?" Curtis sounded stone cold, almost menacing. Curtis could hear Michael asking a question and a female voice answering it.

"Her home."

Curtis swore. "She triggered something. They are on to you."

A vein started pulsating on Michael's forehead. "You better explain that, old buddy."

"Government agencies have internet monitoring trap-and-trace programs. FBI's Carnivore is the best known. These systems use packet-sniffer techniques to monitor specific nodes and data loci on the Internet. Every computer has a unique digital address. If Simone typed in Promise, it most likely tripped a digital trigger device."

"I am not quite following you, Curtis."

"Meaning that Simone's own probing would have activated a counter-probe from whoever killed Danny. Meaning they know who she is and most likely where she is."

"Do you know anything about this Octopus?"

"I don't."

Simone was following the conversation in silence. Michael stared at her, the tension inside him conveyed by his eyes.

"When did she do her search?"

"About a week before Danny died."

"Michael, listen to me very carefully. I'll take the next available flight to New York, but you need to get out right now."

"Okay."

"Take Simone's car to a repair shop for a tune-up, and drive off with whatever loaner car they have in stock. If you are being followed, this is a cheap and easy way to disappear short term without leaving a trace. Find any isolated Bed and Breakfast within a fifty-kilometer radius of New York City and wait. I will call you as soon as I land. Don't tell anyone where you are."

"What the hell did we get ourselves into, Curtis?"

"Both of you are dead fools walking, unless you get the hell out of wherever you are now. Beat feet, brother. I'll see you tomorrow."

"What's promise? What does it mean?" yelled Michael into the receiver.

"Promise is an acronym for Prosecutor's Management Information System. It's spelled P-R-O-M-I-S. Now, go!" It was an order. The line went dead.

In Rome, the door opened just as Curtis hung up the phone. "Mr. Fitzgerald!"

"Oh, hello, nurse. Nice of you to drop in."

"What are you doing?"

"Please tell the good doctor I need to stretch my legs. I'll be back."

"Stretch your legs? "

"Yes."

"Where?"

"America. Tell the doctor not to wait up for me." Several moments later, a tall, well-built man with a limp walked out of the medical facility and flagged a taxi. "Il aeropuerto, pronto." He dialed a number. On the third ring, a woman's voice came on the phone. "American Airlines, how may I help you?"

* * *

A tall, bearded man who was sitting diagonally across the street from Michael and Simone, elbows on knees, hands together, rose slowly, deliberately crossed to a small park and sat down on a bench beside an old man. Both of them looked straight ahead, giving no sign at all that they had known each other.

"Another man in another place seems to know a great deal."

"Do we kill them?" asked the bearded man.

"No, we wait. Let them come to us. There is always time to kill."

The hint of a smile curled the edges of the bearded man's face. He got up and slowly followed a couple out of the park.

CHAPTER 15

Less than twenty-four hours later Curtis stood in his twenty third-floor hotel room, binoculars in hand, studying the traffic. He had given Michael precise instructions: they were to arrive just before rush hour and pull onto the curb adjacent to the hotel, wait there for a minute, then rejoin traffic, driving until the next round-about three hundred yards ahead, then return and pull into the hotel's underground parking. From his vantage point he would be able to follow the pattern of traffic surrounding their mini-van. If they were being tailed, he would be able to tell.

At 4:45 P.M., Curtis saw a silver mini-van approach the hotel, park, and then perform the required maneuvers. Satisfied they were not being followed, Curtis called Michael and told him to come up.

A short while later Curtis heard a quiet tapping at the door. He walked across the room and opened it.

"Michael, it's been a long time."

"And here we are again in the shit soup."

Simone watched as Michael and Curtis engaged in a man-hug and several back slaps.

Michael stepped back. "This is Simone, in case you hadn't guessed."

"Simone," Curtis extended his hand. "It is very nice to meet you. I'm very sorry about your brother."

"Thank you. Michael told me a lot about you."

"He did?" Curtis arched his eyebrow. "I wouldn't believe any of it if I were you."

"Most of it was good." She smiled. "Exactly! Now, let's get down to business"

They listened silently as Simone told them what she knew about Danny's investigation, his papers, what he had told her about a secret account and anonymous safe-deposit boxes.

"But who are they?" asked Michael, sitting on the couch and leaning forward anxiously.

Curtis sank into an armchair by the fireplace.

"At this stage, we can only speculate. Whoever they are, they are a mouthful of acronyms with a damned big stick. From my experience in the field, you have got these in-and-out-of-government agents, former agents, and mafia people, people whose skills are highly valuable and highly lucrative, especially when they go rogue. Independent agents, unknown to each other, but coordinated and deployed through a set of controllers, who are in turn controlled by the real power-players."

"But, what is their goal?"

" We will only learn that when we recover Danny's documents and logs," added Curtis.

" Which means we are back to square one," said Simone, desperation in her voice. "Because whoever has them dares not show their face."

"If they are still alive," said Michael.

Curtis shook his head, closing his eyes, the darkness momentarily comforting the throbbing pain in his midsection. "What if the assumption is wrong? What if everyone is looking for someone instead of a something?"

"What do you mean by that?" asked Michael.

" We are missing a critical piece of the puzzle," Curtis said. Both Simone and Michael listened in silence.

"It has been bothering me since I got on the plane last night. Think about it: What's the simplest explanation? If someone like this Octopus organization is after someone, degrees of loyalty to your brother are utterly irrelevant; this person wouldn't stand a chance. First, they shoot him up with Amytals and his whole life becomes an open book. Then, they would get the papers, kill him, and come after you. But, they didn't. Why?"

"Because they don't have what they need," said Simone.

"Exactly. Which means that it isn't the who we should be after, but the what and the where."

"May I have a drink?"

"Sure." Curtis got up and went to the cabinet. He poured two shots of whiskey for himself and one each for Simone and Michael. "Ice?"

"No, thank you." Simone got up, took her glass and went over to the window.

They sipped in silence, an extended tableau of heavy thoughts, finally broken by Michael.

"Simone, you said it yourself. Danny didn't have many friends, certainly no one he would trust with what he was investigating. But, he couldn't let all that extraordinary work go to waste. That leaves you, his only living relative, the person he most trusted and loved. As long as Danny was alive, he would want to keep you at arm's length. He knew the dangers involved. That's why he turned white when you confronted him on PROMIS. But he would still have taken precautions, in case something happened to him.

"You said it yourself; he made copies and copies of copies of all his documents. These documents were your insurance policy." Michael suddenly stopped. "But they would figure that out, so why haven't they come after us?" he asked.

"Because they know Simone doesn't have them. Remember the counter-probe. What they don't know is who does. So they are watching and waiting," added Curtis.

"Because they are operating under the assumption that it is the He who has it and not the what," added Michael.

"Exactly."

Simone put down her whiskey and picked up a packet of peanuts from a welcome-basket. "So, if it's the what, where is it?"

"The only place in the world where no one would look for it," added Curtis.

"And that is?" Michael sat forward. "Danny's apartment," he answered.

"Curtis, the police have gone through the apartment with a fine tooth comb. They didn't find anything."

"They didn't find anything, Michael, because they were looking for the wrong things."

Michael paused, his mind wandering. His eyes swept across the room, coming to rest on Simone.

"Simone, there are two interlocked elements in this equation – you and Danny on the one hand, and Octopus and PROMIS on the other. And both of these elements share a common denominator."

Simone was struggling with the complementary bag of nuts. "Theories, suppositions, equations. I am fucking tired of this! And how do you open these goddamn peanuts?" She hurled the bag across the room, grabbed up her whiskey, drained it and slammed the glass back down on the table.

After a moment's awkward pause, Curtis said, "Well, thanks for throwing the peanuts and not the glass."

The tension broke and they all had a much-needed laugh. "Simone, what did Danny tell you about PROMIS?"

"He said that with Octopus controlling PROMIS, no data, no matter how secure, could be trusted in its electronic format."

"Wait a minute," Michael interjected. "If you are Danny, you know that this information has to be so well hidden that the assassin would never think to look for it there."

Simone threw up her hands. "We know that."

"It has to be well hidden," Michael said, "but someplace you and only you would know where to look and recognize it when you found it. Think, Simone," he prodded her.

"How would Danny disguise it?" Curtis jumped in. "What interests did you share? What would that something be that would jump out at you?"

"Dante," she replied. "*The Divine Comedy.*"

"*The Divine Comedy*?" Curtis repeated Simone's revelation.

"It is something the killer or killers would never suspect." She took a deep breath, hesitated and then smiled. "Dante."

"Dante?" Curtis frowned in bewilderment.

She turned and looked at him. "An Italian Renaissance writer."

"Yes, I know. What about him?"

"Danny and I both loved Italian poetry, and when our mother died, I bought him a copy of Dante's *Divine Comedy*. He was only sixteen at the time," she said. "It could be inside the book"

Memories rushed to the fore: 1991, an Alzheimer's clinic in San Francisco, the last time they saw her alive. Her pale face in a three cornered hat, walking slowly and heavily towards the camera, gazing out from the photograph, meeting their eyes, but unable to recognize, help or comfort because she is only a photographed figure and cannot see beyond the flat world which contains her – photographed people are already a memory.

"We would spend hours on end reading Dante and imagining the two of us wandering through the depths of the Inferno and the dizzying heights of Paradise. For Danny, it was comforting. He knew every canto by heart and even imagined visiting our mother through Dante in Paradise."

"Simone," interrupted Curtis. "How can you be sure that's where he hid it?"

"I remember now. He said that when the time came, I would know." Simone blinked, the soft flesh around her eyes wrinkling in thought.

CHAPTER 16

It was raining that night in Rome. Angry, diagonal sheets driven by howling winds slammed into pedestrians and cars like an enraged beast. The cold rays of the moon would now and then appear meekly through the cloud veil, persistently trying to assert their natural right to be.

A short, stocky man in a wrinkled, ill-fitting windbreaker was sheltered from the elements by a receding archway leading to a dilapidated courtyard. He stood between two street lamps, across from the heavy ornamental doors of a brownstone apartment building. It was half-past four in the morning. The call would come any moment now. Submerged in the darkness he swiveled his head to the left, then right and then left again. The man heard the slow rumble of an approaching vehicle. The beam of light swung across the darkness, momentarily spotlighting him in his alcove. He froze. Would the call come? Awkwardly, the man adjusted his coat, pulling up the sleeve of his left arm. He checked his watch, bringing the oversized dial close to his face. Four thirty-three. Every few minutes he repeated the action, growing more nervous each time.

He was startled when it finally came at one minute past five in the morning, and almost dropped the phone. "Yes, yes?" he repeated, pushing the receiver into his ear.

The whisper was harsh. "I want you to turn your attention to his sister and her friends."

"Do you want us to kill them?"

"No, not until we find out what they know. I want them alive, especially the woman." There was a momentary pause.

"They might be a bother—" said the man in Rome.

"The woman does not know what she is in for. Neither does her friend. The soldier boy does, but he needs their help to uncover it. Between the three of them, they will lead us to what we seek."

A sharp, abrasive hum erupted somewhere overhead just as the man in Rome put away his telephone. He checked his watch. It was not quite midnight in New York. A call went out with precise instructions to a specialist in the Big Apple. He would know what to do. He had done it before, many times in many places. His real name was irrelevant; he used too many to count, a reliable man who knew how to get into and out of the most unassailable fortified compounds. He was the Invisible Man. The instructions were sent and teams put in place. The man in Rome slowly stepped out from behind the tree and off the curb. First lights now appeared in the windows, two on the nearest side, one in front, spilling its contents inquisitively into the street. There was no point in overstaying one's welcome. Questions might be asked. Anonymity and timing was their game. Too much was at stake.

CHAPTER 17

The brightest part of the day was slowly slipping away by the time the three of them reached Danny's apartment building. Thick banks of cloud obscured the sun, and gusts of wind made their presence felt, weaving their way through the city's streets.

Danny Casolaro had lived on the top floor of a two-story complex in an "upscale" apartment in Greenwich Village. Upscale, because it was expensive. But it was also cramped and noisy. All day long and much of the night subway trains could be heard, creating the impression that the whole structure was slowly on the move. The building had an uninspired façade, except for the windows, carved like the portholes of a ship, standing somewhat aloof amongst a collection of shuttered private houses behind iron railings. Silently, the three of them crossed the lobby. As they climbed to the second floor landing, Simone's mind was reeling. With Danny's death, her entire world had been shaken to its core, and as they approached his home she struggled to gather herself, willed herself not to cry.

"Simone—?"

She flinched and looked at Michael. "I am fine."

The three of them stood in the doorway of apartment 2B. Simone felt as if the ground was being pulled from beneath her; her mouth went dry and her stomach knotted. She ran a quivering hand through her wavy dark hair. What was she feeling? It was difficult to know.

Suddenly, they heard a lock click and a door burst open. A moment later a middle-aged man in velveteen slippers came out into the hallway. Sounds of a game show momentarily spilled after him. The door shut. The man took out his pipe and carefully filled it. With firm, unhurried step he walked down the stairs and into the street.

Danny's apartment was equipped with one of the most sophisticated lock systems in the world. Threat Con Delta, interfaced with audit control key and cylinder compatibility. The audit trail gave you the date and time the electronic key was used.

Simone opened her purse and pulled a set of keys from a metal case. Turning it to the right, she hesitated momentarily, and turned it to the right once more. The multiple security bolts gave way, smoothly sliding across the latches. She pushed the door open with the palm of her right hand.

She gasped, the fingers of her left hand pressed against her mouth. The place was completely trashed. Curtis pulled her out of the way and drew his Heckler & Koch P7, long favored by the Army Rangers. He stepped across the threshold and went into a crouch, pistol at the ready. The suddenness of the movement shot pain through his body. He winced, forcing his head into his right shoulder. "Jesus Christ!"

Michael instinctively moved towards him.

Curtis pushed him gently back and stepped forward, the bandages on his ribcage and chest becoming more uncomfortable. The wounds were not quite healed yet.

"Stay close to the door," he whispered in a barely audible voice, slowly, cautiously headed down the hallway. "If you hear shots, run like hell."

A moment later he came back out. "It's empty," he said as he put H&K P7 back into the holster. He turned to the front door and ran his fingers along the edge examining the frame and the lock. "Whoever was here knew what they were doing." He paused and looked at the two of them. "The audit trail can give you the date and time the electronic key was used." He pointed to the coded side bar. "Except in this case it registers zero, meaning that someone was able to override the system without leaving traces."

"How was Simone expected to get in without having access to the codes?" Michael asked.

"Because her key automatically overrides the system through a microchip imbedded in it."

"We can't stay here. It isn't safe," Curtis said. "We gotta go right now. Did you hear me, Simone? We have to go, now!"

"We need to find the book," she replied.

"That's asking for trouble. They might be back." He reached out to touch her.

"I am not leaving without Danny's copy of Dante," she said, pushing Curtis' hand away.

"Curtis," Michael said and put his hand on his friend's shoulder. "Give us a few minutes to find it. Please." The Ranger stared at him.

"Five minutes, Michael. I'll guard the landing. There is no other way in."

Michael unzipped his jacket. Is it hot in here or is it just me, he wondered to himself, but decided not to ask it out loud. He had a feeling it was just him.

"Simone?" She stepped forward. Everything in Danny's apartment was familiar, and nothing was.

The hall led into a bare and very cramped space. Along each side were two doors – two small bedrooms, a closet, and a bathroom. At the far end of the apartment was the kitchen. The dining area had been converted into a study. There was a yellow-tinged poster of a visiting circus from Volgorod thumbtacked to the wall. A crystal vase sitting on a shelf was the only object left in one piece, on its glassy shell a coating of fluffy dust. The dining room-study was lined with bookshelves, books that Danny was using paved the floor around the chair, and the table was piled high with them. A photograph of Danny was propped up against several volumes of Russian classics miraculously unharmed. He sat in the same pose Anton Chekhov sometimes assumed – head slightly lowered, legs crossed, arms not so much crossed as hugging each other, an aloof expression which he had developed in the final months of his life registered on his face.

"What would you wish for, Danny, if you could get anything in the world?" Their father's velvety voice marked a staccato-like rhythm as he spoke.

"I am saving all my money, daddy."

A pause. A look. "What for?"

"I want to buy a river."

"A river? You can't buy a river. Not yet, anyway."

The next day, his father gave Danny a spool of blue ribbon. "This is a magic ribbon," he said, "If you spread it, it will become as long as a river."

From that day on Danny slept with the ribbon under his pillow, and he dreamt all night long.

"Simone." Michael went to her.

She yanked the bottom left hand drawer of Danny's desk open, rummaging furiously among the papers. "It isn't here! He always kept it in this drawer."

There was an edge to her voice Michael didn't immediately recognize. "Check that large pile of books over in the corner. It has a black leather spine."

Michael began vigorously working the pile.

"Why did you bring Curtis? Please, tell him to go away," she said quietly.

"No, we can't do this without him." Michael replied.

"I don't trust him."

"Don't be so harsh with Curtis. He didn't have to help us."

"Then why is he?"

"Simone—"

"I found it!"

Chapter 18

His name is Paulo Ignatius Caroni," said Robert Lovett, a senior analyst for the State Department. "This is the man who holds the future of the world's financial system in the balance."

"That's quite a statement," said Edward McCloy, senior representative of the world's most powerful banking cartel, a man in his early fifties. He was of average build and average intellect. McCloy was dressed in a long-sleeved white shirt and black cotton trousers. He owed his position to his uncle, John J. McCloy, now deceased, former Chairman of Chase Manhattan Bank, former President of the Rockefeller-controlled Ford Foundation and member of the infamous Warren Commission.

"Not bad, J.R.," snorted Henry L. Stilton, an associate director of the Central Intelligence Agency. "Mustn't be too critical though. Just a bit nonplussed, aren't we? No more Russian bear to bite you on the ass, no more Reds under the bed at night. No, just a crazed freak deep-sixing our plans. Sheer genius. Did he pinch the codes off of you somehow or did he actually break into the system?"

He drew a deep breath. "Henry, we have made some headway, but I need more time," John Reid said, with the odd feeling that he was exposing his bad hand to a Bridge partner.

"Tell me, Bud, if we hired a wet rag, would we have to pay it as much as we are paying you?"

Reid's eyes flashed with anger.

"No need to take it personally. I'm just asking." Stilton sat back in the chair and crossed his legs.

Reid wrinkled his nose, and then blinked a few times. "The system is airtight. Nobody could have foreseen it. It was a fluke. Even if he tried, he could never do it again," he insisted.

Lovett uncrossed and crossed his legs. "He doesn't have to do it again. Because he has already done it. Once … that's all it takes. The consultants with outrageous fees and fancy lingo who set up the systems are up shit's creek without a paddle. You can take that to the bank; that is if you can keep Caroni away from it."

"Thank you for coming, Mr. Secretary." Taylor turned and spoke to the man seated on his right. "The matter at hand is urgent."

The former Secretary of the Treasury was David Alexander Harriman III – a lawyer, investment banker and philanthropist. His gaunt, mask-like face, the result of three cosmetic operations, was betrayed by several deeply imbedded lines around the eyes and mouth. Some believed him to be in his late seventies; others, in his early fifties. In the end, his age was never an issue. He was the point man for some of the world's most powerful and secretive individuals. That was his presentation card. The only one he needed. Although his accent was most definitely Midwestern, he spoke English with the eloquence and lilt of someone who spent a considerable length of time at the world's finest boarding schools. "It might be a good idea if we begin at the beginning, as the good Queen told the little girl."

"Very well, sir," said McCloy, nodding to everyone around the table.

"Mr. Secretary," intoned Taylor.

A hardly perceptible wrinkle of condescension materialized in the crease around Harriman's mouth. Just for a moment and then, it was gone.

"Robert?" Taylor gestured to Lovett; inviting him to speak. "Thank you, Jim."

"Twenty-four hours ago, a former government employee by the name of Paulo Caroni overrode multiple highly sophisticated security systems and came into possession of the funds linked to the off-the-books government-run collateral trading program."

"Secretary, are you familiar with it?" asked Lovett.

"Vaguely, at best. Names are of no consequence to my clients. Only one's deeds and the bottom line. Perhaps, for the purposes of being concrete, gentlemen, you can fill me in … along very general lines as I have purposely stayed out of the loop on this."

"The sanctioned purpose of this particular trading program, Mr. Secretary, was of a macro-economic nature," added Taylor.

"Yes. And?"

"Meaning, the government was recovering dollars of one description or another that had accumulated through the Second World War."

"When defeated nations steal valuable assets during wartime it is called plunder but when the victors grab those same assets they call it recovery," Secretary Harriman said.

"Very perceptive of you, Mr. Secretary," added Taylor.

"How were these funds repatriated, exactly?" asked Harriman. "Through parallel or mirror off-ledger accounts," replied John Reid.

"You have been speculating with the government's money," Harriman added. "Two sets of accounts. One for public scrutiny and another set for private viewing only."

"That is to say J.R. here was running two sets of books," added Stilton.

"Something like that," replied Taylor.

"Do tell me, Bud. Which set of books were you showing me?" asked Stilton.

"I don't remember you ever complaining, especially in view of spectacular profits the Agency was generating for very little, in fact minuscule, risk." John Reid responded.

"So this is what collateral trading is all about," said Stilton.

"Jesus, Henry. You have only been part of this operation for over a decade. Clue in, will you," replied Reid.

"I was told this was a great investment opportunity," answered Stilton. "Few details, little risk, great return on the investment."

"You don't borrow money, even on an automobile, unless someone puts up the collateral, whether you are talking about buying and selling a car or a nation. Everybody wanted to get in on the act," said Reid.

"When you say everybody, would that include CIA?" asked McCloy.

"You might say that."

"FBI?"

"Also."

"The U.S. Treasury?"

"For Christ's sake, everybody means everybody! Every government entity in the country wanted in on the action, including the Federal Reserve, international financial institutions and wealthy investors," said the irritated Citybank's C. E. O.

"How much money might we be talking about?" asked Harriman.

"Ballpark figure? Around 200 trillion."

"Dollars?" chimed in Stilton.

"Yes, U.S. dollars. The actual amount is $223,104,000,008.03." But who's counting.

"I see. And this is the money I presume has been stolen by a former employee of the United States government," asked Stilton.

"Yes," answered Reid.

Stunned, Stilton looked around the room for moral support. "Except for profits, Henry, you have never shown any real interest in it before," added Reid derisively.

"That's because you have never screwed up before." There was a long pause. "And this is the money you lost, Bud."

"We didn't lose it. It was temporarily expropriated. We will break Caroni and get back the money."

"And how exactly are you planning on doing that?" He blew two streams of grey smoke through his nostrils and fixed his companion with hard eyes. "Sorry to bother you, love, I am just a stickler for detail."

"Look, we are working on it around the clock, retracing his steps, tracking the binary codes through the system's back up. The entire operation took no longer than seven minutes. He was obviously in a hurry. He might have made a mistake, in which case we will get the money back."

"If he was able to short circuit the system and overcome every one of the bullshit security flags of a supposedly unbreakable system, what makes you think he will leave you an opening so you can sneak up and bite him on the ass?" Stilton said.

"Look, if you are so damn smart, why don't you book a torture chamber and maybe you could talk him into submission," sneered Reid.

"Enough, gentlemen. In times of crisis we are supposed to hold intelligent conversations and look for common solutions, not squabble like six-year-olds" Throats were cleared, looks exchanged around the table. David Alexander Harriman III was to be taken lightly only at one's own peril.

"Gentlemen," broke in Reid, "there are several problems which we need to address. A percentage of the proceeds generated from this were used to finance a wide variety of clandestine activities."

"You mean the money is gone, but the government's obligations remain outstanding," added Harriman.

"I don't get it," Stilton replied scratching his head.

"To have access to the money the government has to put up something as collateral. The collateral is the guarantee that the money will be repaid. Now that the money is gone, we lose the collateral but are still under the obligation to return the missing money," replied Taylor, and then added somberly, "now do you understand?"

Harriman sat up. He looked over at Taylor. "Let me see if I can fill in the blanks, Jim." He tapped impatiently on the table with the tip of the pencil. "This is the money that would have been used by the government to shore up the American economy, which is about to default on all its obligations to its international creditors, rendering our dollar worthless and effectively condemning us to a third-world status."

The silence around the table was deafening.

"I have been sitting and listening to the five of you describe an operation that has been going on for over a decade involving intelligence networks, government agencies, both public and private money and God knows who else.

"I want to know: what was used as collateral to tap into the government's money and bankroll this entire operation worth untold trillions of dollars?" asked Secretary Harriman.

"The name and the operation I am about to give you remains classified, on the recommendation of the Joint Chiefs of Staff and an unbroken executive order from five successive presidents." John Reid responded.

"That's quite a pedigree, isn't it?"

"I think you will agree Mr. Secretary, once you know what is involved, that the scale of the operation itself and its overall purpose was felt to be in the national interest of the United States government," said Stilton.

"Mr. Secretary, the assets in question are large volumes of gold plundered by the Japanese during WWII. The operation was called Golden Lily. Officially, the government's position has always been to categorically deny any link to this asset base," said Lovett.

"So, let me see if I understand you." Harriman got up and paced. "You have used vast quantities of gleaming gold bars, bearing the triple-A chop as collateral in an off-the-books cloak and dagger operation which has, as creditors, every government agency in the country. And now, that the money is gone, you've lost the collateral. But we are still on the hook for principle and interest payments on $223 trillion dollars..." His voice trailed off.

Everyone nodded silently.

Chapter 19

Back in Curtis' apartment, Simone gently opened the book to the title page. Across the top, something was written in Danny's hand. She scanned the line, her eyes riveted to the page – "Has Hell a geometry?" In the margin, there was a doodle of a cone-like Hell with a tiny figure of Satan in the center. Behind him, in the shape of his wings, a tree grew out.

For a moment, she thought she saw Danny's ghost standing over her in his frayed jeans, twisting his pencil around, moving it faster and faster.

"What are you looking for?" inquired Curtis.

"The Inferno is an intricately planned, rigorously symmetrical narrative poem. It tells of the poet's descent into Hell, and how he passes through the center of the world, and then ascends Mount Purgatory. From Mount Purgatory he proceeds to Heaven itself into the presence of God," replied Simone sounding almost trance-like.

"The poet tells of his travel through the three realms of the dead. His guide through Hell and Purgatory is the Latin poet Virgil, and the guide through Paradise is Beatrice, Dante's ideal woman. Virgil guides Dante through the nine circles of Hell. The circles are concentric, each one representing further and further evil. The end of Dante's trip through the Inferno is the center of the earth, where Satan is held, bound."

"God is the only safe thing to be," muttered Curtis under his breath.

She didn't hear him. For a long time, she stared at the doodle as if in a trance, trying to remember something. "What do you make of this, Michael?" She showed him Danny's doodle.

The silence lasted precisely ten seconds.

"A Tree of Life!" Michael clapped his hands and pointed to Satan's wings.

"Dante's texts are consistent with what might be termed Christian Kabbalah." Michael slipped off his jacket and dropped it on the back of the chair.

Simone unlocked a chain she was wearing and showed the two men a magnificent pendant. "This was my birthday present from Danny. He found a man in Palestine who sold it to him."

"So Danny knew about Kabbalah and mysticism?" asked Michael.

"What is it?" asked Curtis.

"The Tree of Life is a mystical concept within the Kabbalah of Judaism which is used to understand the nature of God and the manner in which He created the world out of nothing." Michael reached into his pocket and pulled out a pen and a scrap of paper. He folded it in half and drew something on it. "Banks or vaults work on a code system. These codes could be numbers, letters or a combination of the two. Unless your brother physically hid a piece of paper with a code within the pages of a book and we just missed it.

"If Danny was aware of the Kabbalah, he must have known the mystical Kabalistic number 142857," said Michael. "It comes from an ancient drawing with nine lines called an enneagram, a New Age mandala, a mystical gateway to personality typing."

"Danny mentioned that the secret account could only be opened with a number-word combination. 142857 could be the number," said Simone.

"I'll bet I know what the phrase is," Michael said smiling at both of them.

"Tree of Life," the three of them said in unison.

"Even if that was true, we still don't know where the money is hidden," said Curtis.

The first rays of mild light were beginning to seep through, moving diagonally, rising like the wall of a distant monastery. Into the cool of morning dripped the smell of yesterday. Someone hurriedly moved across the street, their raincoat bearing epaulets of raindrops. New York was alive as ever, even at this late or early hour, full of sounds. Dawn was coming, and all the trees bowed low to the ground, bending their knees in silent worship. Michael left the window slightly ajar, catching a faint sound of music playing somewhere, not too far off.

CHAPTER 20

D oes anyone outside these four walls know anything about this?" asked Harriman.

"An unemployed former journalist," admitted Stilton.

"An unemployed former journalist is redundant, Henry. Does it imply he was gainfully employed before or after disclosing the facts?"

"He was unemployed, and former because he is deceased. Found dead in his hotel room."

Lovett took out a thin manila envelope from the breast pocket of his tailor-made sports jacket. He opened it and handed it to the Secretary of the Treasury. Harriman studied it, a sigh accompanying his first glance.

"Jesus H. Christ."

It was a photograph of a corpse, slumped in a bathtub full of crimson water. An empty bottle of Jack Daniels was cradled in his arms. Another photo showed the man's wrists exposed, both slashed. Silently he pushed the ghastly evidence back to Lovett.

"The coroner ruled it a suicide," added Taylor. " Was it our operation?" asked Harriman.

"We had a team on the way to capture and interrogate," replied-Lovett. "Except…"

"Except someone beat us to it." There was no reply.

"Someone's gone rogue on us?" The possibility lingered briefly ."Highly unlikely," replied Lovett. "Those in the know are the people in this room. Period," he said, eyeing his colleagues. "And every one of us has too much to lose if this thing were to blow up in our faces."

"What about somebody on the team?"

"Negative. This was sequence operation. Which means they were working blind. Complete compartmentalization of data."

"Still, the journalist is dead," Taylor said.

"How much did he know?" asked Harriman.

"Obviously, enough, or at least that's what someone thought," said Reid.

"Suppose they got spooked," added McCloy.

"Just like that, Ed. Spooked. So they go and kill a man on the off chance he might know something?" Harriman pushed the photograph in the direction of Edward McCloy.

"Let me guess," added the former Secretary of the Treasury. "Nobody saw or heard anything. Casolaro's motel room door was locked from the inside. There were no fingerprints, no signs of a struggle, and no traces of poison in his body. How am I doing, Henry?"

"Batting a thousand."

"Thought so," said Harriman. His reputation was as murky as his gaze was clear.

"Presupposing that none of us are responsible, let's leave whoever did this out of it for a minute." Harriman stood up and walked over to the far wall. "How much did we know about the journalist's activities?"

"He was warned off several times," said Stilton.

"How?"

"The usual methods."

"You said he was investigating. The entire operation or certain parts of it?" asked Harriman.

"It started with the financial aspects of PROMIS and then expanded into derivative trading programs, banking and overseas operations. That's when we clamped down."

Harriman whistled softly. It was a low, swelling whistle, the sound of a man genuinely taken by surprise. "Overseas operations is a giant mare's nest. It involves too many operatives in too many countries."

"Which means he would have needed money," added Taylor.

"Exactly," Lovett said.

"But you said he was unemployed." Harriman looked point blank at Stilton. "What was the source of his funding?"

"Unknown. It looks like he lived hand-to-mouth. We have all of his financial statements, telephone bills, taxes, rent: the whole nine yards."

"Hand-to-mouth journalists don't do overseas. Too deep for their pockets. How often has he been out of the country in the past two years?"

"Not at all. Which is why we believe he acted alone. About six months ago, he tried to borrow twenty grand from First National Bank," Stilton said.

"And?"

"He was turned down." Stilton reached into a yellow folder and pulled out a piece of paper. "No gainful employment."

"Yet someone besides us thought it prudent to take him out and make it look like a suicide."

"In the course of his investigation, do we know how many people he would have contacted?" asked Harriman.

Stilton pulled out another folder, and consulted a sheet of paper. "One hundred and eight," he replied. Harriman silently nodded. "Suppose one of these people learned something, something valuable, something that could bring him untold riches … Are you with me so far?" asked Taylor.

"The kid was known to haul a briefcase full of documents everywhere he went, playing one interested party against the other," said Lovett.

"That's one way to get killed," added Reid.

"You gotta admit the kid had balls," said Stilton. "Dumb fuck, but with balls."

"I can see that virility is an important issue to you, Henry," added McCloy with a smirk.

"According to the police report, the room in Shawnee was empty," interrupted Lovett. "No briefcase and no documents. What we do know is that he made over twenty telephone calls to two people in a span of thirty-six hours before his death." He paused. "The calls went to Langley."

"The CIA?" shouted McCloy.

"That's the breakthrough we have been looking for," grinned Reid.

"We have tried that tack. It's a dead end. The trail goes cold at the gate. A routed line traceable only to a single telephone complex somewhere in Langley, the authorization verified by code, and a call made through internal security. No log, no tape and no reference to the transmission," added Stilton. Lovett slumped in his chair.

"The authorization can always be traced through the code – in this case through the recipient or director of Cons Ops," said Harriman.

"Except that someone went to a lot of trouble bypassing Cons Ops altogether by re-routing it to another entity outside the Agency." Stilton paused, looking down on the pad in front of him.

"Outside the Agency? And that entity would be where?" asked Lovett.

"Pinto Basin," said Stilton, leaning back in his chair.

" What the f—" John Reid suddenly stopped in mid sentence. He looked at Lovett. "Caroni. That son of a bitch."

"That is one angle we haven't examined, yet," added Taylor. "Caroni vanished from our screens. All our planning, all our money, all of our power, our supposed mastery of the game. What of it now? Every nook and cranny where Caroni has been, would have been, might have been are on constant watch. But not a whisper."

"What if Caroni is dead?" asked Stilton.

"If this man is dead and we didn't kill him, then someone else is obviously trying to find the money as frantically as we are," said Taylor.

"As the final note, gentlemen, unless we find the missing money, the world's financial system will collapse onto itself, precipitating the greatest financial crash in history; far exceeding the 1345 Lombard bankers disintegration, which wiped out millions and setback European civilization back a hundred years," breathed Harriman.

They all turned and looked at John Reid. He swallowed hard. His eyes were glassy and he was clearly lacking sleep. "I have a plan." He looked across the room and smiled. It was a slow tightening of the small, thin lips; nothing more.

"Remember, I was there, I know where the rest of the gold is. I need a few more days. I will get this done," he said.

"A few more days," replied Taylor, his eyes resting dispassionately on him. And then, "Thank you for coming, J.R."

Dismissed, John Reid left the room and pressed the elevator button. As he listened to it lurch its way towards him, "The Second Coming" by W.B. Yeats invaded his head:

Things fall apart, the center cannot hold.
Mere anarchy is loosed upon the world ...
Surely the Second Coming is at hand ...
And what rough beast, it's hour come 'round at last,
Slouches toward Bethlehem to be born.

You have one week to find the money.

As the door slid open, he couldn't shake the notion that he was a sacrificial goat, walking blindly into the gaping jaws of that rough beast.

Back in the soundproofed room, there was a thoughtful pause. Stilton cleared his throat. "Dead or alive, we have to find Caroni."

"Get on the blower," said Harriman, pushing his chair away from the table. "I want all our externals up and ready to go. I want Caroni found by midnight."

The others said nothing. For the moment, there was nothing left to say.

The meeting over, David Alexander Harriman III casually strolled over to James F. Taylor. "I gave my driver the day off. Would you mind giving me a ride back to the office?" he asked quietly.

"My pleasure," said the Vice-chairman of Goldman Sachs.

The sedan rumbled down Way Street, a quiet residential area on the outskirts of Washington, slowed down at an intersection, turned left and quickly merged with Washington traffic on the freeway.

"Let's keep Reid around for now. He will come in handy."

"He is a fool," replied Taylor looking over at Harriman. His voice trailed off.

"And a zealot. Somewhere down the line we may need him to sing 'The Battle Hymn of the Republic' as he walks into the cross-hairs for us."

"What about Casolaro's sister and the two others?"

"We wait and we watch. Much can be learned through patience and discretion. There is always time for action."

"I agree. So far, the three of them have nothing," said Taylor.

Harriman shook his head. "I think they do, they just don't know they know it, yet."

"Why do I get the feeling that you know more than you let on?"

"That's all it is for now … a feeling," came the reply.

Taylor squinted, studying the old man's facial expression for clues. "How do you mean?"

"Informants in Rome, how else?"

"I see," said Taylor. He sat back, stretched his legs and looked out the window. Light drizzle was falling diagonally, caressing the roof of the sedan, spattering against the windshield. He glanced over at the old warrior sitting next to him.

"I hear a man from the past, a man who never was." Slowly and deliberately, Harriman started reciting an old nursery rhyme.

"As I was going up the stair, I met a man who wasn't there. He wasn't there again today …"

"I wish, I wish he had come to play." Taylor grinned as he misquoted the last line.

"Let's keep Rome to ourselves for now. Until things get clearer."

A thin smile momentarily appeared on James F. Taylor's face. "F" stood for Frances, his mother's name. She would approve.

CHAPTER 21

The Boss checked his watch. Once the call came, the discussion was over and the finer points of the plan's execution definitively set in motion, it would be destroyed: shredded, and then burned. Tonight. He walked to the door, closing it softly behind him.

11:52 P.M. This would be their last contact until further notice. They were too far along. He understood too well the consequences of being outed ahead of time. It was for his own sake. For the sake of self-preservation. Stilton, he knew, was always more comfortable with black and white solutions. He was not prone to self-examination. On the other hand, he, when he analyzed himself, did so as though he were a detached observer of his own follies and failings. 11:55 PM. Any moment now, it would … the phone purred softly, vibrating gently, spinning on the table like a dung beetle trying to get upright.

"We done?"

"Yes," replied Stilton. "Everything is on schedule. Reid got quite a grilling. Taylor is incensed."

"And Reid?"

"Ready to walk into the cross-hairs."

"Good," The Boss replied. "We are about one third of the way through. Keep low until further notice."

"Will do." Stilton's eyes drifted lazily to a large clock on the far wall. Ding-dong. Midnight.

There was a click.

Stilton picked up a cigar, reached into his pocket and withdrew a brass Zippo. A man, he believed, should never be without a lighter or a gun.

CHAPTER 22

The White House Situation Room is a five-thousand square foot space used by the government both as a conference room and an intelligence management center in the basement of the West Wing of the White House. National Security Council and Department of Homeland Security jointly run it. The people summoned to an emergency meeting that morning, coordinated by the White House Chief of Staff, were top government economists on whose experience and expertise rested the financial structure of the nation.

Larry Summers, Director of the National Economic Council, sat on the President's left. Jim Nussle, Budget Director for Office of Management, was to the left of Summers. Kirsten Rommer, leading economic historian and a Chairperson for the Council of Economic Advisers, took the chair diagonally across from Summers. Paul Volcker, head of the Economic Recovery Advisory Board, sat on the opposite side of the table. As the President stood, a door opened and Secretary of State Brad Sorenson, a tall, slender, conservatively dressed man with aquiline features and silver hair entered and took an empty seat to the President's right.

"Ladies and gentlemen, due to the urgency of the matter, I asked the Secretary of State to join us."

"You look tired, Mr. President," said Jim Nussle.

"I am," agreed the President, resuming his chair. "I'm sorry to bring you all back here on such short notice. I believe you'll agree this is a national emergency."

"Thank you for including us, sir," Kirsten Rommer said.

The President nodded silently. He pressed a button imbedded in the table in front of him. "The first slide, please." The lights were extinguished and a startling image appeared on an over-sized plasma screen in front of everyone. Budapest's cobbled streets – a war zone. Protesters armed with blocks of ice smashing up Hungary's finance ministry. Thousands trying to force their way into the legislature.

"This is real, ladies and gentlemen. For now, the economic collapse is hitting other industrialized countries much harder than America. Around the world, emerging financial markets are imploding at a faster rate than ours. The meltdown has hit turbo charge in Europe as a result of a now three-week old lack of Russian natural gas. Triggered by the economic collapse and compounded by human suffering in unheated, near-zero weather, riots have erupted from Latvia in the North, to Sofia in the South. Around the world, from China, to India, to Europe, industrialized nations are frantically preparing for civil unrest. This is not some piece of fiction. This is not *Atlas Shrugged*. This is about now. It affects all of us."

He pointed to the images on the screen.

"Ordinary people enraged by austerity cuts and draconian wage deflation, fighting for their own survival. Civil unrest now moves from the back to the front burner. Political leaders and opposition groups from as far away as South Korea and Turkey, Hungary, Germany, Austria, France, Mexico and Canada are calling for the dissolution of national parliaments."

"This is madness," someone whispered. There was a deathly silence in the room.

"Let's start with Europe." The President paused. "Kirsten, can you take it from here."

"Yes, Sir." Kirsten Rommer stood up. "Gentlemen, European Monetary Union has left half of Europe trapped in depression. I can only qualify the latest reports as catastrophic for American interests and for the world economy in general," she said squinting at the darkened profiles in front of her. "Events are moving fast in Europe. Bond markets in the Mediterranean region are on red alert. S&P has downgraded Greek debt to near junk and the country's social fabric is unraveling before the pain begins, which bodes ill. The Spanish, Portuguese, and Irish governments are balking at paying their short-term debt, putting at risk the solvency of the financial system." She cleared her throat.

"Next slide, please." There was a click and a multi-colored three-dimensional bar chart went up. "A great ring of EU states stretching from Eastern Europe down across the Mediterranean to the Atlantice are either in a 1930s depression already or soon will be. Each is a victim of ill-judged economic policies foisted upon them by groupss committed to Europe's monetary project and each is trapped." She moved across the room.

"However, the economic aspect of it is just one area. There are others," broke in the President.

"Ladies and gentlemen, this is as much about geography as it is about politics. A new order is being created where geography and money are proving to be the ultimate trump cards because geography is governing economic decision-making. Mr. Secretary, could you take it from here?"

Brad Sorenson stood up and adjusted his tie as a world map appeared on the screen. Someone cleared his throat. Someone else shifted nervously in his seat.

He looked at a piece of paper in front of him. "Geography is giving us our first major political tectonic fault line. From the Baltic south, through Greece, into Turkey, then fanning out across the Middle East is a new frontier of soon-to-be flaming unrest."

"The snake eating its own tail for nutrition. It is the way money works … for now," added Larry Summers, Director of the Economic Council.

"How much money does the government of the United States need in order to keep the U.S. economy afloat and maintain even moderate faith in the dollar?" The President looked at his senior most economic adviser. "Larry?"

"Minimum 2.8 billion dollars a day in foreign direct investment, largely through the purchase of Treasury notes to service our economy, although a more realistic figure is closer to four billion dollars."

"Is there a chance, under present circumstances, that foreign governments will be able to—"

"Snowball's chance in hell, Mr. President." The man interrupted him.

The Commander-in-Chief crossed his arms, leaned back in his chair, deep in thought. Finally he spoke. "I see. What are our options? "Mr. President, less than one month ago we had two options available to us. Troubled Asset Relief Program and Stabilization Fund," said Larry Summers.

"Had implies the past tense. Does that mean that these options are off the table?"

Summers swallowed hard. "Yes, sir. TARP has all been spent on corporate bail out." He turned the page in his notepad. "Stabilization Fund guarantees direct investment into the U.S. economy by the government of the United States if every other option of securing the necessary funds fails. It guarantees that the government will not default on its obligations to its own citizens."

"That was less than one month ago, correct?" Summers nodded silently.

"And now?"

The face of Director of National Economic Council hardened. He looked at everyone in the room. Every pair of eyes bore into him. Finally, Summers spoke. "Now, Sir, the money has gone missing."

"What do you mean, missing?" asked the President in a deceptively bland tone.

"Missing as in missing."

"Why wasn't I informed?" asked the President

"Because we just found out."

"When?"

"Yesterday. That's the reason, Mr. President, I insisted on this emergency meeting in the first place."

Chapter 23

"BS Bank Schaffhausen. Anonymous safe-deposit boxes." Simone had given them the name of the bank without pausing to think about it. She walked over to the couch and pulled a crumpled business card out of her purse. The bank offered anonymous computer source code escrow services and faceless digitized backup. "Which means anyone can just walk in and, using the right combination, unlock the contents," she added. "I always thought it was silly."

"If the number-word combination is correct, I have to get in, unlock the safe, get whatever is in it and get out," said Curtis.

"You mean, we."

"No, I mean me. I can't do it if I need to worry about the two of you."

"I'm going with you." There was determination in Simone's look.

"I can't let you come with me. I don't know what the dangers are and I can't afford to have you exposed … for my own safety."

"We're assuming they'll have the bank covered. But there are just too many banks in this city. How would they know where to look?" Michael asked.

"They will know," Curtis said.

"How?" he insisted.

"From the way they ransacked your brother's place, it's clear they are on to us. Your search of PROMIS guaranteed it."

"How many people do they have working for them?" asked Michael.

Curtis shook his head. "If this is multi-level organization, enough to cover every street corner in the city."

"I think you're exaggerating. They couldn't possibly know where we might be going. There are simply too many variables involved. And if they find us, what are they going to do; kill us, with hundreds of witnesses around?" Simone said.

"You really don't get it, Simone." Curtis shook his head. "They will kill you, yes, but later. First they will kidnap you, unless you and Indiana Jones here possess self-defense skills I'm not aware of. Then they will torture you for information. Finally, after realizing that you really don't know anything of substance, yes, they'll kill you."

Simone spoke quietly but with steel in her voice. "He was my brother, Curtis."

The Ranger came over slowly and placed his large hands on her delicate shoulders.

"I promise, Simone. It will be all right. There is something to be said for the element of surprise."

"If you get the information, we'll need a place to disappear," Michael said.

"Like a hotel," added Simone.

"No. We can't take that chance. All public places will be watched. We need a secluded place to lie low. I have a friend, from the old days."

"Can he be trusted?"

"With my life."

"Even under the circumstances?"

"He was my commanding officer when I first joined the army. It was his recommendation that got me into the Special Forces."

"Then he is military?" asked Simone.

"Which means government," added Michael.

"He is outside the government. Outside, but in a way very much a part of it, on an international level."

"NATO?"

"No."

"Carlyle? Blackwater?"

"He works for Blackwater?" said Simone, incredulously.

"No, he does not work for Blackwater, NATO, or any other official Government organization."

"Who is he then?"

"He is a banker now."

"An ex-G.I. banker? And he is influential?"

"Very much so. He has a high level position in the World Bank."
Simone reached over and touched his arm.

"How much do we tell him?"

Curtis frowned and put his hand over hers. "The bare minimum.
We have to cover our asses."

"With his contacts, he can help us get to the bottom of this," said
Simone.

"The underlying cause of most evil, Simone, is money and the love
thereof. World Bank and the International Monetary Fund is money.
Until we find out what we are up against, let's keep my friend out of
the loop."

Curtis pulled out his Military BlackBerry, VASP end-to-end security, virtually impossible to hack. He dialed an unlisted number and
waited. Finally, on the ninth ring, a man's voice quietly intoned,

"I was wondering when I might be hearing from you. Bagram was
all over the news. But … I have a feeling this is more than just a cour-
tesy call."

"I am here in the city with a couple of friends. We have a problem.
We need a place to lie low. Figure things out."

"Problem solved. When will I see you?"

"Tonight after dark."

"Good. The doorman is off at ten. I will send my driver."

"No, better not. This is a nasty one."

"Paranoia is a virtue in our business. Have it your way."

The two men said their goodbyes. Curtis appeared calm but his
mind was churning. Who are these people? "A World Banker, first name
Cristian," said Michael. "Are we talking about Cristian Belucci? Executive Vice President of the World Bank? The man who has made the cover
of *Time* magazine his personal stomping ground?" Michael was floored.
"You never mentioned keeping such high profile company."

"You never asked."

"We met once, very briefly. What's he like? We hear the stories, of
course. Playing polo in South Africa; attending a Royal ball in London
with the Queen; running with the bulls in Pamplona."

"More like trotting with the bulls. I have never seen him run."

"You're not serious?" asked Simone.

"I am. A three-inch scar across the inside of his right thigh can attest to it."

"Boys will be boys," replied Simone shaking her head.

"How did he make the leap from the army to the World Bank?" asked Michael.

"He comes from a long line of bankers. His great-grandfather put a large bank together back in the mid eighteen-hundreds in Georgia, and I think his granddaddy was president of a big financial something or other in New York."

"He sponsored one of our digs," said Michael. "I believe he was then the President of Bank of America."

"Cristian Belucci may be a banker friend to you, but to the rest of the world, he is a renowned celebrity. Are you sure, Curtis, they won't be able to trace the link?"

Curtis put his hands in his pockets and walked over to the window. "Impossible. The connections go too deep."

Chapter 24

They waited past midnight before setting out. After twenty minutes they pulled up in front of a modest red-stone building, surrounded on one side by a quaint, somewhat unkempt garden and on the other by a miniature playground. Simone and Michael were both taken aback by the austerity of the façade, having imagined the renowned banker living in one of New York's more fancy buildings. They buzzed and were quickly let in. A heavy wrought iron double door, framed unpretentiously with iron piping, shut behind them with a thump.

"Are you sure we're in the right place?" Michael asked. "Appearances are for fools," grunted Curtis. They walked past a wide stone staircase in the center of the foyer and got into an old rickety lift. Curtis pressed "P" for Penthouse. The elevator groaned, jerked unsteadily when they passed the second, slowed down on the third, bumped its way past the forth, accelerated on the fifth and came to a grudging stop, wobbling as it disgorged its three occupants. Simone breathed a sigh of relief.

As if on cue, the heavy door opened and the gaunt figure of Cristian Belucci appeared. He wore an oversized but well-tailored silk robe that dragged on the floor behind him, granting Cristian a distinctly royal look. He was in his mid to late sixties, with long, white flowing shoulder length hair, parted on the right to disguise a rapidly receding hairline.

"Curtis, my dear, how are you? It has been, what, three, four years now!" said the banker in his high-pitched voice as he came towards him with his large hands outstretched. "You look like Hell. What happened to you?"

"It's a long story."

"I have lots of time." He turned and faced his friends. "I apologize. We haven't seen each other for a while. My name is Cristian Belucci. And who might you be?"

"I am Simone Casolaro. This is Michael Asbury."

"The archaeologist?"

"Actually, arcane historian," Michael corrected him.

"Yes, of course, I remember. We met—"

"At a fundraiser in Washington."

"The Smithsonian."

"Exactly."

Curtis looked into a lit space beyond.

"Oh, of course. How rude of me," said the banker. "Do come in."

Simone was first through the door. She gasped. In absolute contrast to the building's shoddy exterior, Cristian's inner sanctum was like no other space she had ever seen. It was exaggerated opulence, with soaring stained glass windows, marble floor, frescoes dedicated to the glories of Venice in the 16th century and creamy gray stone. Niches with statues of illustrious Renaissance artists flanked the spacious rectangular hallway.

"They were going to tear the place down, so I bought it and turned the top four flats into a penthouse. Let me turn up the lights." Dozens of small, well-placed spotlights suddenly put into focus the true splendor of the place.

"You live here?" asked Simone.

"This is my world. In fact, as Curtis can tell you, I have never felt comfortable amongst the multitude. Here I can be alone," he said in a low foggy voice, looking into the distance.

"But you're no hermit. You are always attending balls, fundraisers and speaking at international conferences," asked Simone.

"Part of an expensive act, Simone. It goes with the territory."

Cristian walked over to the wall cabinet and pressed a button. Noiselessly, a fully stocked bar materialized behind him. He opened a bottle of single malt Scotch whiskey and poured himself a drink. "Would any of you care for a libation? I have quite a selection of excellent vintages."

Simone looked over at Curtis. "I would just like a cup of tea, thank you."

"And you, Michael?"

"I'll have some of that Scotch."

"Curtis, my dear, you know the rules of the house. Help yourself to anything you like. As of now," he turned, "that rule applies to you two as well." He playfully wagged his finger at Simone and Michael.

Curtis got himself a drink and poured one for Michael.

"So," Cristian sat down in an easy chair and crossed his legs. "Why are you here?"

All traces of a smile left Simone's lips. "My brother was killed and I couldn't solve it by myself."

"I am so sorry. When did it happen?" asked Cristian.

"Recently, in Shawnee, Oklahoma."

Simone and Michael went over the story, leaving out the part, as Curtis had insisted, about PROMIS and glossing over Octopus.

"But why him?" asked the banker.

"I wish to God I knew," replied Simone.

"That's the key, though, isn't it? Something Danny did know. Something that made others go to great lengths to make sure it never got out." Cristian uncrossed his legs and stood up. "It's a dead end then?"

"We have my brother's papers."

Curtis looked at Simone. " We don't," he corrected her. " What we have are a couple of words and a number that belong to an anonymous safe-deposit box. If we're lucky, and they fit the combination, we might get to see what's inside. Simone feels Danny hid proof of whatever he was investigating in them."

"And you don't?" Simone asked.

"I am not willing to speculate. We still don't know the whole story."

"The secret must be of great importance to someone. Embarrassment, you know, is a potent lever. Second only to fear."

Which reminds me," Cristian reached into his pocket and pulled out a card. "In an emergency, please call this number. Take this cell, Curtis. It is a special phone, actually unique. It uses digital spread spectrum technology."

"Digital what?" asked Simone.

"Spread spectrum was first used during World War II as a method to prevent torpedoes being jammed en route to their target. These signals are difficult to intercept and demodulate. They are resistant to jamming or interference because the signal is spread over a number of frequencies," explained Curtis. He smiled. "What's important is that the bad guys can't listen in on us."

"Exactly," replied Cristian.

The banker looked at his watch. "Sorry to be a party pooper, but I have work to do. Good night my friends." He showed them to their rooms. "Rest, Curtis, as I used to tell you almost a quarter-century ago, is the best weapon. Sleep well."

***

The unlisted phone kept ringing for what seemed like an eternity. A man was trying to reach an important Washington politician, a decision maker of note, who lived in a house at the end of Twenty-fourth Street North in Arlington, Virginia, towering over the Potomac River while keeping a watchful eye on Washington, D.C. The white mansion was set far back from the road, surrounded by red cedar and heavy oak trees. The important politician was a former Secretary of the Treasury, supporter of many noteworthy causes around the world. "The Secretary has a heart for the poor," his staff liked to say. The joke was that by the 'poor' they meant not the hundreds of millions of starving and malnourished people, but rather the 'poor in spirit,' for theirs is the kingdom: the senators, generals, and prime ministers who coasted to the end of Twenty-fourth Street in Arlington in black limousines and town cars and hulking S.U.V.'s to meet one another and pay homage to the god of the purse strings.

"It is 3:17 A.M.," said Mr. Secretary, as he angrily picked up his private line.

"Mr. Secretary?"

"No, it's Hillary fucking Clinton. I assume it is important. Either that or you are in the wrong time zone."

"Trust me, it is. They have been traced to a building in Lower Manhattan."

"Oh?"

"The man they went to see is Cristian Belucci."

"The World Banker? My, my, it is getting interesting. A famous man who keeps secrets. What's the connection?" He cleared his throat.

"Don't know. Our people are working on it."

"I need it yesterday. Understood?"

"Crystal clear."

"We follow the link. How many people do we have on the ground?"

"Ready to go? Six. Three teams."

"Put two men on him."

"That leaves four men to cover the three of them."

"There is a point to this, I suspect."

There was a pause. "The one who survived Rome is staying at Be-lucci's apartment with the grave digger and the fairy, as you call them."

"Well, well. This may just be our lucky day."

"I wish I could share in your excitement, sir. G.I. Joe is a handful and an unnecessary complication."

"The unexpected works. He will lead us to what we seek. And… bring up everything you can on Belucci. I have a feeling he is a walking vaudeville act."

"What's his role in this?"

"Don't know. It's a sequence of events that concerns me."

"What does that mean, Mr. Secretary?"

"Meaning we need to do the math. There is a pattern. We just need to find it. Pull up everything you can on the dead man and map out his relationships with all the contacts. Have the teams in position as of 0600 hours."

"In Belucci, we might have found our dead journalist's financial backer, sir."

"And good morning."

CHAPTER 25

Though it was midmorning, the skies were still dark, drizzle kept the pavement black and slick, with the promise of heavy rain imminent. Curtis looked around him, hyper alert and attuned to any deviations in the normal group behavior of the crowd. He scanned the street. No tail, for now.

Curtis took a cab up 16th avenue, rode for fifteen blocks, then switched cabs and rode eight blocks in the opposite direction before swiftly losing himself among the day-trippers on the subway. He got out four blocks away from the bank, walking at a steady pace westbound, making a few detours, an expression of bored aimlessness on his face, checking reflections in windows to see if he could identify any suspiciously recurring faces. Nothing. He turned the corner and went up an adjoining street, walking past the bank twice before finally approaching it. The first step was to learn the security status of BS Bank Schaffhausen.

The lobby was a high atrium of mitered glass above hexagonal granite tile. Mounted on the doorframe was a glass square that had the glazed, dark look of an unpowered television screen. Curtis knew it was part of a new-generation audiovisual entry system; embedded in the silicate plane were hundreds of micro lenses that captured fractional light feeds from a radial array of nearly 180 degrees. The result was a sort of compound eye, like that of an insect, all integrated by a computer into a single mobile image.

He stood at the end of the line; the look in his eyes was of someone who took orders and did what others, smarter and better than he, told him to do.

Curtis scanned the open space in front of him without making eye contact with anyone in particular: six tellers, separated from each other by mahogany partitions no more than five centimeters wide. Two work stations were empty, the other four occupied by a heavy set woman with bleached-blond hair and large gold-plated earrings; a young girl, obviously a trainee; a tall, gaunt man with glasses; and a beautiful blond woman with large breasts under a skin tight designer white shirt. Eleven people were waiting in line. Four men and seven women. Three more down the hallway, boredom registered on their faces, leaning against the wall, obviously waiting for their respective appointments.

He studied all of them, isolating each, watching their eyes, their body language for inconsistencies – an awkward, unusual reaction, an abrupt glance in an unexpected direction, the sudden involuntary small motion. Someone who looked too bored, too eager, too attentive for no apparent reason, who looked away as if on cue. After that came the clothes, the shoes, the accessories. Did anything stand out? A body posture that betrayed certain tensions or hidden skills? Get to the objective.

Curtis walked over to the sliding-glass doors that gave access to the safe-deposit boxes. There was a fine-mesh metal screen within the glazing. It looked ornamental, but was, in fact, functional. He pressed a metallic button protruding from an octagonal shape on his left. The door panels slid open with a quiet whooshing sound. The room itself was a rectangular space enclosed by a grounded ferromagnetic mesh; the shielding blocked the transmission of any radio signals.

"This way, sir," said the middle-aged official with close-cropped hair. He pulled out a sheet of Schaffhausen stationary with two blank lines centered in the middle of the page. Curtis wrote out "142857" on the top line and "Tree of Life" on the bottom. He handed the stationery to the bank official, who studied it momentarily. "If you'll wait for me in the green room on your right, I will return shortly with your box, sir." He smiled graciously. Curtis watched the body language and listened for tonal cadences. Was the voice unnaturally pleasant? Unnaturally, tense, soft, hard? Then again, this was a bank, where people kept their money. There was always tension, and the more money, the more faux-pleasant the demeanor.

He walked inside the green room, and the man disappeared through an inner door. It was smallish, three meters by five, paneled, and furnished with stainless steel, austerely decorated with two leather armchairs next to each other and a mahogany table pushed against the wall. The door opened again, revealing the same bank official carrying a metal box. He took out a key and placed it in front of Curtis. "When you are finished, just press the button above the table."

"Thank you."

"Will there be anything else?"

"No, thank you."

With a faint head gesture, the official excused himself. Curtis waited for the door to close. He sat silently in front of the dome-shaped box, listening for furtive movement. Nothing. He checked his watch. Quarter past ten. He picked up a key, inserted it into the lock and turned it to the right. He heard a snap. Simone was right; Danny had hidden the codes in a seven-hundred year old poem. He opened the box and examined its contents.

Curtis took out a sheaf of handwritten papers, notes of some sort. Underneath was a stack of financial statements held together by an oversized bulldog paperclip. He carefully took them out and placed them on the table. The next batch of documents was held together with an elastic band, the kind that little girls used to tie their pigtails. He pulled it off and slowly unrolled the contents. A cursory look told him they were copies of gold certificates. He leafed through them and pulled one out randomly. His eyes strayed to the center of the certificate. Suddenly, a number jumped out at him. 750 MT of gold. He leaned forward and read the entire line. "Was issued as the guarantee of the deposit using such as one party of the Gold Metal as much as ... 750 MT." His face assumed an expression of disbelief. How much is that in dollars, he thought to himself. Cristian would know. He randomly pulled out several other certificates, discovering that the first, in fact, was the smallest amount of all of them.

Some of the other objects Curtis found in the box were three DVDs, photographs of people he had never seen, cablegrams and phone logs secured in file folders, numerous diagrams as well as notebooks filled with Danny Casolaro's small, messy and hurried hand.

Later, I will see it later. He placed the contents of the box in two leather pouches, which he strapped to his body – one to his back and the other to his chest, pulling the sweater over the top and adjusting his leather jacket. He felt for the cold steel of his gun. It was in the inside pocket of his jacket, easily accessible if the need arose. He was hoping to God it wouldn't. He closed the box, checked himself, stood up and pressed the button.

Less than a minute later he heard a click and the door opened. "Is everything to your satisfaction?" The official smiled reassuringly.

"Yes, thank you." Curtis stepped sideways, letting the banker pass.

"Please, sir, after you," said the official, slightly bowing his head.

"Straight down the hallway, sir, to your right, through the sliding door."

Within seconds, Curtis was back in the general area. He quickly scanned the people around him. The same bored, expectant expressions, the same postures. As far as he could tell, nothing that upset the natural order of things. He reached for a heavy, oversized brass handle, pulled it towards him and he was back on the street. Curtis turned right.

Then he saw him. A man in a dark raincoat, his right hand inside his coat's outsized pocket, turned the corner just as he came out of the bank. He walked too casually, yet his eyes were hard, watchful, roaming the street. His neck was short and thickly muscled. Without moving his head, Curtis' eyes darted to his left, then right. There was nobody else, for now. Had the killer spotted him looking? Not possible, too far away. Or did he?

The man was walking faster now, but the acceleration was barely perceptible; this was a superbly trained professional. Curtis slowed down, looking straight ahead as he passed him.

Suddenly, the man grabbed his wrist with a large, beefy hand. Curtis pulled his gun, but the man was good. He smashed the heel of his free hand into the gun, sending the weapon flying. Curtis wrenched his wrist around, dropping to his knees just as the man swung with a big roundhouse, missing Curtis's head by centimeters. With his right hand cocked, Curtis threw a hard blow to the ribcage, just below the armpit. The man yelped, his head snapping back, but did not let go, and rammed his knee into Curtis' cheek below his left eye. The left side of his skull seemed suddenly split in two.

The strength of the blow propelled Curtis backwards; he felt something warm streaking down his chin. There was no time to think.

Any moment now others would come, out of the corner of his eye, he caught a glimpse of something black. A pistol! He angled his body to the right, somehow getting to his feet, then swept his left foot off the ground, his heel smashing into the man's arm, knocking the gun out of his hands, a .38 caliber with a perforated cylinder on its barrel.

His right hand spear-punched the man's larynx with a carefully aimed blow. The man coughed spasmodically and went limp, crashing to the ground, both hands tearing at his collar. He was struggling for breath, rolling on the ground, as the ruined cartilage had choked off his air-flow.

Curtis was badly bruised, but nothing was broken. The fight had taken less than fifteen seconds, enough time to draw a small crowd of stunned onlookers. No cops, though. He saw his gun lying against the curb. That was a dead giveaway that he was no innocent victim, but he had to have it. He staggered over and went to his knees, managed to retrieve it, stood up and looked down the street.

There had to be more killers. Where were they? Whoever they were, these people were professionals. A three-point blockade would be standard procedure: at either end of the block, a unit would have been positioned before the operatives descended on the bank. There was only one way out, and that was to break through. He walked away unsteadily, each step painful, his balance nearly out of control. Don't stop.

Then he saw them and his blood went cold. Two vehicles, a dark blue sedan and a white mini-van converging slowly on Curtis from opposite directions. The flanks were covered; the trap was set. They had spotted him, but neither one made a move. The man beside the driver in the sedan spoke repeatedly into a hand-held radio. The crowd! Too many witnesses. Someone would take note of the license plate, call the police. Then he heard the wailing of sirens and the screeching of tires as a police cruiser turned the corner. He couldn't believe his luck. Safety. Will they make it in time? The question was never answered.

Curtis heard a deafening impact, metal against metal, twisting, breaking, exploding into a thousand pieces. The driver's side of the police cruiser rose off the ground, the monstrous impact of a two-ton truck throwing the men inside like rag dolls against the windshield. From the position of their bodies, Curtis knew both were dead.

Screams and the loud, panicky voices of frightened people filled the air. There would be no reprieve. The blue sedan slowly shifted into first gear, crossing the centerline and stopping less than twenty yards away. Jesus Christ. Now what? Curtis could not let them get near him. With the crowd's attention diverted to the wreck, there was nothing to stop the killers from walking up and putting a bullet into him. The crowds and the noise were their cover, escape made easy in the mass confusion.

Without looking, Curtis was absolutely sure that another team was making its way towards him from the opposite direction, threading their way through the crowd, their hands on the deadly steel under their topcoats. There was no time to worry about his rear. He focused on the men in front of him. The two of them were closing in, one from the left side of the street, the second coming towards him from directly in front, closing in like two prongs of pincer attack. The trap had been engineered with extraordinary precision. Two killers ran interference, doing away with the police officers without a moment's hesitation. Unless he did something, he would be next. And then all would be lost. They would kill him and come after Simone and Michael.

The killer in front of him raised his head a couple of centimeters and looked beyond him. Where was he looking? Someone behind him, beyond his reach. The back-up team was in place. He had to act. Take out the killer on the right. Now! Curtis dove to his left, the automatic extended, fired, hitting the man in the chest, the impact of the bullet lifting him off his feet. He collapsed with a thud, as if a rug was pulled from underneath him. One down. Two shots whined over Curtis's right shoulder, lodging themselves in a decorative wooden panel that adorned a storefront.

Curtis rolled. Two more bullets shrieked and ricocheted off the sidewalk in front of him, sending smoke and tiny particles into the air. Curtis rolled over, acquired the target, his left hand steadying his right wrist and fired twice methodically. His aim was accurate, and the man ceased to be a factor.

Two down, two more to go. Where were they? The empty sedan. Get to it. Curtis got to his feet and raced towards the vehicle. One of the killers dropped to his knee, held his gun firmly, steadily and unhurriedly aimed and fired repeatedly, but it was a long shot at a moving target. The bullets snapped through the air in front and to the side of him, breaking one of the headlights and hitting the bumper of the sedan.

Without turning his body, Curtis fired behind him, hoping against hope the bullets would find their mark. They didn't. But he was able to buy precious seconds as the two killers ducked. He struggled to his feet, yanked the passenger door handle and in one swift motion projected himself into the interior of the vehicle: the keys were in the ignition. Bless the bastards, they had made a mistake, thinking they were in control, never in doubt of the outcome. His fingers working furiously, he switched on the ignition, put it in reverse and gunned the motor. The sedan leapt backwards, gyrating wildly. As he jerked the wheel into a 180 degree slide and rammed the gear shift into forward, horrified faces flashed by out of the corner of his eye. That's right folks, they really are out to get you.

Chapter 26

Edward McCloy put his big feet up on the desk, picked up the newspaper, flipped to the sports section of the *Times* and snapped it open. A late morning downpour had replaced the earlier drizzle. He noted pensively that heavy rains always made him feel melancholic. The wetness and dreariness outside reflected the dreariness of his soul, in a perversely comforting way. His eyes shifted to the brass plate proudly announcing his impressive credentials – Senior Representative. Yes, he, Edward McCloy, was the senior representative of the world's most powerful banking cartel. On paper, he was the senior decision maker for the money elite. In reality, he sadly noted, he was a bum boy for powerful people who used him as a once-removed deniable cut-out to hide their crimes and financial transgressions. The ghost of his father appeared in his mind's eye …

"Had it not been for my brother, you goddamned fool, you would be cleaning manure off the streets," his father roared in resentment.

"Dad, I was never good at finance."

"What the hell did you study at that fairy college your mother sent you to?"

"History of Art and Broadcasting."

"And what exactly were you planning to do with that?"

"I love basketball, dad."

"You are a five-foot eight klutz. What position were you planning to play, Tinker Bell?"

"I wanted to be a broadcaster."

"In a town with no basketball team? And what kind of a living is that?"

"Bryant Gumble did it."

"Who the hell is that?"

"The boy from my dorm. He is an NBA broadcaster."

"The nigger? He's got brains upstairs, son. You got shit, enough to start your own goddamned manure business."

His mother's voice chimed in.

"Jack, you are being too hard on him. You are putting too much pressure on him."

"Jesus Christ. Broadcasting and art, my big hairy ass."

"Dad, there are a lot of very respectable people who are patrons of the arts."

"They all come from business backgrounds, you fool. They are patrons of the arts so they can wrap their dirty money in a blanket of respectability."

"What about Uncle John?"

"What about him?" his dad roared.

"He's President of the Ford Foundation. They are heavily involved in the arts. He was respectable."

"Before your uncle got to run Ford, he was a Yale graduate and member of Skull & Bones, not to mention his role on the Warren Commission."

"He minored in Arts."

"He was the clean-up guy on the Kennedy assassination. Remember the three tramps on the Grassy Knoll?"

"Yes," said the son tentatively.

"Within a day of Kennedy being taken out, the three tramps were dead and buried. Your uncle still has the shovel. That was his ticket to respectability. The keeper of the secrets. And you will keep the secrets, too. Or you will be cut loose like a … like a goddamned bait mackerel. Do you understand!"

There was a long pause while his father caught his breath.

"Tomorrow, you will be starting your new job as your uncle's assistant at Chase Manhattan Bank. Don't fuck it up. Keep your mouth shut and do what he tells you, kiss the right ass and you'll go places. You hear me, boy?"

"Yes, Dad."

***

This was why Edward McCloy, senior representative of the world's most powerful banking cartel, felt so dreary on this particularly cold morning. He had spent the past twenty years dutifully keeping his mouth shut and kissing the right asses, mostly against his better judgement. He checked his watch. Ten to twelve. Although his dream career in broadcast journalism went up in smoke, he never missed his dorm mate's show, especially now that he had become one of the most popular television broadcasters in America. McCloy turned the television on to the 24-hour sports channel.

The telephone rang, causing McCloy to shudder momentarily. "Yes?"

"You'd better turn on the television, Ed."

"It is on."

"I don't mean the sports channel."

"Who is this?"

"It's your fairy godmother. Who the hell do you think it is?"

"Henry?"

"I assume we can't be overheard."

"Just a second. What channel?"

"It doesn't matter. Anything but sports. It's on all the news channels."

"What is?" McCloy tuned in to CNN and saw the wreckage in front of the bank. Bloodstained pavement.

"Shit. What happened?" asked McCloy.

"That's what we are trying to piece together."

"Are they ours?"

"That's the funny thing. They are not."

"Then, who the hell are they?"

"Someone reversed the trap on us and inserted their own team."

"What do you want me to do?"

"I want you to talk to your people at Schaffhausen and get a detailed description of whoever was inside. Then meet us at the usual place. Oh, and Ed—"

"Yes?"

"Soonish, Ed." The line went dead.

* * *

By three o'clock, the Octopus cabal sat facing each other around a U-shaped mahogany conference table. The greetings were perfunctory and rather distracted; the handshakes cold, limp and hardly courteous, the recriminations brief; there was no point in going over past errors. It wouldn't do them any good.

"Do we have a photo?"

"Yep, surveillance cameras all around the bank. Name is Fitzgerald. Curtis Fitzgerald. U.S. Army Ranger. Special Forces," said Henry Stilton.

"He flew in from Rome first class," he added somberly.

"That's an eight-thousand dollar ticket. Where did he get the money?" Taylor wondered.

"Good point. He may have worked like hell for his country, but financially, his country has hardly reciprocated in kind." Lovett put in his two-cent's worth.

"Ed, did you get the code he used to open the account?"

"Yes, the bank official thought it was a rather amusing choice."

"What did he tell you?" asked Harriman.

"Name: Tree of Life; Number: 142857."

"What the hell does that mean?"

The former Secretary touched his arm, a pipe in one hand, a lighter in the other. "Rob, get our cyber geeks on this. See if they can spin the disks and decipher the password."

"Whoever orchestrated the trap this morning knew ahead of time what pieces of the puzzle would be in place and when. There is someone out there, somehow, watching and listening and anticipating everything we do and say," said Taylor pensively.

"Which means we are leaking like a sieve." Stilton nodded his head grimly.

"Who could it be?" added Taylor.

They were all briefly silent; then David Alexander Harriman III spoke, his voice cold. "Whoever it is has a direct line into our camp. Whoever pulled it off this morning is waiting and counting on our reaction. Trying to force our hand. It's a sequence of events that concerns us. A pattern. The dead journalist was their kill."

"And Schaffhausen was their fuck up," added John Reid.

"Suddenly, someone seamlessly inserts themselves into our sequence; yet the pattern remains unchanged. There is a shoot-out, except that the prey turned into a predator," continued Harriman.

Stilton gripped the armchair, his wandering eyes intense, probing. "There is nothing to connect, no line of progression, no Fenobacci sequence."

"That would be Fibonacci sequence," Taylor corrected him.

"Shit, damn Italians. You can never get their names straight." Stilton silently cursed both Taylor and Fibonacci.

Suddenly, he slammed his fist against the armchair rest. "Son of a bitch!"

"Christ," Lovett bellowed, so stridently that McCloy braced himself in his chair, "what we have here is a major geopolitical power shift happening in our own back yard. Who the hell is out there on our tail?"

"A lack of pattern doesn't exclude the pattern itself, it just means we can't see it, yet," added Harriman. "What's more, it is someone we most likely are very familiar with, someone who could be walking around with a sign on his chest and we wouldn't see it."

"Is Fitzgerald part of it?" asked Lovett.

"What about the others?" added McCloy.

"Forget the two sidekicks. They are collateral. From our reports, it's an emotional issue," added Stilton.

"We must get to them and kill them," said Lovett.

"Not on a whim," broke in Harriman.

"Are you saying—"

"I am saying, they are twenty-four carat info. We shoot them to the moon—"

"And pick their brains, before we kill them," added Stilton, slamming his fist down.

"I believe the medical terminology is: triggered mental recall under states of external control," said Taylor.

Stilton got slowly, menacingly to his feet. "I am sick of you correcting me, Taylor."

Taylor reclined in his chair, uncrossed and crossed his legs. "Accept my apologies, Henry," he said in a pleasant voice.

Stilton paused. "Still, we are back to the dead journalist," he said grimly.

"So many questions. So little time to answer them all," added Harriman.

Chapter 27

A burgundy-colored limousine was parked in front of a pristine high-rise office building in lower Manhattan. The uniformed driver glanced at the dashboard clock and adjusted his glasses. It was three minutes past five. He reached into his pocket for a cigarette, turned on the radio to the only station he was allowed to listen to, 97.5 FM – Marketwatch. He shifted his gaze to the entrance. Any moment the man he was waiting for would come out and walk rapidly to the car. The voice of the radio announcer was high-pitched and jocular.

"This could be big and it could hurt them real badly. There was nothing about them for days when the crash started three weeks ago. Silence. That told me a lot. It told me that City was in heavy play behind the scenes and under the carpet. City is the one that can pull the plug. You can bet that the people filing this lawsuit have some damn good evidence. The game has been rigged for quite a while now. Those who win in a rigged game get stupid. I wish I had invented this line because it is a darn good one."

"Jonathan," chimed in a second voice, *"can you explain to us today's developments?"*

"What did we see today? Exactly what I anticipated. The global markets are melting down, and it won't be long before the tsunami travels all the way around the world and lands back here again. There is so much history if one studies the Great Depression. Not many of us are left who have seen it first hand, up close and personal. Well, consider yourselves lucky or unlucky because we are about to see it again, except it is going to hit us faster and harder. Ain't progress grand?"

The mammoth glass doors opened and a tall man walked hurriedly towards the car. He was about seventy, wide shouldered, his bearing still erect, his ashen hair carefully coiffed and parted on one side, accentuating his high cheekbones and strong features. The man nodded absently when the driver opened the rear door for him. "Take me home."

"Yes, Mr. Reid." The driver put the car into drive and merged into the afternoon rush hour traffic. The radio insistently spread the bad news.

> "A very short clock is totally on the side of Wells Fargo. The value of Wachovia evaporates every day as depositors close accounts in panic. Citygroup is hoping to avert its death by getting its hands on those deposits. When minutes matter, both sides have agreed to suspend litigation until Wednesday, litigation which had City lawyers banging at a Connecticut judge's front door on a weekend."
>
> "Now let me see, Mark: Wells Fargo is a California company, Citygroup is New York and Wachovia is in North Carolina. Does that sound like a Supreme Court case to you?"
>
> "Jonathan, if this litigates, both Wachovia and Citygroup are doomed. Wachovia becomes worthless and Citygroup implodes."

Reid frowned, momentarily lost in thought, and placed his elbow on the windowsill, resting his chin on his thumb. He reached over to a small box located between the two rear seats, flipped open one of the compartments and pressed a button. Silently, a glass partition went up separating him from the radio of impending doom. Dusk was enveloping the city, absorbing it into the night. Headlights were turned on. Dim light came through the windshield, a reflecting spill, partially illuminating the occupant now and then, bathing him with flashing colors of the on-rushing traffic.

John Reid pulled out his cell phone and pressed the redial button.

"Yes?" The man on the other end of the line spoke softly and quietly.

"I need to see you."

There was a momentary pause. "Under the circumstances, it might not be a good idea."

"I must see you," insisted J.R.

"Things are getting out of hand."

"That's why I must see you."

"When I agreed to work for you, I made a very simple request. Do you remember?"

Silence. "Yes, I remember."

"I agreed to work for you only if I was allowed to dictate the terms of engagement as I saw fit. This is not a good time."

"Now, you listen to me." J.R.'s voice was harsh, full of desperation. "I have paid you a lot of money over the years. I have made you a rich man, so you owe me. You owe me this."

"I don't owe you anything. We both got rich because I am very good at what I do. Good, and discreet. Goodnight, and good luck." The line went dead.

Good night, and good luck. Edward R. Morrow's signature sign-off rang like an ironic bell in his ear. J.R. slammed the hand-rest repeatedly with his fist, unwittingly activating the two-way intercom system. The radio broadcast re-invaded his secluded world.

> *"The shareholders are dumping stock like a flaming bobcat on meth. I shudder to contemplate what might be left of City by the end of the year. Like I said, this will remove all traces of hope."*
>
> *"Then, you are saying, Mark, a real, global melt down?"*
>
> *"Citygroup's demise may not happen tomorrow but here's a clue. I tried to access this story at the Reuters news site one minute after it was published at 4:56 P.M. Eastern Daylight Time. The story was getting so much traffic that it took me two minutes to get a download and another two minutes to save it. The sell orders, shorts and puts must be flying off the screens at breath-taking numbers. A word of warning for the uninitiated. This is major shark territory. Make money on the way up; make money on the way down. The rest, stay the heck out, for your own good."*

"Turn that off," barked J.R., his eyes locked on the driver's eyes in the rear view mirror. He flicked the intercom switch to off and redialed the previous number.

"I want you to listen to me carefully." The voice was menacing and gruff. "Do I have to remind you that I have the entire file? The Agency was extremely cooperative, far more than you are being right now. If I go down, you will go down with me. Get the codes and we get rid of the problem. Kill Caroni and wipe the slate clean. Nobody can trace it back to us. Do you understand?"

"All right," began the quiet voice on the line. "Where?" He was given the address.

"I know we can turn—"

"This will be our last communication."

CHAPTER 28

Staring at Curtis, Simone was appalled, "Christ, man, look at you. We were sure you were dead. It's all over the news."

"You should see the other guys. They're on a slab, by now" he replied.

"We did see the other guys. The body bags, anyway. Should we find a doctor?"

Curtis looked up. "No, don't bother. Just get me some ice."

"Curtis, did you …?" Simone stared at him, eyes expectant.

"Yes, I did." He extracted the automatic under his belt and placed it on the coffee table. Then he unzipped the leather jacket and gingerly pulled off his sweater, detached the two black leather pouches, and handed them to Simone.

Her heart quickened and her mouth felt dry. She looked at Michael. For a moment, she felt Danny's presence as she gripped the two pouches with both hands, holding them briefly to her chest.

She removed the contents and placed them on the table. Somewhere in that myriad pages was a name that linked a man or a woman to Danny's murder. These were the documents that outlined every line of his painstaking, five-year investigation.

Cristian picked up the disks. "I'll print these out." He disappeared into his study.

"It's here. It has to be here," said Simone.

Curtis leafed through the pages of Danny's leather-bound notebook, then handed it to Simone. She sat in the chair by the window, holding it and inhaling its nostalgic odor before turning the pages slowly and lovingly.

It took Cristian almost two hours to transfer the contents of the three DVDs onto paper. By four o'clock they were back in his study to examine the documents and photographs, which were separated and classified.

They divided the material into three stacks. Each stack outlined the lines of investigation: Octopus, PROMIS and Gold. The approach they used was standard, both in the world of academia as well as classi-fied Top Secret information. They read everything rapidly, concentrat-ing on the totality and not on the specifics, trying to get a grip on the general idea and reasoning. There was silence except for the turning of the pages and an occasional comment.

"There is a copy of a 750 Metric Tons gold certificate in the name of Muammar Gaddafi," said Simone.

"How much money would that be?" Asked Curtis.

Cristian lit a cigarette and picked up a calculator. "There are thirty two thousand one hundred and fifty ounces in a metric ton of gold." They all stared at the banker. "At one thousand dollars per ounce," Cristian paused as he checked his figures. "That's a tad under twen-ty-four billion dollars."

Simone's jaw dropped. Michael and Curtis exchanged glances. "How would someone get their hands on so much money?" asked Michael.

"This is not a real person. Every certificate comes with a number of additional documents, all of which need to coincide at the time of sale. Just one missing page would void all the other papers." He paused. "This is designed to protect the identity of the actual holder. The name on the certificate is just a smoke screen. Remember, this is black gold."

"You mean petroleum?" asked Simone.

"No. I mean, illegal, stolen gold. Legend has it, the gold belonged to Egyptian pharaohs. Others say it is rooted in the Fourth Crusade. There is also a modern version placing it somewhere around World War Two." The banker paused. "I don't know which version to believe."

"So, if someone wanted to redeem this certificate for cash—" Mi-chael started to ask.

"It would have to be real gold. Those are the rules."

"Where would someone get 750 Metric Tons of gold?" Curtis asked.

Simone flipped back through Danny's notebook. "Here, 750 MT circled and heavily underlined, followed by the word SOURCE with an oversized question mark. These initials ... CTP. I saw them ... where? Wait a minute. There was something in Danny's notebook on Citybank and something else. What was it?"

She scanned it, the sight of her brother's messy handwriting bring-ing tears to her face. "I ... I," she stammered. Then she saw it. "City/

Reid–CTP/gov.," followed by another oversized exclamation mark. The word combination was circled several times with specific emphasis placed on the mysterious initials.

She looked at Cristian. "Do you have any idea what Danny might be refer—?"

She stopped, reading the look in his eyes. It was clear Cristian knew. He brought his fingers to his face and wiped the moisture that had formed on his forehead, and then shifted his eyes, taking in the three of them, separately. He paused, leaned over, gripping the edge of the table. And then he spoke, slowly and deliberately.

"You are squaring off against a labyrinthine evil so entrenched, you can't conceive what you are fighting." Cristian got up and placed himself in the darkness of a far window. "It's of course about money. So much money, in fact, it will challenge whatever reality you thought you knew about the world of banking, finance and economics." He blew two streams of grey smoke through his nostrils and fixed Simone with hard, bright eyes. "This world is said not to exist in reality. But it does. The shadow world in which CTP lives and manufactures money out of thin air is the dirty little secret of the western economy." He sat down again and faced them.

"What is CTP?" Simone asked.

"It stands for collateral trading program, a highly speculative off-the-books government-run operation.

Every agency of the Unites States government is in on it."

"Christ," Curtis grunted. "Why doesn't it surprise me?"

"You mean the CIA and the FBI?" Simone asked.

"That would only be the tip of the iceberg. Every alphabet soup agency is in on the action, generating spectacular profits for very little risk, and those who are exclusively invited to participate as funders accumulate capital at a shockingly rapid rate. It is a form of money making that is effectively unchallenged by any form of oversight or accountability." Cristian replied.

"Is it legal? I mean, are they—?" she asked.

Cristian shook his head. "Inside trading by the people who control the markets? No, it is most definitely and most highly illegal."

"Are you saying that banks are in collusion with our government in running these programs?"

"And very wealthy and very private individual investors. Banks and central banks that operate the CTP run two sets of books – one set for public scrutiny and another set for private viewing only."

"Do you have any idea who created the program?" asked Michael.

"I don't know. Actually, I don't want to know. I sleep better this way," Cristian said. "Greed only looks good on children at Christmas," he added whimsically.

"What are they doing with the money?" asked Michael.

"Some is being used to rescue many of the world's major banks that face insolvency crises following reckless lending policies and the now infamous subprime debacle. I'll let you in on a little secret. Banks like City, HSBC, Chase Manhattan, Bank of New York, Wachovia, and Goldman Sachs are bankrupt in all but name and stand teetering on the very brink of financial disintegration."

"And the other part?"

"The rest of the money is earmarked for use in sanctioned operations."

"You mean legal operations?" asked Michael. "That would be one way to describe it."

"How much money are we talking about?" he asked.

Cristian shook his head. "The pool of funds created and now held in dormant and orphaned accounts runs to trillions of dollars; enough to pay off the U.S. national debt and every other debt on the planet."

Simone thought she did not hear him right. "How much?"

"No one really knows the exact amount. But it is safe to say we are talking about mid to high trillions of dollars."

"Can such amounts of money exist?" asked Simone.

"Mostly in cyberspace, Simone. You could never physically transfer it anywhere. But then again, you don't really have to, as you can move any amount of cash in a hundreth of a second with a stroke of a key."

"Look at this," Simone said, holding up a heavily underlined document. "This is a 2003 transaction certificate involved in buying the Empire State Building."

Cristian looked up. "March 2003, the Empire State Building was sold by Donald Trump and the heirs of a mysterious Japanese billionaire Hideki Yokoi for sixty million dollars."

Simone carefully removed a paper clip from a batch of documents and turned the page.

"The transaction was negotiated through a middleman." She scanned the page with her eyes. "John Reid."

"Danny has obviously established a City-CTP connection," said Simone. "Do you have any idea where he might have been going with it?" She looked over at several large stacks neatly piled up on one side of the table.

"I don't know. It is a very opaque system, run top down from different countries by different participants who answer to the Board of Directors. The visible head of this Board is John Reid, Citybank CEO, although I doubt he's really in control. More likely he's a figurehead. I wish I could be more helpful," Cristian said, shaking his head.

"Cristian, what are these rows of numbers?" She passed him the page. The banker sat back in his chair, examining the document for several minutes. When he sat back up, there was a gleam in his eye.

"I think, Simone, your brother found proof that CTP is real." The rows of numbers moved from hundred million dollars to a billion dollars and finally to a trillion. "This is one document that whoever runs the operation would love to get back," Cristian replied. "Each operation comes with a code. The code used in Empire State purchase is the same as the code on the CTP transaction sheet. Reid received a time and a sequence confirmation which activated the transaction through CTP."

"And how does Citybank fit into this?" interjected Michael.

"City is the principle vehicle for this operation in the United States. Thirty odd accounts, in almost one solid block at Citygroup." Cristian drank, swallowing more than he intended to, and stifled a watery cough. "So, Danny found a link between Citybank and secret off the books moneymaking government operation," said Curtis, slowly raising himself from the chair.

"What we don't know is how far he got in his investigation before he was killed," added Cristian.

"Still, we know a lot more than we did twenty-four hours ago," Curtis said.

"It's all over the news that City is in financial dire straits because of their lending practices over the past decade," added Michael.

"The real culprits are Wall Street fraudsters responsible for building up a quadrillion-dollar financial bubble of worthless derivatives. Until the early 1970s, the system worked, backed up by a gold standard. Once the gold standard was removed, over the next few decades the Street became the ultimate casino, people gaming the system and creating the illusion of wealth, with electronic money. This speculative floating exchange system bankrupted the world," Cristian explained.

"And that caused today's financial bubble?" asked Curtis.

"The banks built up a huge derivatives bubble in the 1990s. In order to keep the bubble going, the banks constantly needed more money fed into the system. One of the best sources was mortgages, which were used to spawn mortgage-backed securities. The more mortgage money that came in, the larger the profits. Like a junkie in need of another high, the banks began to relax loan standards, and in the end were selling homes to people who could not afford to buy them. Eventually the subprime loans collapsed, bringing down the entire economy in a domino-like effect." Cristian paused. " Without quick injection of capital, the bank would implode, wiping out what little is left of the U.S. and probably the world economy in the process."

"What's the common denominator in all of this?" asked Curtis.

"The man who was there … City's Chief Executive Officer, John Reid," replied Cristian, his eyes steady on his old friend. "Is that why you prefer not to get the FBI involved?"

"I want it to be foolproof before we go external," Curtis replied.

"How do you think Reid is involved?" asked Simone.

Curtis sighed. "I don't know. Reid may be a controller or he might be one of the many of the up-line, answering to someone else, who in turn has his own up-line. All connected by an invisible thread … and all shrouded under a black drape."

"We could get to them," Curtis said, his eyes riveted on Cristian. "What about Reid?"

"It's a start," said Curtis. "He is part of a network. Once we learn who they are, we apply pressure. A deceased journalist has amassed damning evidence that can blow the head off Octopus – names, crimes, gold certificates, phone logs, secret bank accounts, you name it. He had it. Now, we have it."

"They saw us get it."

"We send the message out that this material is for sale. We are in it for the money and are willing to sell it to the highest bidder."

"One asshole at a time," said Cristian.

CHAPTER 29

"Find Caroni and break him," said John Reid, precarious Capo Supremo of Citybank, sitting in his opulent living room overlooking the Hudson River. "Get the codes and we put this whole mess behind us."

"Behind you," a tall, well-built and elegantly dressed man sporting a healthy tan and a pair of alligator boots corrected him in French accented English.

"All right, yes, behind me. Do you have any idea how much money we are talking about? I will reward you. You will be wealthy beyond your wildest dreams."

"I was wealthy before I was born, John. And, believe me, my wildest dreams have long since been realized." He looked at his gold Calatrava special edition Patek Philippe watch. Then the man added, "I assume there is a point to this meeting."

John Reid's features contorted, his eyes glazed, frenzied, "Fuck you! Don't you ever talk to me like you do to your two-bit flunkies!"

"You broke our arrangement and went back on your word."

"This is life and death, Pierre! Or do you not agree?"

Pierre made the deferential gesture of tactful silence. "Why do you think I have come to you?"

"Why have you? I keep asking myself that."

"You have been trained in enhanced interrogation techniques. You know this shit inside out. For Christ's sake, how hard can it be?" He shouted. "You string him up, prod him with names and numbers and access codes, bits and pieces of information … just enough to get a sketch of where he hid it. Then, our computer geeks—"

"You don't get it, do you, John," asked Pierre. "It doesn't work like that. Just so you and I understand each other, prolonged stress from harsh interrogation could impair the memory of a person."

"Fuck him! I don't think you and I understand each other." Reid roared. "I don't get the bank account number and recover the money, I am a dead man. I might be one now, but believe me, I will be damned if I go down alone. Is that clear enough for you?" He pointed his big, fat index finger at the Frenchman.

The Frenchman shrugged his shoulders. "That is not my concern. But this is."

John Reid screwed up his face. "Now you listen to me, Pierre. I have been around for too long and have seen a few things in my lifetime. I was shooting yellow squints in Korea long before your daddy had his first hard-on for your mama."

"I am not an employment agency, John. I don't need to see your resumé. I am an assassin for hire. An assassin with a doctorate degree in economics from the Sorbonne and a minor in philosophy from the University of Lausanne. I believe in the genius of the marketplace and the importance of security. I kill people, yes, but I don't have a death wish and I am not a lunatic."

"Then put them together, Pierre. Put the marketplace and security into one operation. They do the overt, we will do the covert. You and me. Just the two of us."

"A side arrangement, as it were? Without the involvement of the others?"

"Let's cut the crap. Not as it were, like it is," interjected Reid, moving towards the assassin.

Pierre raised his eyebrows.

Reid went on. "We can do it. We must do it. If we don't recover the codes and get the money back, the entire world economy will implode."

"The dark monsters, historical and psychological, don't care about tenderness, they are not subtle or human enough to target what we cherish."

"I am talking about human life! Millions of people will lose everything."

"Don't wrap yourself in the flag of civility, John. Since when do you give a shit about people? What does your friend David Rockefeller call them? The great unwashed, does he not? In any case, hundreds of millions do starve, and who is to say it is such a bad thing? Ghosts don't always get to choose their company." He paused. "Bringing Caroni back in stages might work. Give me a couple of days to think about it."

"Twenty four hours, Pierre. That's all I can give you. One day."

CHAPTER 30

Louise Arbour pushed away the two-hundred and fifty page United Nations Shimada interrogation report and leaned her elbows on a thick, mahogany table, covering her face with her hands. The room floated in darkness. Light from a crescent moon framed her head like a crooked halo. Transparent clouds were scattered about the night sky but did not touch the moon. She lit a cigarette, and inhaled deeply.

"Ms. Arbour, you can't smoke in this building." Her law clerk smiled awkwardly.

"Why not?" Louise said.

"I … I don't know? Stammered the law clerk.

"Sylvia, do you always follow such stupid rules?"

"I don't smoke, ma'am."

"Perhaps, you should consider taking it up. It's good for your complexion and for your common sense."

Slyvia snorted doubtfully.

Louise opened the window. The Roman damp hit her like a clumsy punch, and turned her self-control to impatience.

She picked up the phone and dialed an extension.

"Oui Madame?"

"Quel est le rapport de situation sur notre homme?"

The guard looked at a plasma screen in front of him. "He is sitting up in bed."

"It is ten past five in the morning! What is he doing?"

"Looks like he is meditating."

"How many men are covering him?"

"A dozen, Ms. Arbour."

"I want to speak to Shimada tomorrow. Bonne nuit, monsieur."

"Oui Madame."

CHAPTER 31

In the early hours of a Tuesday morning, John Reid's phone rang.

"Yes?"

"Good day, Mr. Reid."

"What?"

"I merely said 'good day'. There's a crisis that requires your immediate attention."

"Taylor?"

"No."

"Then, who the hell are you?" he yelled into the receiver.

"Someone who has something that you might want."

"Something what? What are you talking about?"

"Octopus, Mr. Chief Executive Officer."

"Jesus H. Christ! " answered Reid in a suddenly hushed voice.

Roger One, thought Curtis to himself. For now he had a name, a new name, a someone called Taylor.

"Well, Mr. Executive, I'm not going to waste your time. Dead journalist. Shawnee, Oklahoma. Dates, places of dead drops, CTP, insider trading, secret bank accounts, the names of the recipients routed through the government people …. And more, a lot more."

There was a long pause on the other end of the line.

"Let me guess," said the banker, "which one of the yahoos you might be. You are not a girl, so that leaves three others. I know Cristian Belucci's voice, and your's is too controlled and too professional to be the grave robber, so, by process of elimination, you must be Mr. Fitzgerald."

Curtis lowered himself into the armchair, his pulse racing. "As I said, a former and now deceased journalist had amassed damning evidence that can blow the head off Octopus. He had it. Now, we have it."

"Why should I believe you" John Reid asked.

"We found the code to open a secret account and extracted the information from an anonymous safe-deposit box. Information from a five year-old investigation."

"How long do you suppose you will be able to keep it before we get it back?"

"Get it back? Are you suggesting it is yours, Mr. Reid?"

"Listen to me carefully. Whatever you have, we want it back."

"We! Oh, no, Mr. CEO, Sir. Not we, they. They want it and they are willing to pay quite a substantial reward for the privilege of blackmailing you."

"They?" asked John Reid.

"They, Mr. Reid."

"Who are they?"

"Let's just say they are a powerful financial conglomerate. A corporation with unlimited resources." Reid bit.

"Who the fuck are 'they'?" he insisted.

"I told you, a conglomerate ... interested in a financial arrangement."

Curtis was back in control and Reid was ready to listen. "Maybe 'they' are in and out of government employment, people, agents, former agents, and mafia, criminals whose skills are highly valuable and highly remunerable when they work for the wrong side. People working independently, unknown to each other, but nevertheless, coordinated and deployed through a set of controllers who, in turn, are controlled top down by their up-line." Use their own terminology to keep him off kilter. "They were wronged once, a long time ago, and now they want to be paid back in spades."

Reid controlled his astonishment. "What does it have to do with me?"

"Very little, except that you just happen to be a part of the culprit organization and one of its weaker links."

"Do you have any idea who you are dealing with?"

"Yes, we believe we do."

"You are insane and a dead man."

"Idle threats don't scare us. And we are insane enough to expose Octopus and trillions of dollars in illegal funds with proceeds laundered through City's accounts. Imagine what that would do for your reputation? How long will Octopus be able to afford to keep you around after that?"

"This is madness. You come out of nowhere and try to bully the Chief Executive Officer of the world's second largest financial institution."

"Who moonlights in his spare time for a powerful cabal of criminals." He paused, and then was back at it again, this time more compromising and understanding. "Please, Mr. Reid. We are just an intermediary trying to earn a living."

"Well, I got news for you. Someone else is horning in on your territory."

"And they would be?"

"That little clusterfuck at BS Bank Schaffhausen? The attack on you wasn't our operation. And if you are suggesting you have another buyer, then someone new has just joined the bidding. Three is a crowd and you are playing a game you can't win," replied the banker.

Curtis was stunned. Was he lying? Not likely. Reid's voice was firm and devoid of emotion. No, he meant it. Schaffhausen indeed wasn't Octopus' operation. Then whose was it? This was a defining moment. Curtis could feel the truth nudging him from somewhere beyond his conciousness. So many threads.

"I think this can be worked out amicably," said Curtis.

"Meaning?"

"We can tie this valuable information into a number of creatively arrived at and mutually beneficial solutions."

"How?"

"Cooperation, mutually beneficial cooperation. You are after certain things, and we might be able to help you in acquiring them, as long as we can rely on you for other things that we are in need of. Remember, Mr. Reid, this is about economic advantages based on privileged information. And you, Sir, are in an ideal position to have access to this information."

"Go on."

"Should the aggrieved party get their hands on what we have compiled, you know the information I am referring to – secret bank accounts, CTP, the names of the recipients, God only knows what they might do with it. Of course, certain damaging bits of information, vital records, if you wish, concerning you, might simply disappear." His voice trailed off.

"An incomplete dossier?"

"As far as our client is concerned, this information might not have been there in the first place. Who is to say? And to tell?"

There was a very long pause. Then, Reid said, slowly, deliberately and grimly, "I might be interested in your offer."

A frightened man ready to change sides. Be careful. Take the eagerness from your voice. Sound detached. You are supposed to be an emissary. "I commend you on your choice. I am in a position to convey your decision to my up-line, who in turn will relay it to others who will reach the appropriate conclusions." Again, Curtis paused, waiting for Reid to make the first move.

"Are you still there?"

"Yes, of course. Perhaps, as a sign of goodwill, you are prepared to volunteer information we might find useful."

Reid was being painted into a corner. He knew it, but under the circumstances he could do little about it. He needed Danny Casolaro's files.

"Perhaps I can help," Curtis volunteered. This was the defining moment. "Octopus ... how many of the others do you know personally?"

Reid said nothing.

No two bluffs are the same, except for the complicity between the deceiver and the deceived.

"What about Taylor?"

"He is new money. A whiz kid."

"What else can you tell me about him?"

"What do you want to know?"

"I want to hear what you think, what you know about him. To prove to us how deeply you have penetrated the organization."

"He is Vice-Chairman of Goldman Sachs."

Curtis had to stifle a rebel yell and the impulse to leap into a victory dance. He took a deep breath, let it out slowly.

"And the others?"

"Board of Directors? Alpha dogs, the former heads of every government agency in the country; FBI, CIA, NSA, ONI, DIA, Pentagon.

It's your classic case of military-industrial complex, which really means military-industrial collusion, when you remove all the chicken feathers."

"Who in particular?" asked Curtis.

"There are several levels. The lower rungs are mid-level government bureaucrats, then the up-line are top military planners and their controllers, then it's the Intelligence Advisory Board."

"The Board? So, what are they? A private company working for the government?" Curtis said.

"They are a front," replied John Reid.

"For the government?" asked Curtis.

"Hardly."

"For whom?"

"For some very powerful people. Most have a lot of local clout. That's how we wanted it."

"Why?" Curtis didn't understand.

"Because it's convenient." Reid paused. "And because most don't know the real story."

Which story? What secret is worthy of such a conspiracy? Curtis wondered silently, then said emphatically, "We know that and you know that," the intonation covering up for his astonishment at what he was hearing. "But others may not feel the same way. Especially, if they ever learn the truth."

"It wouldn't have been an issue had Caroni not stumbled across the bank accounts." His voice sounded snappish and accusing.

Another name. Curtis stared. His jaw had dropped and he knew that he looked ridiculous. Luckily, this wasn't a video conference. He knew instinctively that whoever it was, this Caroni was important. Again, Curtis did everything to hold himself together. "Who is he? How close are you to learning where he … ?" Curtis paused, a quantified pause of a man in the know, who didn't want such valuable information divulged over the telephone line. The rest was left unsaid.

"Closer, not close. Unless we get back what he took—" Reid's voice petered out.

Who was Caroni, and what did he take? The further he walked, the higher went the wire. He could almost hear Niagara Falls roaring under his feet, and feet the wind threatening to blow him into the void.

CHAPTER 32

What did he say?" asked Cristian.

"Let's put it this way," replied Curtis, squinting, his eyes adjusting to the brightness of the room. "What does it mean when the president of the powerful Bilderberger Group, who also just happens to be Vice Chairman of Goldman Sachs—"

"That would be James F. Taylor," Cristian said mechanically, interrupting him.

"Sits on the same Board of Directors as the Chief Executive Officer of CityGroup and both are, somehow, tied into Octopus. Reid also told me that Schaffhausen Bank wasn't their operation."

"Then, there is someone else?" said Cristian.

"Yes, there is," replied Curtis grimly.

Curtis looked at his friend. "They know about you. They know we came here. You are now involved. I have put you in danger."

The banker sat forward, his eyes clouded, focused inward. Then, he struck a match, lit a cigarette and walked around the couch to pour himself a drink. "Most of my reasons to live died with my wife, until now. Don't take this away from me, please." He paused. "In any case, I am too high profile for them to easily do anything to me." He smiled. "Now, what is it about this other group?"

"Someone new who joined the bidding. These were his words. He said that most have a lot of local clout. That's how they wanted it," replied Curtis. "When I asked him why, he said because it's convenient and because most don't know the real story."

"And what does that mean? What story?"

"I don't know."

"Why didn't you ask him to elaborate?"

"I was supposed to know the answer."

"Lower rungs, the up-line, their controllers, then the Board of Directors. The classic set-up of every secret society."

"What do you mean?" asked Simone.

Cristian exhaled noisily, then tapped his cigarette in the ashtray. "The organization is structured as circles within circles, with the exterior layer always protecting the more dominant inner membership that coordinates all operations. All of this, of course, is a euphemism for the creation of global networks of giant cartels more powerful than the very nations they supposedly serve, a virtual spider's web of interlocked financial, political, and industrial interests."

Curtis reflected on the world of greed and corruption teeming with characters whose moral compass was so utterly bent. He wondered how they ever sorted out the bad from the really bad amongst themselves.

"Reid made a curious admission, almost as an afterthought. He said that it wouldn't have been an issue had Caroni not stumbled across the bank accounts."

"Who is Caroni?" Michael asked.

"I don't know." Curtis replied. "Apparently, he illegally came into possession of an uncomprehensible amount of money which wasn't his to begin with. 'Until we get it back he won't get out.' These were Reid's words."

"Got back what … money?" Michael asked.

"I don't know." Curtis replied.

Cristian spoke softly, his words barely audible. "We have to get help. I know people in the government, important senators and congressmen, people in the new administration who owe me favors. They can help us. Let me talk to them."

"No. The FBI, the CIA, Office of Naval Intelligence. They are all in on this. No way. Not until we know exactly what we are up against and who we can trust. One breakthrough and we will know what the real story behind these people is." Curtis did not raise his voice. His deathly tone was enough. Cristian understood.

"I have a suspicion Reid is not the keeper of the crypt, but answerable to someone. The only way we are going to solve this is if we pull them out," Curtis said. "You said it yourself, circles within circles, with exterior layers always protecting the more dominant inner membership."

"And you are suggesting?"

Curtis stared first out the window, then up at Cristian. "The bigger the bait, the bigger the fish," he said after a brief pause. "What we are dangling in front of their noses is working. Reid is worried, and that means so are his superiors. We get the names, we can pull them out individually. I can pull them out. I sensed it when I pinned him into a corner. He reacted as if he was an onlooker, someone high enough to be a decision maker, but not *the* decision maker."

"Welcome to the super-elite Old Boy's Club," Cristian said. "It has taken most of these people over a third of a century of hard work and uncountable millions to get where they are today. Whatever it is they are scared of losing, there is simply not enough time to start again, which is why they will hang together, always working towards whatever common end they have in their sights." Cristian checked his watch. "The rest will have to wait until tomorrow. I have an early morning meeting and it's way past my bedtime. Good night everyone."

CHAPTER 33

Frej Fenniche, Senior Human Rights Officer and Louise Arbour's second-in-command adjusted his tie as he carefully climbed the marble steps to the third floor of a non-descript office building in the center of Washington, a dark blue briefcase in his left hand. He reached the third floor landing. None of the three doors facing him had a brass plate. Frej paused, unsure how to proceed. He put his ear to the heavy wooden-paneled door in front of him, and listened to the muffled sounds beyond.

He heard a muffled click to his right. The door swung silently ajar. Frej turned stiffly, pushing the door gingerly with the palm of his sweaty hand, and sidled into the dim light issuing from inside.

"Hello?" he said unsurely.

"In here," came a reply from somewhere out of sight. Frej Fenniche adjusted his tie again and walked in.

"Hello, Boss, you look grand," he said nonchalantly. He tried to smile, but knew it didn't work.

A man appeared in front of him. He was wearing a well-tailored pinstriped suit. He exuded confidence.

"Did you bring the information?" asked the Boss, his voice flat.

"Yes." Frej opened the briefcase. It held two pieces of paper stamped 'HCM, Highly Confidential Material' across the top of each sheet. They were signed and dated by the UN Commissioner for Human Rights, the Honorable Louise Arbour.

A smile creased the lips of the man in a pinstriped suit. "You have done well, Frej."

"Pleased to serve," came the reply from the UN's second in command.

The Boss reached for a zipper bag and slowly handed it to Frej Fenniche. "This is one part of your reward."

Frej unzipped the bag. It was full of hundred-dollar bills neatly wrapped in packs of ten thousand dollars each.

"Two hundred and fifty thousand dollars, as we agreed."

"Yes, Boss. Thank you."

"Tell me, what are you going to do with all that money?"

"Perhaps retire. Put a down payment on a restaurant or a small hotel on the Riviera." Frej turned around and started for the door, then stopped. "You said, one part of my reward? What's the other part? Perhaps a bonus, for a job well done, dare I say?" He laughed quietly to himself.

"Yes, a bonus. Good choice of words," replied the Boss, turning, a gun in his hand, the silencer telegraphing a discreetly imminent death.

Frej was unable to move. "What, what are you doing?" His voice seemed to be coming from a place far away.

"I must say, Frej, what you lack in vision, you make up for in ambition."

"I gave you exactly what you wanted."

"Yes, you did. Unfortunately for you, you sold out to the higher bidder," he replied.

"I am your loyal servant. I am on your side!" he replied, slowly backing away.

"Who is to say that, tomorrow, you won't offer this invaluable information to Octopus for a higher bid?"

"What? No!"

The Boss fired a single shot into Frej's upper throat, and rang for cleanup.

**

In Rome, the faded spectre of Akira Shimada, the last remaining member of the Japanese Golden Lily unit, sat up slowly, his spindly legs covered up by pajamas too long for his diminutive frame. His sleep had lasted for no more than an hour. The night was smoke-blue, cold and moonless, with light drizzle gurgling and rustling. Thunder, in the distance, swelled in its ponderous velvet folds. The room floated in darkness with a special intensity one perceives only at a certain time of night; the lamp, the desk, carefully laid out slippers; until a small lump suddenly appeared from nowhere, noiselessly and snugly caging itself momentarily within the frame of the solitary window.

Where was he? He lowered his gaze, then, bending lower and lower, silently sobbed throughout his body. The bed gave a subdued creak.

Somewhere, a tower clock with its customary equilibrium solemnly and methodically chimed its message five times. Shame is a wreckage of self, an act that leaves only odds and ends behind. Pain and paranoia. He recognized the scenery, if not the condition.

Shimada got up. He shook his head, restraining yet another onrush of sobs. Weakness. The clock ticked. Exquisite frost patterns overlapped on the blue glass of the window. All was quiet. He pressed his eyes shut, blinking away tears, and had a fleeting sensation that laid his early life bare before him, ghastly in its sadness, ultimately pointless, sterile, devoid of miracles and love.

***

The dark blue sedan rounded the final curve in the sloping road cut out of the countryside, and shot past a mini-van stuck in the mud of the unfinished road. Henry Stilton shifted in his seat, his head arched back into the top of the leather seat, his eyes half closed, smoking, as the familiar scenes shot by him; he looked up at the smoke mingling with the shadows on the glass, one knee raised.

He looked at his watch, then picked up the phone and punched four digits.

"Any messages?"

"No, sir," said the secretary, with a certain ambitious concern in her voice.

"Okay," said the Associate Director of the CIA and pressed the off button on his phone, anger and confusion clouding his thoughts.

Less than four minutes later, Stilton's telephone rang.

Without ceremony, "I am worried about Shimada. Interpol's security measures will be formidable," said Stilton, the crevices on his face more pronounced in the moonlit night.

"Don't worry. Shimada is ours."

"How can you be so sure?"

"The privileged have deferments, Henry. We simply change the rules of engagement."

"We have a direct line into their camp," said a voice on the other end of the line.

"But—"

"Oh, by the way, Henry ... I trust Octopus doesn't suspect?"

A shiver ran up and down the back of the Associate Director of the CIA.

"You can bank on that, Boss." He swallowed hard.

"No, you had better bank on that. Good night, Henry. Sleep well."

CHAPTER 34

A slight rain fell. Pinkish-orange sky was giving way to a more somber grey. Somewhere on the outskirts of New York a bang resonated across the sky, sending the startled pigeons upward.

"Interrupt him," demanded a gruff voice, breathing heavily into the receiver.

"Yes, sir, right away sir."

"Boss?"

"What happened at Schaffhausen?"

"What we thought was tied up, came untied."

"Meaning?"

"Curtis Fitzgerald is alive."

"I know that! What do you think I am, an idiot?"

The Colonel swallowed hard, like an old prizefighter, riding out a punch: his eyes closed for a second. "We can still—"

"Forget Fitzgerald. I want Shimada."

"But we don't—"

"He is in Rome. Villa Stanley," said the Boss. "Use the same crew we used in Colombia." The line went dead.

***

"Pick me up at the usual place within the hour," said the voice.

John Reid nodded his head in relief. "Thank you. I knew you would agree with me."

"Thank you for making me see it, John."

"I'll make the usual transfer tomorrow morning."

"Absolutely. You have always been very generous with the money."

"You deserve it. You are the best."

In New York, a black Mercedes S-600 silently pulled up to within seventy-five yards of an entrance gate, separated from the loading area manned by a sleepy and underpaid security guard. His view of the car was obstructed on the left by bulky freighters cargo to be loaded the following day and on the right by the shadows of a stationary crane. The area was deserted, the row of warehouses dark, the wattage low by municipal decree. The guardhouse, made of dark brown wood with forest-green shutters, looked like a modified A-frame. Diagonally, no more than one hundred yards from where the Mercedes was parked, was the door to the pier's warehouse office. It was padlocked, the lights were off inside, its oversized loading doors grimly facing the deserted pier.

The man behind the wheel turned off the engine, but did not make any move to get out. Less than sixty seconds later, there was a tap on the passenger window. The driver unlocked the door and the man quickly got inside.

"It's as cold as a meat locker," said the man, wiping the moisture from his lenses.

The driver extended his hand. "Glad to have you on my team." The man silently took it.

"Tell me, what made you change your mind?"

"Your persistence." The Frenchman inhaled deeply.

"There was no other way, Pierre," said John Reid.

"Tell me, John, have you told anyone else?" Pierre folded his glasses and put them away.

"Who the hell am I going to tell? I don't know who to trust anymore."

"What about the Board?"

"No, something isn't right there." He was silent for a moment. "There is something I have been meaning to ask you. Shortly after you left, I got a phone call from a man claiming to have accessed the dead man's papers and documents. He said that someone else was willing to pay a lot of money to blackmail us. Why would he say that?" He stared pointedly at the Frenchman.

"It's obvious. Caroni has the money, and this someone else has the documents. Your grand strategy is falling apart at the seams."

"The strategy is sound!" Reid banged on the armrest.

"Is it?"

"It's not what you think," Reid said, breathing heavily. "That's only a part of it. There are two other conditions."

"I am quite aware of them, John." Pierre interrupted him.

"Impossible. You are not a part of the—"

"Board? Octopus?"

"Then how—" He stopped in mid-sentence, and stared at the Frenchman.

"Who better to know your every move but an ex-Agency psychopath who broke into your impenetrable system and got away with trillions of dollars? PROMIS is alive, and only Caroni could have made this happen. He is our plant."

Reid was stunned, but immediately recovered, his right hand surging forward, aiming for the Frenchman's neck. But he was old, slow. Pierre easily deflected the punch with the palm of his left hand while delivering a powerful uppercut to the chin with his right. Reid yelped and slumped momentarily into the seat. Pierre then pulled out his Heckler & Koch P7 mounted with a silencer.

"What promises did you make to the man on the phone?"

John Reid focused on the weapon. "What are you doing!" he screamed. "What are you saying?"

"You don't think we know? Your mutually beneficial cooperation based on privileged information puts us in a rather awkward predicament, John. If one betrays the principles the others betray him. In a word, you have become unreliable."

"It was a ploy, a strategy to draw him out. I would never betray the Board."

"I am not concerned about the Board."

"Who are you?" cried Reid, hatred in his voice, clenching his large fists.

"Guns beat fists," replied the Frenchman, holding the gun steady, pointing it at his head. "I could never accept your assignment because Caroni knew my face," the Frenchman said raising his voice. "I fulfilled the contract on Daniel Casolaro."

"And you got paid for it," Reid said breathing heavily.

"Twice." He smiled. "It would only be fair to tell you before you die that I work for a different paymaster. The only thing new in the world, John, is the history you don't know."

As a last act of defiance, Reid rose off the seat and lunged forward, his eyes spouting impotent fire. The muffled shot was barely audible in the soft interior of the luxurious Mercedes. Reid slumped over the wheel, eyes owl-like, death softly beckoning from just beyond. The Frenchman leaned over and softly whispered into his ear. "My name is—"

But Reid was dead, his body slumped forward, head rolled to the side, his eyes wide, staring at his executioner.

CHAPTER 35

Simone Casolaro greeted the cold New York morning by stretching in bed, still bearing the pillow's imprint on her cheek. Her nerves were raw, after a restless night.

With Danny gone, she was in a kind of limbo. How she missed him, yearned to see him, if just for a day, maybe just for a fleeting moment. Unhappy families. Tolstoy's adage is wrong. They are all alike, caught in a predictable, dreary circle of misery, remorse and sadness; families in mourning anyway. Happiness has variety, pain is repetitive, forever wearing the same stiff, stubborn face.

Click. From the living room came the sounds of music – a bongo, a xylophone, then a flute. Click. Dog barking, then piped laughter. Another Click. A slightly husky voice was announcing the arrival of a Russian circus. Click. "Oh, so you haven't heard?" the voice said in surprise. Canned laughter. Pluff ! Sounded like a slap. More canned laughter. "Why would audiences want to be told when to laugh?" Simone thought to herself. Click. "It's a winner! The new instant bestseller from Justin Underhand, *The Hand of Justice*, is not just a spy thriller, it's a literary triumph! An inside look at the invisible heroes who fight the War on Terror. Full of seduction, hard-core action, and imagery that will take you on the virtual ride of your life!" She cringed.

Art, she thought, as soon as it is brought in contact with politics, nearly always sinks to the level of ideological trash. *Underhanded* trash. Simone grinned, laughed quietly to herself … then laughed louder when she realized she could still laugh, and got up to get dressed.

"Well, good morning!" shouted Michael, TV remote in hand, feet up on the table, grinning ear to ear. "Did we wake you? Haven't seen one of these things for a while," he said, pointing at the television set.

Curtis appeared, adopting the ingratiating posture of an uptown waiter. "Good morning, Simone. There's coffee on the table, freshly squeezed orange juice, along with fresh fruit, a variety of cereals, bacon, pancakes, sausages and nuts," he crooned and simpered.

She smiled at Curtis. "Coffee is fine. Black, please and very strong." Click. "From the creators of Spasm IV, comes Rawhide Ride, more action-filled, more dangerous, more fantasmalicious!" Click. "Who do we love? Jesus! Who? Jesus! Jesus is Lord! Praise the Lord! Praise Jesus and give him your life—" Click. "... brings you the latest update on last night's shooting."

Suddenly all eyes were glued to the TV, as the camera moved in on a Mercedes 600 and the name of the victim crawled across the bottom of the screen. "John Reid, the well-respected and powerful CEO of CityGroup, one of America's leading financial entities, was shot and killed last night, begining what is sure to be a headline-grabbing investigation. NYPD has so far declined to comment on the death. Sources have stated on condition of anonymity that City has been involved behind the scenes in major emergency cash negotiations with a yet to be named financial entity to cope with steep losses across its leading investment divisions. A spokesman said there was no link between Reid's death and the group's current activities, but declined to give further details, saying the investigation was in progress." The camera moved in on a body bag as it was wheeled to a waiting ambulance. The screen was suddenly filled with gory images of the inside of the Mercedes with Reid's corporate photograph appearing in the top right corner of the screen.

"What's going on?" Simone asked.

"Someone got ahead of John Reid," Curtis replied.

"Whatever it is we are dangling in front of their noses is working," Michael added.

"No, not working," grimly added Curtis. "We needed Reid to smoke them out. He was prepared to trade information for our silence. I have to call Cristian."

"Hello?" Cristian picked it up on the first ring.

"Reid is dead."

"I know. I can't talk right now. I am waiting for a call from the President."

"The president of what?"

"Of the good old USA."

"Oh, that President."

"Exactly. But I will tell you that the unnamed financial entity City-Bank was negotiating with? That's us. The government is overstretched beyond limit and they wanted us to lend City a pile of money with the government's personal guarantee as back up."

"The World Bank lending money to an American Corporation at taxpayer's expense? I can see the headlines."

"All hell has broken out here. Someone leaked a preliminary document to the *Times*. If it gets out, our ass is grass. That's why the President is calling. I'll call you back." The line went dead.

Curtis shook his head. "So, Danny was about to expose Octopus, a cabal of twenty-plus people who control most of the world's wealth. And he was killed. Reid was ready to cooperate. With his help, we would have pulled the Octopus out of its hole. Now, Reid has also been killed. Ah! ...." He looked at Michael. "Remember what Reid said?"

"Most don't know the real story," replied Michael.

Curtis checked his watch. "Almost ten o'clock. Cristian is right. It's about associations. To pull them out we need to float some bait in front of them ... but first we need more Intel."

"What do you want us to do?" Simone asked.

"I need you to go the Central Research Library and pull all the archives on Reid. Everything. Names, dates, photographs, old microfilm footage. Anything you can get your hands on."

Michael peered at Curtis. "What's the bait?"

"Not what, who."

"Okay, who?"

"Me."

Chapter 36

As always, it happened at night. A cargo plane touched down in the darkness, its lights doused to avoid detection, lumbered across a pocked and rutted runway, and came to a stop by a hangar at the far end of the strip. The horizon was seabed-flat save for what appeared to be colossal grey gravel heaps in the furthest distance. The plane's rear ramp lowered, revealing a dozen men dressed in military fatigues emerging like aliens in the red-hued light of the cargo hold. Thirteen men. A baker's dozen. Reticular placement, standard configuration at Special Ops. Each operative had a connection – visual, audio or electronic – with at least two others. A coordinated response, and protection in case any of the participants were taken out of action by enemy fire.

Each was equipped with a Heckler & Koch G36 military assault rifle. A thirty-round clip of 5.56 x 45mm high velocity, lightweight black polymer ammo, usually reserved for members of Special Forces units. The optical sights used a red-dot reticle. Assaulted by the cold, northern winds, their heads were covered with bandanas, their breath visible in the frigid air of a Roman winter. This particular airstrip was neither a civilian nor a military airport. In fact, it was not on any map issued for public scrutiny.

A canvas-topped Jeep pulled up alongside the cargo plane and a man stepped out. "Colonel," a soldier said. He was dressed in a T-shirt that said, 3rd Signal Battalion: The Signal Dogs. "The TOC is in place. Serial 93 is on the way."

TOC stood for Tactical Operations Center, the headquarters of a military unit. Serial 93 meant the group of reinforcements. The man who was addressed as a Colonel pulled out a military version of a BlackBerry device and typed something in. End-to-end RASP data security. It was standard equipment for clandestine operations.

Several military transport trucks pulled up alongside the cargo plane. Assault rifles and other military equipment were off-loaded into them. The whole process lasted just under ten minutes.

As the last vehicle pulled away, the big bird lurched, the fuselage trembling as the plane began its race down the runway. Within seconds, it was airborne. The two remaining figures on the ground followed the plane's trajectory for several seconds, then slowly walked across a thick, sturdy bridge, barely wide enough for a single vehicle. The two figures were dressed like the others, military fatigues and bandanas covering their faces. Each turned his face away from the blasts of wind that buffeted him. They walked rapidly, circuitously, through the trees to a small clearing, where stood a Jeep-like vehicle, but much larger and heavier, with balloon tires of very thick rubber.

The taller of the two men pulled out an electronic communicator, a small model in a hard grey plastic shell, but with a powerful signal.

"This is Alpha Beta Lambda. It's a wrap." The response was inaudible. Less than ten seconds later, the departing rear lights of the Jeep disappeared into the night.

CHAPTER 37

The New York Times Reference Library on 620 8th Avenue has one of the most advanced research libraries in the world, not to mention one of the most extensive electronic collections of out-of-print magazine and newspaper back-issues in the country, dating back to the early 1850s. Donated to the city by the Astor family and conveniently situated across the street from the Astoria Hotel, it is the library par excellence for researchers and professional investigators alike. With grandly arching windows deeply set in Purbeck limestone, adorned with spindly wrought-iron balconies and a partially enclosed courtyard, it offers researchers the quiet intimacy so necessary to their line of work.

Michael and Simone mounted the stairs to the first floor and turned down a hallway that led to the huge reading chamber dominated by enormous rectangular tables set in rows of six, each mounted with flat-screen computers.

Less than three hours later they had pre-selected a sizable file of material on John Reid, now deceased Chief Executive Officer of the once mighty CityGroup. These files documented that in the eleven years as City's top man, Reid had shown a gift of always being in the right place at the right time, while carefully husbanding the company's prestige and credibility.

There was family: loving wife, adoring children. Harvard moments, activities, school group shots. Reid as a young man with confident looks, shoulders thrown back and chest puffed up for the photographer. Later, there were fundraisers, photos with presidents, foreign leaders, disadvantaged children, sporting events sponsored by City. Reid was there. Front and center. Right place at the right time. That was for public consumption. A brilliantly interconnected lie. It was a life assembled from a thousand real-world fragments, a stream of vivid episodes transformed into a steady stream of puff pieces in leading periodicals. A slate constantly erased and rewritten for public consumption.

Michael and Simone decided to go further back in time, to Reid's beginning. Where did he come from? Was Reid in the war? Which one? Whom did he serve under? Where? For how long? Over the next two hours, a different profile emerged. A profile of a man who fought under the leadership of General MacArthur. Area of operations: Pacific Theater. Reid was severely wounded. He won a Congressional Medal of Honor for "doing something foolhardy, like saving another soldier's life," according to Navy News from 1956. It wasn't a story of battle alone. Reid's war was mainly a jungle war, and its principle effort had to be the safe transportation of troops and supplies. Rigid secrecy had to be maintained. Then. But now?

She stopped, pushing one of the volumes away and tentatively looked at Michael. "Driblets of drivel," said Simone, rubbing her eyes, her dark hair flowing across her collarbone.

She leaned back, flipped off her shoes, dangling her feet carelessly to and fro.

Suddenly, she remembered. Danny, running through the snow-covered field. The snow still falling lightly, but with the elusive suddenness of an angel, it would change direction and then again, and again. Simone's demeanor changed, hardened.

Someone trundled by with a metal trolley full of books. The trolley had a wonky wheel as it whistled past them down the linoleum floor.

"We had better get back to work," she said in a subdued tone. Michael glanced at her, but failed to catch her eyes.

They dug deeper. Late spring 1956, Reid was part of a secret group of soldiers trained in Australia and then sent on a clandestine mission in the Philippines. What did Curtis say? Old Boy's Club. Sixty-year-old story. Japan, Korea.

Reid, MacArthur, Australia, Philippines? How do they fit into the picture?

Curtis had gone back in his memory, recalling every piece of conversation, every name, date and place since getting involved in this mind-boggling lunacy. He had written it all down, key names on the left side of the page, apparently insignificant bits of information on the right. Since then, he had been trying to clear his head, ending up within two blocks of the Research Library. They were supposed to call at four. He checked his watch. Twenty past. What the hell was taking them so long? He shook his head.

The phone rang. Curtis picked it up on the first ring.

"We are up to our eyeballs in governmental duplicity."

"Give me a name, Michael. Give me something, anything to go on."

"Reid served in the Pacific Theater. Twice. Once under MacArthur in Korea, transporting troops and supplies; the second time, as part of a secret group of soldiers trained in Australia and then sent on a clandestine mission into the jungles of the Philippines. We found a declassified intelligence report titled Golden Lily."

"What was the nature of the mission?"

"Don't know. The system was airtight."

"When?"

"1952, and 1956."

Curtis frowned and clucked his tongue. "Who wrote the report?"

"Someone by the name of Stephen Armitage."

"Reid, MacArthur, Korea, Philippines, alphabet soup agencies."

"We need to find Armitage. He may be the missing piece of the puzzle."

"That shouldn't be difficult. Since retiring, Armitage took up a teaching position at Hudson."

Curtis put away his phone, buttoned his jacket and pulled the lapels up around his neck. The dusk of twilight dimmed everything around. Golden Lily. The words were still a hazy shadow slithering out from under a rock. But they needed to step on that shadow to keep it from retreating, from disappearing again into a misty oblivion of dead souls.

CHAPTER 38

H udson University is located on the Upper East Side of Manhattan, on 74th Street between Central Park and the East River. Around 22,000 souls attend Hudson, with nearly one thousand faculty and staff. One of them was Stephen Armitage, professor of Oriental studies and deep-cover agent for the Central Intelligence Agency.

"Stop over there," Michael said, opening the cab door before it came to a full stop. The two of them walked across the park, opened the wicket gate and cut across the road that led to Carl Sagan Hall.

He approached a pair of young men striding down the cobbled steps, worn smooth from many decades of use.

"Excuse me. I'm looking for the Department of Oriental Studies."

"Up the steps and down the hall to the right," said a frizzy-haired youth, pointing to the entrance.

They swiftly mounted the stairs and headed down the corridor through an archway leading to a maze of offices occupied by some of the leading eminences in the field. Twenty-six Rhodes Scholars and forty Nobel nominees were listed on Hudson's teaching staff. Armitage's door was the last one on the left, hidden from view by a protruding rectangular pillar.

The two of them approached the door, stood for several moments listening and finally knocked gently. They heard the muffled sound of a chair sliding across the floor and, seconds later, footsteps. The door opened.

"Stephen Armitage?" Simone asked.

The man in front of them had a rumply, wilted look about him with a head of hair like the later portraits of Beethoven. He emitted a throaty rumble, knitted his impressive brow and blew his nose.

"Dr. Armitage, yes. Dr. Stephen Armitage." He said, as if confirming the fact to himself. His hands trembled perceptibly. "How may I help you?"

Simone looked to her left, her eyes taking in the space down the hall, then pinned the professor with her eyes. "Golden Lily."

There was a brief, shocked silence silence, then Armitage spun away. "I am sorry, this must be some kind of a misunderstanding. This is the Department of Oriental Studies. You must be looking for Professor Lilem from Weill Medical College."

"No, I believe we have come to the right place. Gol-den Lil-y," repeated Simone slowly. Armitage turned back, attempting nonchalance, then abandoning the posture.

"Who are you?"

"People who need some privacy."

Another intense pause, then Armitage finally gestured with his head for them to come inside. The room had an unmistakable smell of academia. Armitage's table was cluttered with stacks of colored folders and bright yellow envelopes; on top of them, old newspapers, some of which had fallen to the floor and been kicked under the table. An overstuffed chair sat piled with exam papers sat against the far wall; it was authentic, not a hastily set up space for appearances only, as was so often the case in secret service operations.

"Why did you come here?" asked Armitage, shutting the door.

"We want to ask you a few questions about a report you wrote on Golden Lily."

Armitage smiled, his thick, purplish lips flat until he spoke. "Golden Lily. Sounds like a Victorian saloon singer." When nobody laughed he snorted nervously, moved behind his desk, and sat down. "Please forgive me. I am getting old. My memory is not what it once was."

Simone leaned into the desk. "We're not here to spar with you, professor. My brother was murdered, and I think his death and Golden Lily are somehow related. Time is short and so is my temper."

Armitage leaned back in his chair, hands on the armrest. His face was pale in the dim light of a cold, late winter afternoon. "Many have sought access to the secret over the years. Few have survived, and those who have would rather crawl into a deep, dark hole than speak a word about it."

Michael's mind was spinning, racing, and processing the confirmation that Golden Lily was real. "Simone's brother uncovered a terrible conspiracy, washing up at the feet of some of the most powerful people in the world. All of these people have several things in common: World War Two. Late forties, early to mid fifties, Japan, Korea, the Philippines, present financial crisis and gold."

Armitage paused, his palms outstretched. "A group of powerful men." Again, he paused. "In the United States?"

"It seems to be international."

"Do you have a name for this conspiracy?"

"One seems to be the 'Octopus,'" said Simone.

"Octopus? That's just like the Agency." The scholar shook his head. "Use all the banal trigger words you can come up with."

"What?"

"It's in the CIA manual," said Armitage. "Someone at the Agency thought that if you used provocative names for code words, you would make the operation itself sound more legitimate." There was a pause. The bridge of silence was accentuated by the hum of a large ventilator somewhere nearby. Simone looked intensely at the scholar, as the old man looked out the window. Finally, the silence was broken.

"Golden Lily is a poem written by Japanese Emperor Hirohito."

"A poem? What does a poem have to do with a secret so terrible?"

"Between 1937 and 1942, a highly secret unit led by the Emperor's younger brother was tasked with the methodical plundering of Southeast Asia. It was called Golden Lily. The sheer quantity and value of plunder gathered by Golden Lily was mind-numbing. The whole of Asia under Japanese control had been combed for treasure. In fact, the amount of gold stolen in those six years far surpasses the combined gold reserves of the world's central banks. It is, without a doubt, one of the greatest conspiracies in the history of mankind; not by its span, neither by the sheer amount nor by the audacity of the operation but rather by what it hid.

"Because if the actual amounts of gold and money at stake ever see the light of day, it would reveal a secret far more sensitive." He raised his index finger and looked significantly at Simone. "That the amount of gold buried in the Philippines alone during World War II is ten times greater than the official figure of 140,000 metric tons of gold supposedly mined in human history. The fact that such quantities of gold exist outside of official channels is astounding. That this secret is officially protected is even more shocking."

"You said between 1937 and 1942?"

"Beginning in 1943, most of it was shipped to Prince Chichibu's headquarters in the Philippines."

"What happened in 1943?"

"Stalingrad. The turning point in World War II in Europe, when the Russians stopped Hitler short of the Caucasus oil fields. The Germans lost a million men: killed, wounded or captured. The beginning of the end for the Axis powers. The most astute German and Japanese commanders understood that right away. It was simply a matter of time. Moving the treasure to Japan was no longer an option. Plans had to be changed, if only as a temporary measure. The Japanese army shipped the gold to the islands and was forced to leave it there, with the vain hope of returning after the war and recovering the loot in secret. A group of officers, with the help of a special brigade of engineers, began to bury the treasure. It took them months to excavate and construct complex systems of tunnels large enough to store the trucks and sometimes deep enough to run below the water surface."

He stopped for a moment and walked over to a cherry wood cabinet. "I need a drink. Will you join me?" Armitage pulled the handle. A door opened to reveal a fully stocked minibar.

"Perhaps later," Michael replied.

Armitage shrugged his shoulders and poured a healthy shot of brandy. He took a sip, held it in his mouth, savoring it, and then swallowed. "I have drunk the hemlock far too many times, Michael." He gulped down the rest, wiping his mouth with the back of his hand. "To understand this story, to truly appreciate its immensity and horror, you must visualize it, taste the sweat and smell the rot. Without a visual perception of what it must have been like for the prisoners digging those tunnels under the watchful eye of the Japanese master sergeants and howling winds, up to their eyeballs in mud, starving and half naked, insects the size of your fist gnawing at you, realizing you had a snowball's chance in Hell of making it out alive, this sordid episode cannot truly be understood for what it was." He nodded his head at nothing in particular, then scowled.

"The vast amount of gold and other treasures were divided into 172 caches of various sizes. Most of it was buried in the Philippine Islands before the end of World War II. Here, bullion, platinum diamonds and valuable religious artifacts – including a golden statue of Buddha weighing one ton – and collectively valued by Golden Lily accountants at $190 billion back in 1943 – were buried together with live Allied prisoners who had been forced to dig the tunnels."

"What happened to it? Where is it now?"

"Please, don't jump ahead." He coughed, wiped his mouth with the red napkin and poured another snifter of brandy. "The Japanese cartographers made maps of every hiding place and the emperor's most trusted accountants marked each cache with a three-digit number representing its value in Japanese yen. One of the 172 caches was marked with a "777," the equivalent of more than 90,000 metric tons of gold; or 75% of world's official gold reserves and valued at 102 trillion American dollars in the year 1945, when the yen was exchanged at 3.5 on the dollar, an amount that dwarfs the current global debt."

Again, Armitage paused.

Simone's jaw dropped. "You are talking about trillions of dollars by today's exchange rate."

"Actually, quadrillions of dollars, an amount so preposterous, it defies reality."

"It's impossible to keep such a conspiracy hidden. Someone must have known."

"Very much so. By late May of 1942, the United States had cracked Imperial Japan's secret communications code, and had prepared its own plans to get its hands on the booty. Do you remember Roosevelt's famous speech about unconditional surrender for the Axis powers?"

"Casablanca Conference, January 1943," Michael said mechanically.

"To those panicky attempts to escape the consequences of their crimes we say – all the United Nations say – that the only terms on which we shall deal with an Axis government are the terms 'unconditional surrender.'" The old man laughed. "The great humanitarian didn't have victims on his mind when he surprised Churchill with his precipitous words."

"So, the government knew."

"Roosevelt knew. Understand the gravity of the situation. It was never made public. All those soldiers officially missing in the line of duty, and for what?"

"And Churchill?" Armitage shook his head.

"The Americans broke the codes, and they kept the information close to their vests. American intelligence agents carried out a clandestine recovery operation in the Philippines between the years 1948 and 1956. It had taken the CIA tracking team four months to find the first treasure cave, located more than seventy meters below the ground. The Japanese engineers had developed a sophisticated technique using unusual rock formations and other topographic signs as signals to reveal their location."

"So, then, what did they do with the gold?"

"One part of the twice-looted gold became the basis of the CIA's off-the-books operational funds during the immediate postwar years, used to create a worldwide anti-communist network. To ensure loyalty to the cause, the CIA distributed Gold Bullion Certificates to influential and well-known people throughout the world."

"What did they do with the rest of it?"

"They left it in the jungle, for safe keeping. It is still there."

"The Philippines. Ferdinand Marcos. Didn't he know?"

"He sure did. Way back in 1953. That's when he found out. Of course, he was but a lowly hoodlum and a hustler then. But he had limitless ambition, something that the American government underestimated. Between 1953 and 1970, with the help of Japanese prisoners of war captured in the Philippines, Marcos unearthed slightly over 600 metric tons of gold… that is until he found the map at the end of 1971 and really went to work. By the time he was done, Marcos had unearthed over 32,000 metric tons of the hidden treasure."

"How did he find the map?"

"One of the Japanese prisoners. He was part of the original Golden Lily. In exchange for his freedom, he drew Marcos a small section of the map, the part he committed to memory back in 1943."

"Twenty-eight years. What happened to him?"

"They found him in a jungle hut, arched back in his chair, his throat surgically punctured."

"That was Marcos' idea of gratitude?"

"I guess."

"What happened to the Philippino gold?"

"Our government confiscated it when Marcos was deposed."

"When did the United States government find out Marcos got his hands on the gold?"

"About a week before he was deposed in a popular uprising, if you believe in fairy tales."

"Did anyone else know about the existence of the treasure map?"

"Our government sure the hell didn't know. At least not back then."

"What about the prisoners?"

"I doubt it. Most of those who were unlucky enough to form part of Golden Lily were buried with the treasure. The ultimate keepers of the crypt."

"Even the Japanese soldiers?"

"Not one Japanese soldier or prisoner of war survived the ordeal. I have the 1982 Congressional subcommittee report on that." Armitage sat back in his chair. "Still, it is an interesting question. With the chaos of the dying days of the war, a few of them might have slipped through the claws of the Imperial Japanese Executioners. Do you know something I don't?"

"It's just a hunch, but then as you said, the chances are slim."

"If someone did survive, they would be in their late eighties or even early nineties by now."

"Why was the gold only hidden in the Philippines?"

"I never said only in the Philippines. Chests full of gold, platinum, precious stones and priceless religious artifacts were also buried and hidden in the jungles of Indonesia. Virtually unknown to contemporary history is the fact that Indonesia's President Sukarno, along with a number of other Third World leaders had planned to set up a secret non-aligned bank back in 1955, using trillions of dollars in contraband gold as a guarantee."

"What was the West's reaction?"

"The establishment of so powerful an entity whose gold reserves dwarfed those available in the West would have sent shivers of fear through Western governments as well as the European and American banking fraternity. They sent a high-level delegation to Indonesia, under the auspices of post-war reconstruction, trying to talk Sukarno out it. In return, they promised greater cooperation, protection against all enemies, low tariffs on Indonesian goods, blah, blah, blah. It was Kissinger's first foreign relations assignment – and first unofficial fiasco."

"What did Sukarno have to say to this?"

"After listening politely, he showed them one of the secret repositories. It was so high-tech, even by today's standards that it made Fort Knox look like a day camp for boy scouts. There was stack upon stack and row upon row of beautifully made original precious metal storage boxes, all containing one-kilogram Johnson Mathey Hallmarked Gold or Platinum bars, each bar with a unique number and certificate bearing J.M. identification stamp. Bank certificates indicating gold and rubies on deposit; thousands of tons total. Vault Keys and Depositor ID cards made of gold. It was like the Arabian Nights. After they recovered from the shock, he told them to pound sand. Kissinger exploded and personally threatened Sukarno with an assassination."

"Why didn't any of the aggrieved parties sue for the wealth? There is a 40-year period in which a country can reclaim its stolen property."

"The governments? And expose the entire conspiracy? Who would dare? Get it through your head, young man, there was no intention on the part of the people involved to return any of the plunder to the Asian Nations – Burma, Vietnam, Cambodia, China or Korea; be it Marcos, Sukarno, Roosevelt, the CIA or any of the leading banks who stuffed the treasure into their secret vaults." Simone arched her eyebrows.

"Who controls the accounts?" Michael asked.

Armitage shrugged his shoulders. "That's one thing I don't want to know. Believe me, I have actively refrained from learning the identity of these people, and after all these years, I still prefer the damp comfort of my academic cave to a cozy, velvet-lined coffin six feet under."

Hunching over, covering his eyes with his hand, Michael lapsed into thought, and before him bright, speckled images passed by impregnated with thousands of details, and yet the lineaments were now vividly clear to him. "We are very grateful to you, Stephen," Michael said.

The old agent studied the much younger arcane historian. "So, you figured it out, whatever it is. Good for you. Time is a precious thing, Michael. And the years teach much that the days never knew. Maybe Life had in mind something totally different, something more subtle and deep. The trouble is that I am too old, and I shall never understand why evil is ultimately more fashionable than good." He propped an ear on his trembling, white hand, cracking his finger joints with the weight of his head. "Some people don't know what to do when their belief system collapses."

Simone shut her eyes and seemed to go to sleep for a moment. She opened them and lifted her hand to Armitage's face.

"I want to thank you from my brother who couldn't finish what he started."

"You are welcome. Now will the two of you get the hell out of my office, I've got work to do!"

Michael opened the door.

"Stephen." The scholar looked up. "We are in your debt."

They walked out of the building and into the night, their hearts pounding. Golden Lily. Simone wished she could step on the stench emanating from it again, to keep it from vanishing into a misty oblivion of dead souls.

CHAPTER 39

T he Captain stood still, his hands on the windowsill, looking out at the garden, his face near the glass. The shift from darkness to dawn framed the surrounding countryside in all its splendor, the slanting light spreading a film of milky blue across the sandy terrain.

"What exactly are we getting ready for, Captain?" asked one of the guards.

"As much as we can," the man grimly replied.

Beyond, on the opposite end of the estate that faced a ravine, another group of men gathered. They too were getting ready.

"Remember, tear gas will be on my remote; pipe bombs on Billy's. They are on a five-meter kill radius."

"Are you boys ready for some action?"

"Let's go," said the Colonel dressed in combat fatigues.

Villa Stanley was situated five miles north of Rome, in the midst of a series of foothills covered in olive groves. Unseen beams of trip-light threaded the wall of the compound on the south, east and west sides. The wall on the northern side surrounding the enormous estate was more for effect than protection; it was just under four meters high, but far higher from below, only accessible through a ravine heavily overgrown with bramble bushes.

The first commando crouched as his partner put his left foot and then his right on the man's shoulders. The commando silently and effortlessly rose to his feet just as the second man gripped the top of the wall, and quietly pulled himself up over the ledge. The others followed.

Thirteen men. A baker's dozen. They fanned out like shadows quickly gliding off into the night, blending with the surrounding countryside.

A tall man with a bald head and ears like ping pong paddles slid down off the exterior wall to the slanting ground at its base. He crawled forward some ten meters and stood up, listening, his eyes darting in every direction, scanning the darkness.

"Echo Lambda One to Base, over."

"Go ahead Echo Lambda One," came a reply.

A twig snapped. Three soldiers came by talking.

The commando clung to the wall, the wind strong, and waited until they passed above.

"I am inside."

"Report Echo Lambda One."

The first commando scanned the terrain through his TIG7 Thermal Infrared goggles. The large expanse of manicured lawn, leading from the main gate towards the sweeping circular drive some eighty meters away, was dotted with cypress trees, planted in long, neat rows and providing an important sculptural feature in this primeval landscape.

Two heavy chains suspended from thick iron posts bordered the path leading to the front entrance. At fifty meters out, on either side of the main house, the terrain eased away and eventually leveled out into a wide undulating green, spotted here and there with elm trees and spreading pines.

Through the thick branches of the tall overlapping pines, flickers of light shone from the main house.

"Two men at the entrance, three guards at your two o'clock, one at your twelve o'clock and another two at your nine o'clock."

"What about the main house?"

"Four on the first floor, six on the second."

"Shimada could be anywhere."

"We'll find him."

"Roger that."

Muffled sounds on gravel moving towards him, slowly and methodically; a toe of someone's foot touched down and pressed gently against the surface, keeping the weight evenly distributed. Toe to heel, in a smooth, continuous motion.

"Danger close, two o'clock, forty meters," crackled the voice in his earpiece.

"Activate decoy," ordered the Colonel.

Rising to a crouched position, the man picked up a couple of small rocks, making his way toward the gravel road that led to the circular drive. The line of trees prevented the guards stationed at the house from seeing him. "Twenty meters, eighteen, seventeen."

He threw one of the rocks near the guard, who turned around, finger on the trigger, crouched, feeling the panic of uncertainty, and slowly made his way towards the sound. "Twelve meters at your one o'clock," the voice murmured.

He threw a smaller stone almost at the guard's feet. The guard spun around. The instant he did, the second commando pulled himself up, clamped one arm around the man's throat, choking off all sound as he plunged his jungle knife deep into the man's chest. The man gasped and his lifeless body slumped onto the ground. The commando pulled him out of sight.

"Team two you are up," came a metallic voice.

Instantly, two men rose from the dense, concealing undergrowth on the west side of the estate, and walked on a wide arc north that led them past the western side entrance and then back towards it, situated on a narrow elevation. One of the two commandos glanced at his watch. It had taken them forty-eight seconds to get in position. Two minutes later, the two guards came into view, some seventy meters away, as they walked up the path from the gate. Up ahead, team three were side by side, crouching below the wall, waiting for their signal, staring at a prearranged point, their concentration absolute, their bodies primed and trained to move instantly. "Ten seconds," came the voice. "Nine, eight, seven."

The two guards were less than thirty meters away, casually talking to each other, blissfully unaware of the waiting deathtrap.

"Teams two and three in position. Six, five, four."

A searchlight suddenly swept the ground about thirty meters to team two's right.

"Three, two—" prompted the voice from his earpiece.

Team two, positioned on the higher ground, cocked their weapons. Sound triggered instinct. One of the two guards started to raise his head.

"One, fire!" came the command, as bullets from high-powered assault weapons with infrared scopes and silencers shredded the men's torsos. Team two descended the elevation just as team three surged up from below.

"Pipe bombs and tear gas in place, over."

"Roger three. Team four, you are up."

A metallic splat, then another. One of the guards on the southern perimeter collapsed as if a rug was pulled from under him. Shadows. One, two, three. A dull thud, then another. The shadow evaporated. The second guard ran forward and to his left, tripping on something solid under his feet.

Two bodies. Now, he understood. One of the snipers was covering him, God bless his soul. He dropped to the ground, his eyes scanning the underbrush.

The guard whipped his head back as the razor-like edge of the blade sliced the flesh on his cheek. The commando was working his blade in a skillful, semi-circular, compact motion, protecting his body with his left hand while the knife-wielding right pounced at the victim. The guard lashed his right foot out – just as the blade was coming back for another go at his head – catching his attacker in the kneecap, then instinctively crossed his wrists and blocked the steely edge. The commando spun to his left, freeing the blade and changing the grip. For a moment, the two men stared at one another. Then, the commando, his eyes ablaze, flexed his mammoth right arm, the heavy, jagged piece held blade down, shot up slicing the flesh under the guard's chin. The guard grimaced, sucking his breath between his clenched teeth and staggered several feet away from the attacker.

Light reflecting off steel. A gun! The guard lurched to the ground, rolled over and rolled over as the commando kicked the gun away from him, trying to stomp on his head. The commando sprang forward, slicing the blade toward the guard's forearm. Still on one knee, the guard grabbed his arm, twisting the commando's wrist and crashing his shoulder into the assassin's body. The guard ripped the knife from him and whipped his arm with all the force he could muster, sending the long, jagged blade with desperate force into the commando's neck, blood matting his blond hair instantly. The commando gasped, then exhaled audibly and went limp, falling backwards on the grass.

Breathing heavily, the guard reached for the transmission switch on his radio. He winced, wiping the blood from his face and forcing himself to concentrate.

"Ascolta! C'é un'emergenza ... !"

"What?" came the steely voice of his Captain.

"We got company."

"We are ready." A shadow. Or was it a premonition?

The Captain threw himself down a split second before a quadruple burst shattered the central window-pane in his second floor makeshift office.

"Activate the pipe bombs in the western and northern sectors," came a gruff reply.

The explosion was massive, blinding and deafening. Flames erupted into the early morning sky, a throbbing, immense wall of fire, destroying a fuel tank and sending the debris up into flaming sky.

"Alpha team hold your fire and your positions," shouted the Captain to his men positioned on the second floor of Villa Stanley.

"Team two, path!" shouted the Captain, in a hoarse voice. "We will split them up if we can pull them into the western sector."

"They will go in through the front door!" shouted one of Captain's men.

"Exactly!" replied the Captain. "Team two, ready?"

"I am going with you Captain!" shouted one of the men in the elite unit protecting Shimada. "You are short staffed."

Seconds later, more explosions began, first in the northern sector and then in the western sector of the Villa.

"The communications back-up center is out, sir," shouted one of the men.

"Captain, they are using—!"

Another explosion, this one much nearer the main house. The man's head slammed against the concrete, and he let out a low moan. "Pronto!" screamed the Captain into his radio. "They are using heat-seeking missiles. You two—"

"Sir?"

"Cover me, we've got to draw them out."

"Too dangerous, Captain."

"Cover me. That's an order. On three, two, one, go!" cried the Captain, slinging the strap of his Uzi over his shoulder as he leapt down the stairs, taking them three at a time, followed by two barrel-chested men with short, cropped hair.

As he came out, the gravel erupted all around him; he zigzagged wildly towards the protection of a Jeep. Pain! The shock waves shot through him like a lightning strike.

He grabbed his shoulder. The Captain spun around the edge of the van, his weapon exploding, firing at the military fatigues in front of him. One down, and then another. His muscles were spasming in agony. He pressed automatic fire. One, two, three, four, five, six; the shells flew in the air … and then they stopped. The explosions replaced by the sickening sound of a jamming click as the round in the chamber failed to eject.

The Captain reached for his Beretta pistol, his left arm limp and bleeding, his right arm clutching the gun as if it was life itself, his two sentries on either side of him. He fired at a rapidly moving figure some thirty meters in front of him.

There was another explosion, then another, then the third and finally the fourth, much louder and nearer than the other three.

"They are attacking the western sector, Captain! We must pull back."

"No," shouted the Captain over the general mayhem. "They are trapped. Now, they have to go through the main entrance. That's their only way in or out."

Four more explosions in rapid succession could be heard from the northern side of the perimeter. The thick fifteen-foot wall on the northern side blew up with such force that the earth shook, sending stone fragments high into the air.

"Colonel, we're trapped. We have to evacuate," the short guard said with a harsh bark.

Silence. "Colonel?"

"Evacuate Echo Lambda One. It's over," replied the Colonel. Automatic gunfire burst from the shadows just beyond the gravel path killing one of the snipers on the roof protecting Shimada, his limp body collapsing and plummeting to the ground.

Suddenly, a massive explosion blew out the front gate, as a Hummer lurched through the black smoke and debris towards the eastern end of the estate. Several commandos were running toward the vehicles. In seconds, they would get away.

"Cut them off !" shouted the Captain.

Another explosion blew away a large section of the wall as the vehicle rolled through the gaping hole and sped away. The Captain raced out through the hole, emptying his weapon, then hurling it after the receding taillights in impotent fury.

CHAPTER 40

Michael and Simone passed through the lobby, nodding at the doorman, who sat in his stool behind a wooden counter at a brightly lit desk, reading a newspaper and listlessly smacking his lips. The thought occurred to him, God, I love her.

Simone, glancing at Michael, reflected that, by some kind of collusion between them, their romance had followed a pattern of unfulfilled expectations and dashed dreams. It occurred to her how insignificant these longings were compared to the sublime anticipation, the enormous excitement of the actual moment. She realized that, ultimately, reality is beyond our ability to truly express it. At the same time she felt a transfiguration of her self, a healing radiance. After all, what is love, if not a sublime surprise of mutual discovery, a chance amazement of the senses.

She pushed the apartment door open and stepped across the divide, bridging the gap between then and now. A gust of wind blew several loose sheets of paper onto the floor, some flat, others crumpled. Michael walked over and stood for a moment by the window, observing the dim light drifting in. Despite the rain's having stopped hours ago, it was still wet. She sensed his gaze upon her, but her swift glance failed to catch him; only the right corner of his gently joined lips was slightly raised.

She came from behind and slid her hand under his shirt. A tremor invaded Michael's back as the instantaneous surge of enchantment rippled through his chest. He turned and caressed her neck with his lips, then bit her softly, his teeth threatening the skin of her throat like a playful cat. She fitted herself to him, her eyes blazing, the fabric of her blouse rising and falling in rhythm with her breath, her fine breasts heaving, her nipples stretching with desire. They fell back against the window pane. Without taking his eyes off her, Michael slipped his hand under her top and felt the firmness and warmth of her breasts. She cried out, her hands clasping his body, clinging to him for dear life.

In a sort of staggering dance, they collapsed on the couch. Michael closed his eyes in order to concentrate on the golden flood of swelling joy, and the sweet despair of desire. He lost himself in her endless dark hair, her bow-shaped pink lips, parted slightly, her healthy hot flush, the softness of her skin and the long, pure line of her throat.

His heart thumped alarmingly, one hand caressing her between her legs, their mouths locked, as she arched in absolute urgency.

Suddenly, Simone pushed him away, and sat up.

"What?" said Michael.

"Let's get rid of the masks."

She pulled off her black silk bra, and pulled down her skirt. "This time is for real."

Michael threw off his clothes and looked her in the eye. "Yes."

She shuddered as she lowered herself to him, and began the rhythmic beauty of true man-woman bonding, sinking deeper and deeper into the quicksand of the magic moment. Her hair flew across his chest like the leaves of a willow tree. She glued her mouth to his ear. He gave her his all, and more. An eternity passed in a matter of moments.

Afterward, as they lay entwined in each other, the long beams of late afternoon sunlight slanted in through the French window, glowed in seeming harmony with their newfound truth, and from afar, down in the street came the sounds of music – a lonely saxophone. Russian rhapsody. All was beautiful and the day overflowed with life, love, and the promise of hope fulfilled.

CHAPTER 41

A black convertible, a Lincoln Continental, and a hulking SUV pulled up to a house at the end of Twenty-fourth Street North in Arlington, Virginia. Their headlights shone on the circular drive in front of wide slate steps that led to a heavy oak entrance door. The white mansion was set far back from the road, surrounded by red cedar and oak trees. It was dusk; the streetlamps had already started to glow, bathing the house in rich ochre. Smooth, transparent clouds blanketed the sky, promising a clear night. Everything was still. Everything was ready.

Robert Lovett gently pressed the doorbell as the others moved in behind him. He blew his nose into a handkerchief, a yawn suddenly overcoming him. The door opened.

"Gentlemen." It was more a command than an invitation. The four men silently walked into the study. David Alexander Harriman III switched on the light, shining a dull tawny tint on the rosined linoleum and the wood-paneled shelves lining the walls with the spines of books huddled in tight ranks. Beyond the plate-glass windows, the soft light of a half-moon shone through, reflecting the soft incandescence of the evening. A night to remember.

"You've heard?" Harriman said, as he threw a late afternoon edition of the *Washington Post* on the mahogany coffee table. He looked over at Lovett. "I suppose you'd look better with some sleep."

Lovett sat down in a soft easy chair and again blew his nose. "It has been a long several days," he said.

"I read about Schaffhausen this morning. They are actually calling it a mugging gone wrong," said Ed McCloy shaking his head with a snort of disdainful amusement. "Are they the same people who took Reid?" he asked, tugging on his ear.

"No, Ed, we took out Reid, and unless you know something we don't, Schaffhausen was someone else's operation," replied CIA Associate Director Henry Stilton, leaning forward and pulling a cushion from underneath him.

"In the meantime, we have business to attend to." Harriman picked up a glass, tossed in a couple of ice cubes and filled it with Bourbon. His voice was casual and unhurried. "Robert?"

The four men held their breath. Robert Lovett, officially a senior analyst for the State Department, was better known to the men in the room as deep cover for the Political Stabilization Unit, a branch of the U.S. intelligence known as Consular Operations. "One hundred and four of Casolaro's contacts have been analyzed and discarded for various reasons; three because they are dead, natural causes, and the rest did not know or suspect anything of substance. We have painstakingly gone over their phone logs, credit card charges, bank account statements, personal and professional relationships, anything that might, inadvertently show some foreknowledge of the real situation. Nothing."

"And the remaining three contacts?" asked Harriman, his intelligent eyes penetrating and searching.

"One was Caroni. The other one is Barry Bachrach, a United States attorney. Straight as an arrow. God, flag, country."

"A real patriot," added Stilton. "I know the man. When the Agency tried to buy his silence for certain transgressions of little consequence, he put a few of our best men in jail."

Harriman got up slowly, shaking his head, a mean smirk on his face. "There is always a confused soul who thinks that one man can make a difference; and sometimes you have to kill him to convince him otherwise." He stopped and looked at Stilton. "That's the hassle with democracy, Henry."

"I left the best for last," said Lovett.

"Who?" insisted Harriman.

"Remember how we couldn't find him because he used a routed line bypassing Cons Ops? The authorization was verified by code and a call made on the basis of internal security." Lovett unbuttoned his half-brown wool and polyester suit jacket.

"No log, no tape and no reference to the transmission. Yeah, I remember," added McCloy.

"We found a chink in his armor." He looked smugly around the room. "Routed lines with code authorizations have 28A-40J level of clearance. That's their technical designation. Only people with Three Zero and Four Zero clearance have them."

"Except for security purposes they are not identified as names, but rather as numbers," said Stilton. "How did you get around it?"

"We isolated all potential Three and Four Zero candidates and checked their whereabouts at the time of the call. That provided us with zero-knowledge pass code for purposes of verification. There is a system for limited-access intranet verification in cases of National Emergency developed for collaborative operations with other agencies. Through it, we got an abbreviated personnel listing which provided us with a Top-level confirmation. A simple request to the Joint Intelligence Services got us a digital photograph of the only two people who might have made that call. One was in surgery. An emergency appendectomy verified by the medical staff at Bethesda and CCTV cameras."

"And the other?"

"The other is a Four Zero clearance at the most unlikeliest of places."

"You know, Robert, I almost understand what you just said." Harriman tilted his head. "His name, please."

"Mike O'Donnell." Lovett pulled a photo out of his manila folder.

"Cristian Belucci's senior staff member," added James F. Taylor.

"My, my!" replied Harriman, his eyes roving the room. "I hate owing. Always prefer to be owed." He was addressing McCloy. "We'll just have to pay him off for his services, Ed. God, flag, country."

The former Secretary of State reached for his phone and dialed.

"Oui?"

"This is David Harriman. I have a matter which requires your immediate attention."

"I am at your service, Mr. Secretary."

"You will be given a photograph of a man. Find out what he knows, then put him to rest. Do it as soon as possible."

"C'est fini."

Harriman picked up a remote and turned on the TV. CNN erupted into the room.

> "Stephanie, what are you hearing from your White House source"
>
> "Lou, if there was any doubt in anyone's mind that this voracious bear market is going to be with us for a long, long time – this week's events should have erased them all."

"Is there a bright spot in any of this Stephanie?"

"Well, let's see. General Motors shares plunged 22% to $1.56, touching levels not seen in 71 years and putting its market capitalization below $1 billion. That's gotta hurt."

"What about banking?"

"Bright spots in banking, Lou? Bank of America shares hit a record low and Citygroup stock slumps to a 28-year low as the two financial giants face extinction in the face of government's inability to steady the sinking ship." "Thank you Stephanie.

In international news, Latvia's coalition government collapsed today, plunging the Baltic country into political turbulence at a time when its economy is mired in a severe crisis and investors are increasingly concerned about the situation in Eastern Europe.

"The capital Riga was rocked by protests over economic policy in January. The government collapse in Latvia comes only weeks after Iceland's government resigned over the devastating crisis that has wrecked the island nation's economy and less than a week after Lithuanian President and Estonian Prime Minister have resigned after a vote of non confidence."

Harriman punched the off button and dumped the remote. "Unless we find the money, none of it will make a damn bit of difference," he muttered, his hands clasped behind him, anguished exasperation in his voice.

"We are doing the best we can," said Edward McCloy, shrugging his shoulders.

"Ed, we have spent the better part of the past decade buying up companies all over the world through mergers and acquisitions, using misleading front companies as surrogates, cornering the world markets and manipulating prices. With the world economy tanking, our initial investment has lost most of its value and our collateral has been requisitioned because a former United States government employee broke into a secret account containing trillions of dollars in slush funds. We have to do better than that."

CHAPTER 42

I t was past midnight when the exhausted Executive Vice President of the World Bank walked out of his office located at 1818 H Street in Washington, flagged a cab for a short ride to the airport and boarded a company jet. Less than one hour later he touched down at LaGuardia airport in New York.

Cristian went to his car and pulled out of an executive parking lot attached to the east end of the airport's national terminal one, reserved for government officials and corporate elite. He put his Bentley into fourth gear and raced through the intersection just as the light turned red. To say his day had been brutal would definitely qualify as an understatement. Someone at the World Bank had leaked a preliminary draft document to a senior financial columnist at the *New York Times* that showed the bank was lending money to CityGroup, brokered by the White House. The government leaned on the *Times'* Chief Executive Officer, who was made to understand that foregoing reporter-source confidentiality, in this case, was in everyone's best interest. The senior financial columnist, under threat of instant dismissal, had given them the name of Mike O'Donnell, an affable Irishman and Cristian's most senior staff member. This put Cristian under instant suspicion as the man behind the leak, causing the President of the United States to cancel his telephone call.

Additionally, O'Donnell was nowhere to be found. He had a business lunch with a Goldman Sach's executive which he skipped, no explanation given, and a 6:30 P.M. interview which he cancelled by way of a brief text message, saying only he was detained, leaving no telephone number where he could be reached. From what Cristian knew about O'Donnell, that omission was extraordinary, especially at this time of financial disintegration of the markets and pressing money problems for the newly elected President. There were too many people who might need his advice, approval, signature or information at any given moment. As Belucci's senior aid, few knew the inner workings of the World Bank better than O'Donnell. It was not logical he would sever that cord. It was also a screaming alarm bell that, the night before, he had cleaned out his desk and removed all personal items. Was he given a heads-ups? By whom? If O'Donnell was the source of the leak, then Cristian would, for obvious reasons, want the culprit out of the way and as far from the premises as possible.

***

Curtis buttoned his jacket and pulled the lapels up around his neck. The dusk of twilight dimmed everything around. Something was wrong. It simply didn't make any sense.

CTP was real. One part of the pool money, trillions of dollars, created by the collateral trading program was being actively used to rescue many of the world's major banks, who faced insolvency crises as recession bit deeper and harder. That's why CTP was put into motion in the first place. Notwithstanding, the crisis was deepening by the minute, with the government stuttering along at best and paralyzed at worst, unable to get it right.

Why would the government ask the World Bank for a one hundred billion dollar loan if they had access to trillions through the program? Unless, of course, they didn't have access to the money. If not, what happened to it?

Still pondering, Curtis ambled down the road, hands in his pockets, past the post office, the supermarket and several beggars with stooped shoulders and hands outstretched. He distributed a few dollars to each of them, as a propitiatory, sacrificial gesture, and proceeded across a miniature park with stone benches, two of which had been spray-painted by someone named Joey, proclaiming his eternal love for Sarah in big, bold, crooked letters.

***

Cristian's Bentley turned left, effortlessly climbing a steep ramp as the garage doors silently opened. Less than thirty seconds later he had parked his car and locked the door. He checked his watch. Five minutes to two. A shadow stepped out from behind the pillar, an elongated object in its hands. Cristian spun around, looked at the shadow, then at the object. Suddenly, he realized what it was. "Don't do it, please. If you want money, I'll give it to you. I can pay." He took a halting step, then another, hands out in surrender.

"I am already well paid, but thank you for such a kind offer."

Two muffled pops in rapid succession. Cristian felt a searing heat as he fell on his back, left hand still holding the attaché case, right hand on his stomach. He heard footsteps, slow and deliberate. The shadow was over him now, stooping, examining his victim from above. He laughed. "D'accord, mon ami. Au revoir."

A gust of wind blew by. Cristian heard it, but, oddly, couldn't feel it.

***

Simone sat next to Michael at Cristian's living room table, reading one of the travel magazines. Her attention constantly strayed; concentration escaped her. She checked her watch. "What's taking him so long?" She put down the magazine and poured herself another cup of tea, glancing over at the door for the third time in less than a minute.

Suddenly, Michael's telephone emitted two sharp beeps. Michael reached for the phone. "Hello?

"I've been shot … I'm in the garage."

The ride down seemed interminable. The elevator doors opened and the two of them cautiously stepped out. "Cristian!" they both whispered in unison.

"Here," the voice was barely audible.

"Oh, God, what happened!"

"No time to explain." He was leaning against the front wheel, driver door ajar, his cell phone in his left hand. He pulled himself up with difficulty, his head jerking in short movements as he raised his eyes to meet Michael's. "Call ambulance, hurry," he said, his voice still a whisper, his lips barely moving.

Michael dialed, spoke to someone. "Ambulance will be here in five minutes," he said.

Less than twelve minutes later Cristian was nimbly wheeled into the Emergency Medical Service ambulance by two paramedics. Simone and Michael climbed in beside him.

Michael's phone rang.

"Michael, it's me. Sorry for calling so late. Are you two asleep? What happened? You got something?"

"No. Cristian's been shot."

"What!? How?"

"In his garage. Police are trying to piece it together; we're on the way to the hospital."

"How?"

"Someone obviously knew his schedule and was waiting for him."

Curtis' mind went into overdrive.

"Michael, this is getting more and more dangerous. Reid was right. There is someone else, another player, bigger than Octopus, and they have their hooks sunk into both them and us."

"All right," said Michael, his voice faint. "God help us."

"I wish I could believe He can. Or, maybe God just doesn't give a damn anymore."

CHAPTER 43

White House Situation Room

The President got to his feet. Biting his nether lip and pondering something, he turned and faced the others.

"Ladies and gentlemen, I have asked you to attend this meeting because, as the President of the United States, I have moral responsibility and a Constitutional obligation to lead this great nation," he said, in a somewhat tentative but still resolute voice. "The scope of the crisis, as we are discovering, is simply beyond one's comprehension. Our efforts to address an entirely new set of life-threatening issues run the risk of being seen for what they are; not lipstick on a pig, but lipstick on a corpse.

"Our immediate priority has to be the missing money. Find it. I don't care what Devil you make a deal with, but find that money. Larry, how much time do we have?" The President stood up.

"Three days, one week tops, Mr. President," replied the Director of the National Economics Council. "Whatever is coming is coming at us at light speed and we may not have the luxury of an organized retreat. The system is broken. It's broken for reasons far greater than what used to be called corruption. And it cannot be fixed when an unprecedented economic collapse is smashing down every wall between humanity and the unthinkable."

"Jesus Christ." The President cupped his face with both hands and sat motionless for several seconds. "Then what?"

Kirsten Rommer, leading economic historian and Chairperson of the Council of Economic Advisers stood up. "First stage? Systemic breakdown that will cripple our economy. The country comes to a screeching halt. No welfare checks, no social security, no healthcare benefits, no food stamps for the poor and no money to pay the three-and-a-half million government employees." She paused. "The scenario

I foresee is that panic will, within a few days, drive prices significantly skyward. And as supplies can no longer meet demand, the market will become paralyzed at prices too high for the wheels of commerce and even daily living. The trucks will no longer pull into food stores. The shelves will be all-but-empty. Hoarding and uncertainty will trigger violence and chaos. Police and military will be able to maintain order for only a short time, if at all. Consumers will stop paying their bills and going to work. This would be the second stage. The poor will be the first to suffer and they will suffer the most. They will begin to die. That's the final stage," she said quietly, her voice on the verge of breaking. "It is very hard and very painful to accept this reality. Mother Nature does not grant time-outs."

The President nodded. "So much emphasis has been placed upon false priorities that the true issues have been obscured and politics has come to mean crafty and cunning selfishness, instead of candid and sincere service. Politics is not an end, but a means." The President paused, then continued. "I want clear-cut solutions," he said, suddenly realizing that his head was throbbing and his back was aching.

"Sir, I believe identifying mission-critical systems is an absolute imperative at this moment," said William Staggs, coordinator for the Office of National Preparedness. "Knives are coming out and points of no return are fast approaching. In short order we will know whether the United States and the rest of the world lives or dies. More, we will know whether civilized society is an option in the long run, or an untenable dream. If it is not, then the barbarians will break down the gates, and they will bring with them mighty appetites."

"What are you saying?"

"The problem is, Sir, we have no Plan B, and it is now also too late to come up with a Plan C or Plan D. Finding the missing money is our only hope."

Vice-Admiral Al Hewitt cleared his throat, his figure rigid in his chair. "Mr. President, I believe that in the name of national security, we must begin real-time preparations for martial law. Progress is what brings light out of darkness, civilization out of disorder, prosperity out of poverty. All of these essentials are being challenged and threatened."

"Al, if we simply go to martial law, democratically elected civilian government bodies would be closed down and taken over by the military, possibly including us," clarified Secretary of State Sorenson.

"We must protect the country. There is no room for dissent when America is under attack!" replied Hewitt.

"The job of the democratically elected government is not to declare war on the people of the United States!" shot back Sorenson.

"The job of the government is to maintain law and order, even if it requires the enactment of martial law."

"Christ, Al, you are advocating a Homeland Security State and setting the stage for the militarization of civilian institutions."

"We are creating conditions necessary to keep the country out of harm's way!"

"Wherever war is called peace, where oppression and persecution are referred to as security, and assassination is called liberation, the defilement of the language precedes and prepares for the defilement of life and dignity!"

"Brad, I think you have picked the wrong profession. You should have been a speech writer for some wack-a-doodle liberal. You'd have made a fortune."

"Fuck you, Hewitt! Remember who you're talking to."

"All political power is primarily an illusion, Brad. Don't puff yourself up too much."

The president stepped in. "I'm President of the United States. Now, that may be temporary, but it's no goddamn illusion. This barroom brawl stops now."

Everyone fell silent; they looked at each other, then turned and faced the President. Secretary of State Sorenson frowned, a questioning look in his eyes.

The President nodded slowly, massaging his temples with his palms. "It is said that one of Voltaire's disciples once asked him, 'I'd like to create a new religion. How should I go about it?' To which the master replied, 'It's very simple. Just get yourself crucified and then rise from the dead.'" Again he paused, but it was a different silence. And when he resumed speaking, it was a different tone. "That might be easier. Perhaps we should ask the dead."

A few minutes before four o'clock in the morning, the meeting was over and everyone left the White House Situation Room. The Secretary of State and the President were the last to go.

"Brad, I commend you for what you said in there," said the President, his hand on Sorenson's shoulder. "You are one of the few relics who actually read the Constitution and understand what civilian authority really means." They walked silently for a few moments, each deep in thought, fighting his own demons.

"How long have we known each other, Brad?"

"Forty years, give or take a few months."

"Forty years. Going all the way back to high school. Christ, you used to let me copy your math exams."

"I'll hold it over you forever, sir!" Sorenson smiled.

"No, you won't. You are too ethical." Again, they walked for a few more meters immersed in silence. "What happens if they're right? If there is only one option open to us. What then? The aftermath scares the hell out of me."

Sorenson nodded silently, but did not reply.

"Listen Brad, Hewitt is a son of a bitch, but he is very good at what he does. We need him. I also disagree with his methods and his principles, but this is not about personal likes or dislikes, it's about doing the right thing at the most crucial period in the world's history. And what we need right now is to ensure we have the means to fight this. We need time, and Hewitt just might be able to buy it for us." The President paused. "Let him play toy soldiers. That's what he does best. But in the end, the soldier boys couldn't run with it—"

"Because they have no concept of politics," interrupted the Secretary of State.

"Exactly. Remember, until the very last minute, the decisions are still made here, at the White House." The President looked at Sorenson with a calm, thin smile. "I'll keep him on a string while you look for the money," continued the President as they turned towards the exit, "How do you think they did it?"

"Through a highly sophisticated computer system."

The President raised his eyebrows. "A computer program?"

"*The* computer program, sir. PROMIS."

***

The elevator stopped on the third floor, the bell rang and the door opened. "To your right sir," said a dull looking man with a waxy bald spot. The hallway was a glistening pristine white, the floor was rose-colored marble, which was altogether proper as Mount Sinai Medical Center had established a reputation that was second to none.

Curtis turned right and continued down the hallway, noting that each of the rooms he passed was the size of a junior hotel suite, far in excess of normal hospital standards. But then again, Mount Sinai was no ordinary hospital. It was a wellness center for the world's richest and most powerful, where they paid outrageously for services rendered. One of the two well-spoken guards, wearing the uniform of a private security firm, in reality part of a government-owned entity, checked Curtis' name against a manifest, and with a polite "This way, sir," let Curtis through the door made of thick varnished oak with a blinking red light above its top frame.

"… remained faithful to starched collars and cuffs," Simone was saying, licking her lips and setting the glass back on the table, the scent of coffee suffusing the room.

"Faithful to whom and where?"

"Curtis!" Michael jumped up, strain registering on his pale face, yet obviously relieved to see him.

"I was telling Michael about my dad."

Curtis mechanically glanced over to his left. The bed was empty. A prickle of apprehension and alarm ran down his neck.

"He's in surgery. They told us to wait here." There was a pause. "Another ten minutes and it would have been too late."

Curtis stared into space, his eyes intense.

"Just look at us," said Simone trying to cheer everyone up. "We look dreadful."

He looked at a plasma screen in the corner of the room. "Was there any coverage of the shooting in the news?" asked Curtis.

"A special bulletin on CNN, few details, calling it a mugging," replied Michael.

The rest was left unsaid, as he moved away from the table and leaned against the far wall.

"The markets plunged another eighteen percent today." Curtis closed his eyes as if in a trance. "There's something we're not seeing." Curtis pushed himself off the wall and walked up and down the room, hands behind his back. "Cristian said that on the request of the United States government, the World Bank was ready to lend CityBank money. Why would they do that?"

"Danny had proof of a link between the secret trading program and Citybank," said Simone, looking hard at Curtis.

"Which, according to John Reid, was a multi-level system involving the military-industrial complex," added Michael, leaning forward and looking past Curtis at the window and beyond.

"I wonder how high your brother got, Simone, before they felt threatened enough to neutralize him," Michael added.

"Military-industrial complex," Curtis repeated slowly. "They would be after control, right?" And then without waiting for an answer, "Except they couldn't hope for military control until the money part was taken care of."

"It all comes back to the same thing," Michael said.

"Someone is pulling the plug on the world's economy," replied Curtis.

Stunned, Simone sat rigidly on the edge of the chair, struggling to keep her eyes open. Curtis sat on the windowsill, focusing on something elusive and just out of reach. "What's the 'common denominator' in Danny's investigation?" he asked.

"CTP," said Michael.

"End result? Money," Curtis added. "Gold? Money. Octopus? Cornering the world markets through control of money supply. United States government? An entity that uses money to further its objectives. PROMIS?"

"A computer program to keep track of it all," added Michael.

"Bingo."

Almost an hour later the door opened, revealing a pale-faced and unconscious Cristian wheeled in by an orderly and a nurse, and finally a doctor. The doctor put his index finger to his lips, indicating silence. He nodded to Simone and motioned for the three of them to come outside.

"It was a close call, but he will live. He is heavily sedated and very weak. He should wake up any moment. When he does, I'll give you five minutes with him, and not a second longer."

The three of them sat in complete silence for twenty minutes before Cristian opened his eyes. He saw a face, but it was blurred and out of focus. The anaesthetic fog in his mind had not lifted entirely. He made a strangled noise, and the three of them sat up.

"How do you manage to look so good with two bullet holes in you?" Curtis asked softly.

Cristian winced, then looked away. Finally the words came. "Don't make me laugh. I can barely breath," he replied out of the corner of his mouth. He could hear his voice; it was weak, but he could hear it.

The doctor put his right hand up. Five minutes. He and the nurse silently let themselves out.

Curtis waited for a few seconds, listening to the noises outside. Muttered sounds, hushed voices.

"Did you see who shot you?"

Cristian tried to move his body but the strength wasn't there. "Not clearly."

Curtis stood motionless over him, his tone controlled. "Did you see anything at all?"

"A shadow – and he spoke French." The wounded man winced. "Curtis," he said in a barely audible tone.

The big man squatted next to the bed. "I'm here."

"The money is missing," Cristian whispered in a hollow tone.

Curtis held his breathe. "What money?"

"CTP."

Curtis checked his watch. The five minutes were almost up, and he knew there would be no point in arguing with the doctor. "How much money?"

"All of it … I think," came a reply. "I think I know who has it."

Cristian found the strength and opened his eyes, but just barely, his lips widely parted. "You must … If not …" And then he could not speak any more. The door opened, he heard light, cautious footsteps fading away … whispers … and then nothing.

CHAPTER 44

In every large city, each new wave of ethnic immigrants has its own little home-away-from-home. Brighton Beach Avenue in Brooklyn is the heart of the Russian enclave, where the dilapidated buildings are classic New York, but the sounds and the smells evoke the old country. The signs come in two languages, and the store windows have that musty Soviet-era look, with last season's tacky holiday lights surrounding samovars and matrioshkas and the occasional undusted plastic plant. Women with high-strung temperaments and colorful aprons "talkaet" at the top of their voices in a peculiar patois of Russianized English.

One hour after leaving the hospital, Curtis, Michael and Simone strolled by Uncle Vanya, a small, smoke-filled restaurant offering all kinds of vodka, blini and caviar, past Rego Park, crossed the boardwalk, and stepped onto the wide sandy beach facing the sea.

"It doesn't make any sense," said Curtis. "Simone's brother Danny, Octopus, Japanese World War Two witnesses, gold, Golden Lily, CTP, John Reid, and now Cristian Belucci with a calling card from a French psychopath assassin. But there is no logic that ties any of these distinct events into a common cause. John Reid is part of the cartel."

"Was part of the cartel," Michael noted.

"Reid was part of the cartel along with some very powerful pissheads, but someone thought it was expedient to take him out. Nothing makes sense." He glared at nobody in particular. "And then, Belucci, World Bank's Senior VP and one of the richest men in the world gets shot in his garage in the middle of the night. His Bentley was untouched, so mugging is out of the question."

"Yet the press are playing up the robbery-gone-wrong scenario," Simone added.

"Exactly. It's the sequence of events that bothers me. Although Reid and Belucci are poles apart, one shooting followed another."

"Two bankers. Both wealthy, both high profile. What was it? A matter of hours?"

"Less than twenty-four. Whoever killed Reid probably also shot Belucci. But why?" Curtis asked.

"All right, Curtis. You've asked for a thread. I'm not sure I can give you one, but maybe a thread of a thread," Michael said.

"Danny was on the verge of tying some of the richest people in the world into a web of criminal activities that have spanned the past sixty years. A few among these rich folks would have wanted him silenced, wouldn't you say?"

"That was the premise, all right," agreed Curtis, nodding. "It's why I called Reid, trying to pull others out, never expecting to find what I did. A global cartel made up of government people, intelligence agencies, mafia and rogue criminals. And above them the Octopus. That's what Danny called them."

"Eight tentacles, eight hearts. Can't be killed and can't be starved to death. I like the symbolism of it."

"So I told Reid there was another group interested in the information, capable of blowing the head off Octopus."

You pretended to be the middleman and that you were in it for money," stated Michael.

"Reid was ready to turn. Then suddenly he's killed." Curtis said.

"It's as if someone was watching and listening," added Simone.

"Obviously, they couldn't allow it to happen. Reid must have known way too much."

"Then Cristian gets shot less than a day later," Michael said.

"If Reid was part of the Board, and the Board is part of Octopus, then another group is using us to take over Octopus' business. Tit for tat. Reid and then Cristian," Curtis said.

"They have us exactly where they want us, except we don't know anything about them, and they have all the principle and secondary players mapped out," Michael concluded.

"Who the hell is more powerful than Octopus?" Curtis asked.

"Just hear me out. For now, it's just a theory. This is where my arcane knowledge of symbolism comes in handy. You're Special Forces, right? I mean, that's your training?" Michael asked.

"10th Special Forces Group."

"What's the symbol on the unit coin?"

"A Trojan Horse surrounded by three arrows spinning in a circle."

"What were you engaged in?"

"Interrogation of the most hardened Al Qaeda prisoners and sympathizers. HVS: High Value Subjects." He paused. "Operation Trojan Horse."

"Remember the symbolism," Michael said. "A Trojan Horse surrounded by three arrows spinning in a circle. Now project its symbolic image into a verbal meaning."

"A Trojan Horse surrounded by three arrows spinning in a circle … Jesus Christ! The logo of the Trilateral Commission. World government. The Commission's purpose is to engineer the creation of global financial cartels more powerful than any single government on the planet."

"Exactly. Three arrows spinning in a circle representing three markets led by the five permanent members of the United Nations Security Council. The Americas. Which is the United States. Asia. Which would be China, and the European Community represented by Russia, Britain, France."

"As the world economy collapses into a heap of shit, you control populations on three fronts – the Americas, Asia and the European Community, and through three markets – Hong Kong, Wall Street and the European Economic Area. That would be the first level of control." Michael said.

"Presidents and Prime Ministers control individual countries. Individual countries under three markets of the Trilateral Commission are truly operated by Fortune 500 companies," added Curtis, clearly thinking out loud. "That would be your World Company Limited. Second level of control."

"The more powerful a Fortune 500 company is, the more powerful its market share."

"Market is the Octopus," Michael interjected. "Three. The sacred number of the trinity."

"A mega-conspiracy theory," Curtis added.

"The media uses the epithet 'conspiracy theorist' to stigmatize anyone who discusses it. This is different because we are dealing with real people and real crimes. After everything you had said about Octopus, I did some checking. The three markets combined under the Trilateral Commission. What does it mean to you?"

"The theory of the New World Order," added Curtis. Michael nodded.

"In order to control each market you would have to own or heavily influence four things: Intelligence, Armed Forces, Banking, and Artificial Intelligence. Acquiring all four legally would be hard—" Curtis said.

"Unless an Octopus of men working towards that goal were formed," interrupted Simone, suddenly remembering Cristian's words.

"Every alphabet soup agency is in on the action generating spectacular profits for very little risk .... It is a form of creating money that is effectively unchallenged by any form of oversight or accountability. However, whoever set it in motion had to have been somebody at a pretty high level."

Curtis continued, "However, you couldn't do it through force alone."

"Nor would you need to," replied Michael.

"Not with the world's most sophisticated artificial intelligence at your fingertips," added Curtis.

"PROMIS," Simone said.

"That's really what it's all about, isn't it," said Curtis, closing his eyes and massaging the back of his neck with the palm of his right hand. Scenarios flitted by in his mind – imagined, prodded, considered, explored, and rejected, all within seconds.

Around them, on Brighton Beach, people laughed and flashed smiles and held hands, made witty small talk and shopped and jostled, ate hot dogs and sugar-coated buns. It was as if a veil stood between them and the nightmare confronting the three friends.

"We need to find whoever created PROMIS," Curtis said.

"I don't expect it to be a problem," replied Michael. Curtis' eyes found Michael's, and he prepared to listen to the rest.

"What do you know?" Curtis asked, hand in pockets, head tilted to the side.

"The man behind PROMIS has been living on borrowed time."

"They call him the invisible man."

"His name is Sandorf. Alan Sandorf. That's the name I found in Armitage's Golden Lily report at the reference library."

"There were several references in the Armitage report. We didn't see it first as the entire report references over one hundred people."

"There are several third-person references to Sandorf but no direct quotes. Except for one place when Armitage quotes another person in reference to this technology. This person was footnoted as 'name withheld,'" Simone added. "It has to be the same person. The invisible man hiding in plain sight."

CHAPTER 45

Curtis rounded the corner, walking rapidly and turned onto Blight Avenue, a small dead-end street parallel to 135th Street, the heart of Harlem. He checked the number Michael had given him. One block up. The building was old, but in surprisingly decent shape, all things considered. Curtis put his hand on the railing and swiftly climbed the seven steps to the landing.

The name Sandorf, A. was under the fifth mail slot, a bell beneath the letters. Discretion was called for. Curtis checked the street. No cops. He reached into his pocket and pulled out a thin key, flat but for five tiny elevations between the cuts. It was a "bump key," designed to hit spring-loaded stacks in the keyhole column hard enough that the top pin bounced clear of it for an instant, high enough to go past the shear line. In that same instant, before the spring pushed the top pin down again, the key would turn.

Curtis positioned the bump key in front of the hole, inserting it halfway, and banged it with the palm of his right hand, forcing it deeper as hard as he could, and then twisted it the instant it was in. The lock clicked and the door opened. He silently walked in, then shut the door behind him. He could not use the elevator as its sound might alarm Alan Sandorf.

They call him the invisible man.

He took the first, cautious step. The old staircase creaked. He went up swiftly, taking steps two and three at a time. In less than thirty seconds, he had reached the top floor. Sandorf's apartment was at the end of the hallway. He stood still for several seconds catching his breath. He was about to ring the bell situated to the right of the door but thought better of it. If Sandorf for whatever reason decided not to let him in the sound of the doorbell might draw unwanted attention. Curtis moved to the door and gently knocked.

From beyond, he heard an odd sound growing louder and louder. Someone came to the door. Then the sound stopped. Someone was standing inside the apartment and listening. Curtis heard a click and the door opened.

"Yes?" said a short black man. He had a low-pitched voice that could have easily belonged to a baritone opera singer. He was in his mid-fifties, with a slim build but a pronounced beer belly. He looked slightly sleep-rumpled and was wearing a silk dressing gown with green sheep stretched tight across his plump midsection.

"Alan Sandorf ?"

"That depends on what ya looking for."

"Wisdom."

"Wisdom?" He pushed the door open. "Look around you. Can't you see, you've come to the wrong place?" Curtis stopped on the threshold of the apartment. It was a large, cluttered loft, giving the impression of a flea market rather than someone's living space.

"It has character. Looks like the war room at the headquarters of the *New York Times*," said Curtis,

"Is that what you read?"

"Sometimes."

Sandorf snorted. "Reading the *Times* is like attending funeral services for a notorious grammarian," replied the strange black man.

"Is that your appraisal of me?"

"Appraisals often contain germane facts." He turned around and faced Curtis.

"I—"

Sandorf held up his hand. "Have a chair, son."

Curtis stared at the black man with curiosity. "PROMIS. How much of it is real and how much is a myth?"

Sandorf leaned back against the wall, studying his visitor. "Who are you? What do you want?" he asked in a whisper.

"They call you the invisible man, Alan – the genius behind PROMIS." Curtis paused. "Please, I need to know what it can do. What it has done."

"You should know that you have involved yourself in an extremely sensitive government operation, that's the bottom line."

"My scars can attest to that."

"It's your funeral." He shrugged his shoulders nonchalantly, as he shuffled his way towards the center of the room.

"Myths, by definition, cannot be proved, but facts can be understood and integrated," he began, lowering himself with ponderous relish onto a couch. "What would you do if you possessed software that could think, understand every language in the world, provide peep holes into the innermost secret chambers of everyone else's computers, that could insert data into computers without people's knowledge, enter via the back door of secret bank accounts and then remove the money without leaving a trace, that could fill in blanks beyond human reasoning and also predict what people would do – long before they did it, within a one percent margin of error? You would probably use it, wouldn't you?"

"What was it used for originally?"

"I designed it to track cases through the legislative, judicial and executive branches by integrating computers of dozens of U.S. Attorneys' offices around the country. The more data you uploaded, the more accurately the system could analyze and predict the final outcome of the cases."

"How does it work?" Curtis asked.

"Actually it's quite simple. All information on someone is fed into the software – educational, military, criminal, professional background, credit history, basically anything you can get your hands on, then the software is tasked with making an assessment, then rendering a conclusion based on the available information. The more information available, the better the software will predict the outcome." Standorf laughed softly. He got up, limping into the kitchen. "You want some coffee?"

"Sure, why not. Black, please."

"PROMIS can literally predict human behavior based on information from the person," he shouted from the kitchen. "The government and the spooks immediately recognized the financial and military application of PROMIS, especially the National Security Agency, which had millions of bits of intelligence coming into its facilities every day, with an antiquated Cray Supercomputer Network to log it, sort it, and analyze it." He brought over a cup of coffee. Curtis took a sip and almost gagged.

"Good coffee, eh?" asked Sandorf.

"Great," replied Curtis with a forced smile.

"Don't be shy, there's more in the kitchen." Sandorf blew his nose into a handkerchief, folded it into a square and put it away. "The long and the short of it was that whoever owned PROMIS, once it was fused with artificial intelligence, could accurately predict commodities futures, real estate, the movement of entire armies on a battlefield, not to mention every country's purchasing habits, drug habits, stereotypes, psychological tendencies, in real time, based upon the information fed into it."

"Interesting, but not what you had in mind when you build it, is it?"

"My program crossed a threshold in the evolution of computer programming. A quantum leap, if you like. Are you familiar with block-modeling social research theory?"

"Should I be?"

"It describes the same unique vantage point from hypothetical and real life perspectives. For example, pick an actual physical point in space. Now, in your mind, move it further out than you ever thought possible. PROMIS progeny have made possible the positioning of satellites so far out in space that they are untouchable."

"The ultimate big picture."

"Now you are getting it!" Sandorf laughed. "There is another advantage and it is awesome." He drank greedily. Curtis had never seen a person drink with such profound, concentrated relish. "I love a good cup of coffee! Anyway, Geomatics. The term applies to a related group of sciences – all involving satellite imagery – used to develop geographic information systems, global positioning systems and remote sensing from space that can actually determine the locations of natural resources such as oil, precious metals and other commodities."

"Sounds like a perfect con."

"It is, especially if you have enhanced PROMIS software with back-door technology."

He rose and headed for the window. "By providing the client nation PROMIS-based software it would then be possible to compile a global data base of every marketable natural resource. And it would not be necessary to even touch the resources because commodities and futures markets exist for all of them. An A.I.-enhanced, PROMIS-based program would then be the perfect set up to make billions of dollars in profits by watching and manipulating the world's political climate."

"You know that for a fact?" asked Curtis.

"Subsequent research clearly demonstrated that a similar remote hypothetical position would eliminate randomness from all human activity. Everything would be visible in terms of measurable and predictable patterns. As you said, the ultimate big picture. The other thing to remember is that where mathematics has proved that every human being on the earth is connected to every other by only six degrees of separation, in undercover operations the number shrinks to around three. In the PROMIS story it often shrinks to two."

"It really is a small world."

"But PROMIS is not a virus. It has to be installed as a program on the computer systems that you want to penetrate." He limped over to the bookcase. "Look on your right there. Top shelf, red leather spine, a notebook written by a guy named Massimo Grimaldi, the greatest computer mind in history. I put it there over five years ago, don't figure it moved since then." Curtis pulled down a heavy, musty volume covered with a thick layer of dust. Sandorf found the page and showed it to Curtis. "You see this?" Pointing to a drawing.

"What is it?"

"Elbit Flash memory chip. It was Grimaldi's idea."

"What's so special about it?"

"PROMIS is fitted with an Elbit Flash memory chip that activates power to the computer when it is turned off."

"How can you do that?"

"Because Elbit chips work on ambient electricity in a computer. By combining another newly developed chip, the Petrie, which is capable of storing up to six months worth of key strokes, with Grimaldi's creation, it is now possible to burst transmit all of a computer's activity in the middle of the night to a nearby receiver – say in a passing truck or even a low flying Signals Intelligence satellite."

"Incredible."

"There is something else about PROMIS you should know – the trap door. The trap door allows access to the information stored within the database by anyone who knows the correct access code. Intelligence and banking records accessed through the Trojan trap door allow unrestricted access to governments—"

"Which ensures the survival of the U.S. dollar abroad and at home," added Curtis.

"So you are not a dumb chump, after all. Take it as a compliment, son, I mean it." Sandorf put the Grimaldi volume on a rickety table in front of him.

"Sold to foreign governments, the PROMIS A.I. software could later be accessed by our government without the foreign government's knowledge. Remember, these are not nice people, these are financial thugs at their worst."

"What you are describing goes beyond economic hanky-panky. What's the objective?"

"Look around you, son. The world is going to hell in a handbasket faster than you can say 'God have mercy.' The goal is to penetrate every banking system in the world. These people could then use PROMIS both to predict and to influence the movement of financial markets worldwide."

"I have been made to understand that in order to capture each market you would have to control, own or influence Intelligence, Armed Forces, Banking, and Artificial Intelligence."

"That's what they say. But why would one need to go through all the trouble now of monitoring all of a foreign country's intelligence operations and military? There's an easier way to get what you want. Fit PROMIS with a Trojan door version on every computer you sell to Canada, Europe and Asia, both civilian and government to monitor their military, banking and intelligence operations. You access their banks, and you know who's getting ready to do what."

"This places all data at constant risk of exposure."

"Exactly."

"Are governments aware of it?"

"I doubt it, but even if they were, there is little they can do about it at this stage in the game. These are mission-critical systems requiring years of development, not something you whip up in a jiffy at a hot dog stand. Forcing every nation on Earth into cooperating with whoever has the system could easily be done once PROMIS software is on line."

"Because software would control national banks, intelligence agencies and military," Curtis added.

"Exactly. By cornering, via unlimited access, banking, intelligence and the military, the mere threat of force is all that is needed. A weapon is only good if someone knows what it's capability is. Prior to using the atomic bomb it was irrelevant."

"The Nagasaki Syndrome. But how did the world allow this to happen?"

"They didn't. You see this book? It was stolen from Grimaldi. He was killed, and they made it look like an accident."

"How did you get your hands on it?" asked Curtis incredulously. "It was a gift from the people who killed him," replied Sandorf matter-of-factly.

"What happened?"

"According to the official version, he hit his head in the bathtub and drowned in two inches of water. Christ, Grimaldi was an Italian Jew. His shnozz was longer than Pinocchio's. How the hell do you drown, face down, in two inches of water?"

"So, no one knew."

"Governments had been provided with modified PROMIS software which each one of these nations then modified, or thought they had modified, again to eliminate the trap door. But unknown to all of them, the Elbit chips in the systems bypassed the trap doors and permitted the transmission of data when everyone thought the computers were turned off and secure. This is how you cripple everything Canada, Europe and Asia do that you don't like."

"Can you stop them?"

"Me? You are kidding me, ain't you, son? Look at me," he said.

Sandorf rolled up the sleeve of his silk gown exposing his deeply scarred left hand. "I'm a junkie. Some days, I can't even pull my pants down in time to take a piss." He paused. "And even if I weren't, it's too late."

"What do you mean."

"You really don't get it? It's fourth and goal on the two-yard line with ten seconds to go in the game."

"I have another question for you." Curtis' words were clipped.

"I thought you might. Didn't figure you had gone to all that trouble for some background noise."

"Suppose someone wanted to use PROMIS to break into an unbreakable system. Can it be done?"

Sandorf sat back, deep in thought, his hands crossed, resting against his large belly. "It would have to be someone mighty good. And there's only one person who fits the bill. Paulo Caroni."

"You're saying he knew about PROMIS?"

"Yeah. One nasty son of a bitch. Resident demon of the labyrinth." He uncrossed his arms, awkwardly pulled himself up and moved within inches of Curtis' powerful frame, grabbing his forearm with his long, bony hands. "I will give you a piece of advice, son. You gotta' count your fingers every time you shake that guy's hand.

"There are very, very few who can touch him, maybe a hundred in the whole world." He looked at Curtis. "I guess you know about the missing billions."

"You mean trillions."

He smiled. "That's what I mean. The penetration and looting of the money was the White Sands proving ground of the PROMIS economic atom bomb."

"How did he become involved in it?"

"He was brought in by the government to help create a more brilliant AI system out of PROMIS. Caroni already had his own system, so the marriage between my baby and his immediately produced a hybrid. This hybrid was used by the United States government to collect financial intelligence and monitor bank transactions."

"For whom?"

"For the CIA, initially, among other entities. It was a conspiracy, a full-fledged military-industrial complex conspiracy. It went all the way to the top. Their own private stomping ground."

"Who were the top men involved?"

"Does the name Henry Stilton ring a bell?"

Curtis' eyes widened. "Second in command at the Agency?"

"That's the one. They engaged in a conspiracy to steal my software, modify it to include a trap door that would allow those who knew of it to access the program in other computers, and then sell it overseas to foreign intelligence agencies. I began to smell a rat when agencies from other countries, like Canada, started asking me for support services in French when I had never made sales to Canada."

"Caroni. What can you tell me about him?"

"When he was just ten years old, he wired his parents' neighborhood with a working, private telephone system that bypassed Ma Bell."

Sandorf limped over to the balcony, opened the door that led to the terrace. To Curtis' surprise it was ... well, a Zen garden. A plot of ground perhaps four meters in length by five in width, with a very simple arrangement of rocks and stones, sand, gravel and pebbles. "This is called the Karesansui in Japanese. It means dry water and mountain, the illusion of water is done with the way sand is raked across the ground, creating a pattern of ripples while the rocks and stones are scattered to replicate mountains and islands."

"That's quite a sight," said Curtis.

Sandorf grinned. "There are fourteen rocks and stones here. Legend has it that when a person achieves the highest form of Zen enlightenment, the fifteenth rock becomes visible to them."

"Why does someone like you live here?"

"Security," said the black man.

"Here!"

"Can you see a white son of a bitch trying to rob me in the 'hood?"

"You could disappear. Go live somewhere else."

Sandorf shook his head. "No, I can't. They'd know it in a jiffy." And without waiting for Curtis' reply. "I have a microchip in my right triceps. The government is keeping me on a short leash." He paused, lowering his voice. "And because I'm a junkie." Sandorf leaned against the wall, head arched back, his eyes half closed, lips trembling. He cleared his throat.

"Shortly after producing a hybrid between PROMIS and Caroni's model, I was kidnapped, and every few hours I was injected with world-class heroin. That was their insurance policy. When they finally let me go, over three months had passed. I think it was a government-run clinic somewhere out west, judging by the climate and vegetation, but I can't prove anything." He looked into the distance. "At one time, I was the hottest property in Washington. Now look at me," said Sandorf in his low baritone, rubbing the crown of his head.

"Why are you still alive?" inquired Curtis.

"In case the system breaks down and there is nobody left to fix it," replied Sandorf bitterly.

"I can help you fight this."

"You realize the ideal solution for the dark forces is the possibility that the target, if subjected to the most personally embarrassing and socially reprehensible kind of false allegations, might self-destruct and thus negate the necessity for further character assassination."

"Bastards. This is standard ammunition for the Agency's counter-intelligence operations as a means of quieting those who threaten them," said Curtis in disgust.

"God forbid you have any kind of vulnerability or skeletons in the closet," added Sandorf.

"How many have been taken out by suicide, devastated mentally or emotionally, or sought escape in drugs and alcohol?"

"Many lives have been destroyed in one way or another in the pursuit of truth – by false accusation."

Curtis limped over to a worn out couch and plumped heavily on it. "I am in your debt, Alan. If one day you want to crawl out of this sewer—"

Sandorf raised his right hand. "I want no part of your fucking merry-go-around of guilt. Go feel guilty somewhere else," he said, sitting up in the cushion, straightening his back and shoulders. "Don't take it the wrong way." And then he added, "This is just one dead man talking to another."

Curtis lowered his gaze and exhaled heavily.

Sandorf looked at him one last time and turned his head away. "You take care, son."

***

On the outskirts of Washington, along one of the more deserted stretches of the Potomac river, a bruised and bloody corpse with a broken right arm, eyes bulging out of their sockets, the livid face knocked out of shape by death, was removed from a white van. Inside, a well-built figure with an impressive tattoo of a dagger on his right forearm picked up the car phone and dialed a number. "It's done."

"What did you find out?" came the reply.

"Nothing. For a man who didn't know much, it sure took him a long and painful time to tell it."

"Get your car and remain outside the hospital. You'll be relieved at midnight by another team. Report any movements immediately. Don't move in until we give a signal. Don't fail me."

"Understood, Mr. Secretary."

Chapter 46

Simone looked over at Cristian, then at the monitor. His vital signs were steady, his breathing constant. She then looked over at Michael.

"I will never stop looking for them, Michael. Never. I understand how insignificant I am to them. No matter how many ways I try to distract myself, I still lie in bed at night going over every detail of our last day together, and wonder how I could have misunderstood or not foreseen how bad things were." Her voice trembled. "Sometimes, I can almost convince myself that it is all a mistake, that Danny will come through that door any minute now. But, he doesn't and he won't, ever.

And after all that, someone who loves you comes along; who actually loves you and whom you love, and you think of what might happen if it didn't work out and how big pieces of your soul will be lost forever. And I shudder at the thought of losing you." She inhaled, what seemed to be all the air in the room. "Oh, God I am so tired. When will it be over and done with. When? If only I had listened to my heart and not let him go."

"Simone." Michael came up, spinning her around, forcing her to look at him. "Danny knew exactly what he was doing when he enrolled in journalism school. He knew exactly what he was doing when he met his first contact. He knew exactly what he was doing when he followed the beast into the lion's den. He was who he was. He loved what he did."

"Michael."

"That load isn't yours to carry."

She looked into his face, studying it as if it was a face of a stranger. Michael leaned down and kissed her gently.

"I believe tiptoeing out the door would be most traditional, but, unfortunately, I am somewhat tied up." Cristian had woken.

"Cristian, we were just—"

The banker raised his hand. "There is really no need to explain."

Simone poured him some water. "Here, you look thirsty."

He smiled. "Thank you for showering me with little attentions. Where is Curtis?"

"Meeting an invisible man."

"Where?" he asked in a bewildered voice.

"It doesn't matter. He thinks he can kill two birds with one stone." A flash lit-up the window blinds followed by a loud thunderclap six seconds later. The weather in New York was cold and restless, enormous flame-colored clouds skimmed overhead.

Michael's phone rang. He pressed the loudspeaker button on his outdated model.

"What happened?"

"It's about PROMIS," Curtis said. "The trillions of dollars created and held in dormant accounts were stolen through PROMIS. Sandorf told me as much. Cristian must have realized it, too. This stuff is plutonium. Anyone who comes near it gets killed."

"Let me catch up," Michael said, shaking his head.

"The Collateral Trading Program was a government operation created to save the world's financial system from imploding in case of financial Armageddon. Except that the Octopus were using that money to generate spectacular profits for very little risk, remember?"

Banks and central banks that operate CTP run two sets of books – the one set for public scrutiny and another set for private viewing only. "Who stole it?" asked Michael.

"Someone by the name of Paulo Caroni. He was brought in by the government to help create an upgraded AI system out of PROMIS. He already had his own system, so the marriage between Sandorf's system and his produced a hybrid. Once Octopus had the hybrid, they dumped Sandorf."

"Why?"

"Because Caroni was one of them, at least initially, and Alan Sandorf wasn't. He told me the penetration and the looting of the money was the test run of the PROMIS economic Atom bomb."

"Do you remember what Cristian said?" Michael asked.

"He said such amounts of money could only exist in cyberspace," replied Curtis, "because you could never physically transfer it anywhere."

"He also said that you didn't have to, as you can move any amount of cash in a millionth of a second with a stroke of a key."

"That's where PROMIS comes in," answered Curtis.

"A large chunk of it was deposited in thirty accounts, in almost one solid block at Citygroup."

"Whose Chief Executive Officer, John Reid, is now pushing up daisies."

Curtis quickly went over his visit to the strange world of Alan Sandorf, explaining how the conspirators would force every nation on Earth into cooperating with whoever had the system, and how it could easily be done through PROMIS, because PROMIS A.I. would control national banks, intelligence agencies and military.

"Why are they doing this?"

"Fanaticism," Curtis replied coldly. "Without the CTP money being injected into the system, the world economy will be wiped out. But it will come at a price. Perhaps the puppet master himself, whoever he is, knows what that price is, but others, those who blindly follow orders, don't. This fanaticism has blinded the conspirators to the true consequences of their shenanigans. Events of this sort could never be contained. They are playing with fire and will be consumed by it in the end when riots, on a scale without precedent, will overrun every country in the world, ending the old order and establishing a new order, a New World Order with the help of the most powerful artificial intelligence in the world, PROMIS."

Michael stared at nothing. There was no need to reply, the thoughts filled him like a deepening shadow.

Simone walked over to the door, turned the handle and opened it. "I'll go get us something eat."

CHAPTER 47

Afternoon in the Big Apple. Simone stood at the curb and slowly inhaled the pungent city air. The wet remains of snow lingered on the sidewalk, and drops of water flowed in slow succession into the gutter.

A black sedan glided quietly up alongside Simone. The sliding passenger door opened, a powerful arm encircled her waist, yanked her off her feet and pulled her inside. The door shut and the sedan sped off. Somebody pressed a gun firmly into Simone's temple, its message unmistakable.

"You have no right ..." She stopped, the foolishness of her remark apparent. She tried to sit up. It was not to be. Someone pressed a soft, wet, acrid-smelling cloth into her face just as the driver turned on the radio.

> *"First it was Eastern Europe's credit rating which less than two weeks ago was downgraded to 'junk' and now it's Western Europe's financial woes that have taken center stage."*
>
> *"That's right, Larry."*
>
> *"Italy's credit default swap spread reached their widest levels on record after Standard & Poor's Ratings Services cut that country's credit rating to 'junk' status. Earlier today, S&P warned in a separate report that 'all the ingredients of a major crisis are in place' in Western Europe. On top of that, Moody's Investors Service placed France and Austria on review for a possible downgrade due out early next week, citing political uncertainty and concerns about the banking sector. Yesterday's collapse of Italy's coalition government spread worldwide concern that it could create a domino effect among the rest of Western Europe's economies."*
>
> *"Thank you, Marian. At home, the nation's largest banks are so close to collapse and the world economy is coming unglued so rapidly, a major Wall Street meltdown is now imminent.*

Specifically, it's now increasingly likely that virtually all of the dire forecasts of recent months could come to pass in a very short period of time, including a full-blown stock market crash: A swift plunge in stocks to about 3000 on the Dow and 300 on the S&P ... or lower."

"David, this is beginning to look more and more like economic Armageddon and the day of reckoning. Give us your short-term predictions."

"Short term is right, Larry. We're talking days or weeks, not months ahead. First of all, corporate bankruptcies: A chain reaction of Chapter 11 filings or federal takeovers, including not only General Motors and Chrysler, but also Jet Blue, Macy's, Saks Fifth Avenue, Sears, Toys 'R' Us, U.S. Airways and even giants like Ford or General Electric. Next, megabank failures: bankruptcies or nationalization not only of Citygroup and Bank of America, but also JP Morgan Chase and HSBC. Third, a nationwide epidemic of small and medium-sized bank failures. Fourth, insurance failures.

"What remains to be seen is how the new President is planning to honor all the pledges his government has committed to over the past two months."

"How much money have they promised, David, is anyone keeping track?"

"Marian, counting the $300 billion dollar gift to AIG, we are looking at a grand total of eight trillion dollars."

"Do they have that kind of money? I guess we will find out shortly."

Michael moved to the window, because it seemed a good place to think. He glanced at Cristian, who had willed himself into a deep, escapist sleep. Michael walked over to the coffee maker. He made coffee. Black. No sugar. He drank some, both hands around the mug. He checked his watch, again. Thirty minutes. Where is she? He took another pull of coffee, stared at the floor and sipped again. Then he called her. Forty-five minutes. It rang, but she did not answer. When he called again, it went straight to voicemail.

"Hey. Where are you? Are you okay? But even as he spoke the words, he knew she was not.

CHAPTER 48

In Washington D.C., the rain lingered with diminishing strength over the capital. The President's eyes strayed beyond the bullet-proof library bay window to the White House lawns. They looked gray in the fading afternoon light, on this unseasonably warm winter afternoon. Clad in an open-necked three-button shirt with gold cuf-flinks and a pair of black trousers, he was deep in thought. A nation at war with itself, nations at war with each other. A war for survival.

How he missed the snowy winters of his childhood. He closed his eyes, transporting himself back to his seventh Christmas, remembered the parlor of his family's house, surrounded by a paradise of multi-col-ored fallen leaves, books with gilt-edged pages, the Christmas tree ... The image lingered in his mind, filling him with warmth ....There was a buzzing from his telephone console. The memory soundlessly crum-bled, fading fast into the unredeemable past. What am I doing? He glanced at his watch: a quarter past five.

"Yes?"

"Mr. President, Secretary of State Sorenson would like to see you, sir."

"Let him in," he replied curtly. He cleared his throat.

The door opened and Brad Sorenson stepped into the room.

"We may have a lead in the PROMIS affair. A man came to see someone who apparently worked on developing the software."

"When, and who?" The President stared at his Secretary of State, then turned and sat down in his plush leather chair.

"Yesterday. From the physical description and intelligence reports, Mr. President, the man's name is Curtis Fitzgerald. Ex-army Ranger, member of U.S. 10th Special Forces Group." He placed a manila folder on the President's desk.

"Physical description?"

"A report from one of our undercover agents who was badly hurt in an altercation with the subject."

"Go on."

"Sir, the man who developed the original software lives in Harlem. His name is Alan Sandorf. It is our understanding that Fitzgerald went to see him."

"This Fitzgerald," said the President, opening the folder and scanning Fitzgerald's enviable resume.

"One of ours?"

"Perhaps. At this point, we can only speculate. There is no telling who he's working for, or how much he knows," said Sorenson.

The President looked hard at his Secretary of State, anger and frustration finally surfacing. "Brad, with everything we have on our plate, this is one complication we can do without. You think he or they are somehow connected to the theft of the money?"

"Alan Sandorf is being questioned by our people as we speak."

"And Fitzgerald?"

"No, sir. Our people are waiting for your instructions."

The President paused, then spoke firmly, his voice cold, his eyes penetrating. "For Christ sake, have him brought in for questioning. We are weeks away from a complete meltdown and you are twiddling your thumbs, waiting for instructions! Bring him in now!"

"Yes, sir. Right away, sir."

***

Curtis's phone rang. "Curtis, it's me."

"What happened?"

"Simone has disappeared." "

What?"

"You heard me. Simone has vanished into thin air."

"Are you sure?"

"How long has it been?"

"Over an hour. She went to get something for us to eat. I might be overreacting, but I don't think so."

"Maybe she stopped off somewhere on the way?"

"She would have called."

"I will be there ASAP." The line went dead.

CHAPTER 49

Curtis entered into his Special Forces training mode, concentrating upon the work before him. Find Simone. As he started walking towards a block of apartment buildings across the street where Simone was last seen, Curtis had the distinct sense that he was being followed. Abruptly, he turned around the corner, walked past a red awning and up an adjacent street, acutely aware of his surroundings while adopting the air of an aimless stroller. In the next fifteen minutes, he had turned up and down several streets, at random, only to find the same short, stocky man with a droopy face and a shopping bag trailing in his wake.

Something bothered Curtis about the tail. If the man was following him, he was making it too easy to spot him. That meant that he was a decoy. Then where was the real tail? Curtis turned left at the end of the block, onto a much narrower pedestrian walkway, then a quick right into an alley, listening to the sound of quickly approaching footsteps. Just as the droopy-faced man appeared, Curtis whirled him around and pinned him against the wall.

"Put your hands up!" the fat man said, wheezing hard.

"You are kidding, right?" asked Curtis.

"I am afraid he is not," came a voice from dark end of the alleyway. Curtis' head snapped to his right as he pushed the man away while reaching for his gun.

"Gun down! You move, you're dead!" The voice he heard was used to barking out orders, short, clear orders. Special Forces training type of orders. He heard a set of footsteps, slow and deliberate, then another and another.

"Turn around, face the wall and spread your legs! Move! ... Now!" Curtis had no choice but to do as he was told.

***

Simone sat listlessly in a bentwood armchair. Leather belts held her hands and feet in place. Out of the half-open window she could see pastures. She must be on a farm somewhere. The odor of chloroform lingered in her nostrils. With a return to consciousness, the image of a sedan and a powerful hand pulling her inside kept rising within her like a hot wave, ready to swallow her, again and again.

The door opened and someone slowly walked in. Simone squinted. A man came into focus. He was tall, well built and elegantly dressed, sporting a healthy tan and a pair of alligator boots.

"The most merciful thing in the world, Ms. Casolaro, is the inability of the human mind to correlate all its contents," said the killer, walking across the room toward a metal kit on the table.

"What do you want?"

"The codes."

She didn't flinch. Simone found her calm center. She had learned to do that when their mother died and she became the parent, the big sister, the confidant and the troubleshooter rolled into one.

"I don't know them."

"The best lies are told face to face, with a touch of arrogance," the killer said slowly. He spoke with crisp condescension. "What you lack in arrogance, you make up for in pride." His eyes narrowed suddenly. "As things stand, I think I believe you."

He handed her the telephone. "Dial."

"Dial who?"

"Curtis. Tell him you are scared to death. Weep, if you can. Then tell him I will let you go in exchange for the codes." He paused. "And tell him to come alone."

"And if I don't?" The change in atmosphere was like a sudden drop in temperature. He stared at her unblinkingly. Not a muscle on his face moved. To Simone's overwrought nerves, the silence was piercing in its intensity.

"Do you ever feel, Ms. Casolaro, that your life has consisted of a series of rehearsals for a play that never opened?" Simone didn't respond.

"Well, the curtain is going up. Tell the Ranger to meet me within two hours at First Presbyterian Church of Newtown. Tell him if he does as he is told, I will let you go. Alive and unharmed. He has my word."

CHAPTER 50

Three Marines and a tall man between them reached the bank of elevators as a fourth Marine, a sergeant, pressed the button and waited, gripping a key in his hand. The door to his left opened with a soft clanking sound. They entered, he inserted the key in the lock release above the blue panel with the letters SR , twisted it, and pressed the lower button. The doors shut with a soft buzzing sound and the elevator shot directly down to the underground level. The doors opened and the four Marines walked out.

"Move!" one of them barked the order to the tall man standing between them and pushed him forward. They proceeded down the long hallway to a large steel door with a metal sign in the middle – "Situation Room."

"Turn around." Curtis did as he was told, putting his hands behind his back. "In front," the marine barked out the order. The man was almost as tall as Curtis, heavily muscled, his smooth-shaven head a stump-like extension of his thick, powerful neck. "Hands clasped in front of you where I can see them." Curtis clasped his hands and raised them to his chest. The sergeant shoved him against the wall and held Curtis with a grip of steel. "Now, you listen to me. I don't know who you are or what you have done and frankly I don't give a shit. But you get this, cowboy—"

"It's Army Ranger, U.S. 10th Special Forces Group," replied Curtis staring point blank at the Marine.

The man took a step back, but quickly recovered. "Oh, a bad-ass mofo. I don't care if you're—"

"Sergeant." The door opened and the President of the United States walked in. "Please wait outside. I will shout if I need you."

"Yes, sir. Thank you, sir."

The President waited for the Marine sergeant to leave and shut the door behind him. "Welcome to the White House Situation Room, Mr. Fitzgerald. You are probably wondering why you are here."

"The thought has crossed my mind, sir."

"You are Curtis Fitzgerald, Army Ranger, U.S. 10th Special Forces Group?"

"Yes, sir, I am."

The President nodded. "Then you are the man I wanted to see."

"There are easier ways to get me to come to the White House, Mr. President."

"Oh?"

"You could have simply asked."

"Would you have come?"

"Probably."

"Without wanting to know why?"

Curtis paused, studying the President's tired and lined face. "Probably not."

"That's what I figured. What was your business with Alan Sandorf?"

Curtis straightened up.

"A now-deceased investigative journalist uncovered a conspiracy stopping at the feet of some of the most powerful people in the world. He dubbed these people the Octopus. We have discovered, sir, that the key element in the conspiracy is the PROMIS Artificial Intelligence computer program."

"So you know about PROMIS."

"Yes, sir."

"That's one of the reasons I wanted to see you, Mr. Fitzgerald." The President paused. "What did Alan Sandorf tell you?"

"That PROMIS crossed a threshold in the evolution of computer programming, a quantum leap into such fancy sounding areas as block-modeling social research theory and geomatics technology, which Sandorf claims would eliminate randomness from all human activity."

"Everything would be visible in terms of measurable and predictable patterns. The ultimate big picture," said the President. "Yes, we know. Did he also tell you how PROMIS would predict and influence the movement of financial markets worldwide through control of national banks, intelligence agencies, and military?" The President asked.

"Yes, sir, he did."

"Did he tell you anything else? Mr. Fitzgerald, please think careful-ly before you answer." Curtis remained silent, studying the President's face. "Sir, I am not the only person who has access to this information. If you are—"

The President raised his right hand. "Mr. Fitzgerald...may I call you Curtis?"

"Yes, sir, you may."

"Curtis, the government has no intentions of hurting you or your friends. If we did, I can assure you, I wouldn't be here speaking to you right now.

"I believe you and the government of the United States are after the same people. We also believe you are in possession of certain infor-mation, bank codes actually, that can save the world from imploding. Without this information, and the thought should frighten anyone possessing a scrap of sanity, the United States and for all intents and purposes, the world as we know it, is doomed to extinction."

Curtis leaned forward. "Should I accept this at face value, sir?"

"Under the circumstances, knowing what you know, and what you have been through, I probably wouldn't. My only means of convincing you is the word of the President of the United States of America." He walked over to the console at the other end of the room and sat down.

"I would like you to see this. Then you can decide for yourself whether the word of the President is worth something or not." He pressed another button, the lights were extinguished and startling images instantly appeared on half a dozen over-sized plasma screens mounted in a row on the wall in front of them.

"This was taped three days ago. For security purposes, all internal meetings are automatically video and audio recorded."

A scene familiar to the President played for Curtis' benefit. Buda-pest's cobbled streets – a war zone. Protesters armed with blocks of ice caught on film smashing up Hungary's finance ministry. Images of thousands of enraged people trying to force their way into the legisla-ture were projected on six screens at once.

"You might have seen these on the nightly news, Curtis." He paused awkwardly. "What nightly news broadcasts didn't show you is the following."

Out of the darkness, Curtis heard the voice of the man who now stood next to him.

"This is real, ladies and gentlemen. For now, the economic collapse is hitting other industrialized countries much harder than America. Around the world, from China, to India, to Europe, industrialized nations are frantically preparing for civil unrest. This is not speculative fiction. This is not *Atlas Shrugged*."

The President pressed a button on the console, moving the sequence forward. He lowered his eyes and spoke in a disembodied tone of voice.

"Now, watch this."

"How much money does the government of the United States need in order to keep the U.S. economy afloat and maintain even moderate faith in the dollar?"

"Minimum 2.8 billion dollars a day in direct foreign investment, largely through the purchase of Treasury notes to service our economy, although a more realistic figure is closer to four billion dollars."

Curtis was enthralled, awe stricken.

"The amalgamated pool of funds created and now held in dormant and orphaned accounts run to trillions of dollars."

"The money is missing …. You must find that money. Find it. If not—" Suddenly, his gaze fixed on the President, Curtis spoke in a monotone.

"Paulo Caroni. Sandorf told me it was his operation."

"Yes, we are aware of it now."

"Who does he work for?"

"We don't know. Any more than we know the whereabouts of the funds." Speechless, Curtis stared at the President. "Why don't you simply print more money?"

The President shook his head. "We can't. It would take us a year to print 200 trillion dollars. At best, we have one week."

"Two hundred trillion dollars? Am I hallucinating, sir?"

"No, your heard me right. Two hundred trillion dollars."

"That's insane! What about gold?" Curtis said quietly. "I know about Golden Lily."

"That gold is no longer ours. It has been put up as collateral against the trillions."

"What are you saying?"

"Until we find the money that gold is no longer ours. And we can't exactly take out an advertisement in the newspaper—"

"Because you are dealing with stolen gold deposits from World War II."

"Exactly. Can you see our predicament?"

"What about the people behind the Octopus? The Board of Directors?"

"The perpetrators," said the President. "Then, you know about Stilton."

"Of course, we know about Stilton. We also know about Reid, Harriman, McCloy, Lovett and Taylor."

"Harriman?" Curtis' jaw dropped. "As in former Secretary of the Treasury David Alexander Harriman III?"

"The one and only."

"He of the super-wealthy Eastern Establishment family? Church going, God-fearing Harriman?"

"Going to church doesn't make you a Christian, anymore than going to a carwash makes you a car."

"Jesus! That son of a bitch."

"Sociologists call this condition elite deviance, a condition that exists when the elite in a society begin to believe that the rules no longer apply to them."

The President looked at the Ranger. "As I said, we have reasons to believe that you and the government of the United States are after the same people." Then he sank into his chair. "I walked away from a reasonably stress-free life to one where I wake up in a cold sweat in the middle of the night. I haven't had the luxury of a night's sleep for the past two months. And the thing is that sometimes your world and my world intersect because both of us have a job to do; of looking after the normal world, the everyday world of everyday, normal people who work nine to five and have barbecues and picnics with family and take their sons and daughters to Saturday morning football games and afternoon birthday parties. The safety of the normal world depends on making sure the bad guys don't succeed. Sometimes that means looking the other way or playing ball with your enemy's enemy and even your enemy's best friend. They are extraordinary measures, Curtis, which make me question my sanity more often than you can ever imagine."

Curtis sat in the armchair to the President's left.

"Mr. President, you said we had the bank account codes that could save the world from imploding. I am sorry, sir, but I really don't know what you are talking about."

"Once the government realized Caroni had cracked the system and stolen the money, we worked back to map out a web of his relationships within the past six months." The President paused. "One of his contacts was an unemployed journalist."

"Danny Casolaro?" Curtis asked.

"Caroni gave Mr. Casolaro a cryptographically-strong pseudo random string of a thirty-two number combination because, as he told him, he feared for his life. Caroni told Casolaro that this number, along with an error-trapping routine used simultaneously with the protected mode memory, was the key to unlocking a phantasmagoric amount of money from its hiding place."

The President looked at Curtis and reached for his drink. "But there was something that Caroni didn't know about Casolaro – his high proficiency level with computers. Casolaro must have known that cryptographically-strong pseudo random strings of a thirty-two number combination were used for virtual dead-drops in illegal activities by banking institutions through corporations such as Swift CHIPS online financial clearing house interbank payment system." The President put down his empty glass.

"I'm sorry?" Curtis said.

"It's a financial messaging network which exchanges messages between banks," replied the President. "And that's where Caroni had hidden the two hundred trillion dollars worth of contingency funds."

Madness. Possibilities not previously considered were suddenly brought to light. Then, Curtis spoke. "You are absolutely right, Danny must have had them." Curtis stared at the President, the blood draining from his head, his eyes steady, unblinking.

"Casolaro got curious or greedy or both and did something he wasn't supposed to. He hid the number without telling Caroni."

"How do you know this?"

"Because we have had Caroni in our crosshairs for quite some time. When Danny Casolaro called him, we recorded the conversation. Caroni's plan had backfired."

"So he killed Danny."

"The government doesn't think so."

"What makes you think we have it?" asked Curtis.

"BS Bank Schaffhausen, Curtis. We are not quite a banana republic, yet."

"Sir, we have gone through all of the documents and didn't find anything remotely resembling this number."

"Check again," interrupted the President. "Recheck again. Go through his records, logs, files. Don't look for something missing. Look for something that's there, but something you are not supposed to see. It has to be there." The President pounded the table with his clenched fist. "Somewhere amongst his papers, there is a ticking time bomb, ready to explode. We have to find it and deactivate it. We have one day, Curtis, tonight, to be exact!"

Curtis looked at the President, now studying him. "I think, Mr. President, you have earned a vote from this American in the next election."

The door abruptly opened. "I am sorry, Mr. President,"

"Brad?" The President looked quizzically at his Secretary of State. "You had better see this." Frozen images on a large plasma screen in front of them suddenly disappeared and the familiar face of a television pundit covered the screen in its entirety.

"It's now time to make things real simple. First of all, an epidemic of defaults by thousands of cities, states and other issuers of tax-exempt municipal bonds in the past twenty four hours; stock market shutdown across most of Asia. Remember, it is early in the morning in the Orient. Credit market deep-freeze: A virtual shutdown in all debt markets except U.S. Treasuries, which is rumored to have enough cash to stave off its own shutdown for another two days, max. An avalanche of selling – and virtually no buyers – for corporate bonds, commercial paper, asset-backed securities, municipal bonds and all forms of

bank loans. Government bond collapse: A ninety percent decline in the price of medium-and long-term government securities, as the U.S. Treasury bids aggressively for scarce funds to finance a ballooning budget deficit. We are looking at a chain reaction of debt explosions, a free-fall in the financial markets. There are no ifs, and, or buts. This is it, folks. The financial clock on the world's collapse is ticking."

The President pressed a button on a console. "You will be flown home, Mr. Fitzgerald. Please get in touch with me tonight."

"Sir, before I leave, I have a favor to ask of you."

"If it has anything to do with saving the world, consider it granted."

"When your men took me, I was looking for someone. I have reasons to believe she was kidnapped."

CHAPTER 51

The driver checked his watch, then flipped the power switch and pressed the transmission button. "Come in Roger One." Static erupted, words following.

"The next shift has just arrived. You have ten minutes to pick up the package. In and out."

"Understood, Mr. Secretary."

He turned and faced a man in the passenger's seat. "It's show time." The assassin adjusted his nametag, then opened a glove compartment, removed the cylindrical instrument, spun it into the short barrel, and then examined the grooves of his silencer. He gave it a final, wrenching turn, depressed the magazine release and checked the clip.

***

A guard leaned against the wall, rubbed his eyes and looked at his watch. "Ten minutes."

His name was Dougie, although everyone called him Gordon due to his uncanny physiognomic resemblance to Buster Crabbe as Flash Gordon. He was a young man in his early twenties, closely cropped blond hair, blue eyes. He and his partner had been at their post for nearly six hours. The man they were assigned to protect was obviously someone important, because the firm's usual policy was one man per operation.

The guy who ran the firm on his family's behalf was a cheap-ass prick, but they needed the work, especially in this downward cycle, as one of the managers at the company called it, whatever that was. One man per operation. Keep costs down and multiply the benefits.

The man in the room was now their responsibility, the assignment of guarding him understood, the reasons behind it withheld – which was not the smartest thing to do, they jointly concluded, because human nature had a way of piquing one's curiosity. After somewhat lengthy deliberations, they concluded that the man was neither a famous athlete nor a well-known movie star. With that realization, their interest in him waned considerably.

"Ten minutes and we are out of here."

"Man, I'm bored." Dougie yawned. So did his partner, J.J. "You want a Coke? I owe you one from last week."

"Diet. I'm parched." J.J. patted his belly. "Parched, how about that?"

"I love it. You're a regular dictionary."

Two killers walked up the marble steps past a glass-partitioned reception counter, down a long narrow corridor that led to another door some meters away. They wore Monocrys body armor hidden by expensive, tailor-made, pinstriped grey suits. Immediately to their left was an efficiently manned coat-check station. Then came the offices of the hospital's general managers and staff, then a glass door and the hospital's interior courtyard. The stockier of the two men stopped, his head turning in all directions, his eyes darting to the people around him. He looked at his partner. The second man returned his gaze. "Let's go." They circled the landing on the second floor and climbed the staircase to the third. There it was! The stockier man carefully opened the door, glanced up and down the hallway. To his right, someone wearing a uniform was fishing something out of a Coke machine.

"Excuse me?"

"Yes?" The man looked up.

"We have a few things to discuss, you and I," said the stockier of the two killers pointing his gun at the security guard. He spoke quietly, his eyes over the guard's shoulder.

"And you would be foolish to withhold anything," added the other. He pulled out his weapon and pressed it against the man's temple, feeling the exhilaration of holding the man's life in his hands.

The guard, breathing heavily, blinked rapidly.

"Cristian Belucci. Where is he?"

"Down the hallway, third door past the elevator on the left."

The killer pushed the weapon into the man's temple, letting the cold of the heavy steel make its presence felt.

"How many guards?"

"Please, I don't know anything. I won't tell anyone. I don't know who you are! Please, I want to live."

"How many!?" The killer yanked the guard up again slamming his back against the wall.

"Two. Me and my partner," he whispered, terrified.

"Who do you work for?"

"The government."

The assassin shook his head. "That training is not what it was, paisan." He fired two shots into the man's head.

Dougie stifled a yawn and scratched his head when suddenly he heard the crash bar on the hallway's heavy metal exit door carefully pushed into the opening position. He looked to his right, in time to see two men round the corner and continue down the hallway towards him, their walk casual, devoid of all urgency.

Dougie pushed himself off the wall and faced the two men. "Can I help you, gentlemen?" He smiled.

"We are here to see Mr. Belucci," said the stockier of the two killers.

"We're co-workers," added the other.

"Co-workers?"

"Yes, sir. He is a very important man. Such a tragedy." They both shook their heads.

The guard scanned the guest list. "I'm sorry, I don't have anyone listed at this time. You will have to clear it with the security company. We have strict orders where this man is concerned."

The stockier man smiled. "We understand. We are here for a symposium."

"Just for a day," added the other killer.

"Just today," repeated the stockier assassin. He pointed to an identification tag.

Dougie glanced at the man's tag. "The World Bank?" he said. The face on the tag matched the man wearing it. "I don't know." He looked down the hallway. "We're off in a few minutes, perhaps you could come back when the next shift takes over."

"We would love to, but unfortunately we only have a few minutes."

"It's a surprise."

"My partner will be back in a second. I think—" It happened with the impact of a single furious thunderclap, the kind he loved to listen to on his farm back in Iowa. The killer extended his hand, Heckler &

Koch MP5K materializing out of nowhere. There was a glow of light, a spit, Dougie's knees buckled and he began falling.

***

Cristian sat up in bed. He could hear several muffled voices, slow and monotonous. Then, he heard a thud. Someone was outside those doors, someone who wasn't supposed to be there. Cristian leaned in the direction of the door, holding on to the metal railing with his right hand, listening. There was a metallic click as the heavy metal handle was turned, but the door didn't give. It was locked! Cristian reached for his telephone and began dialing. He felt a stab in his midsection, momentarily gasping. Another sound, then another. Where were the guards?

Suddenly, an explosion blew away the lock. Time stood still. The next moment, Cristian saw the monitor explode – blossoming into a cloud of glass fragments – even before he heard the popping sound that accompanied it. The explosion of light was so bright it pained his eyes. The pin-striped figure burst into the room, his partner behind him carrying the lifeless body of a security guard.

The stockier of the two men smiled. There was no trace of self-doubt in his dark blue eyes. "Mr. Belucci, I presume.

"What are you going to do?" asked Cristian.

"Correct a mistake," answered the assassin. Cristian realized he was still holding his cell phone in his right hand. Press the button and the call will go through. He sat up. "Like many a dark venture—" He casually pressed the green button. "The one thing it will not survive is exposure to light." Cristian knew the blow was coming, and he felt the pain in his temple explode even before he registered the motion of the man's hand.

"Pull him up by the waist," ordered the first killer.

Something moved behind the figure standing to Cristian's left. A shadow. Cristian heard two muted spits and the start of a terrible scream. The skinnier assassin lunged over Cristian's bed, gun drawn. Too late. Three more shots exploded from deep inside the room. The man plummeted to the floor, his throat ripped open.

Cristian groaned and pulled himself up on his elbow.

"What the hell took you so long?"

"Sorry, Boss. Unexpected trouble. All settled."

CHAPTER 52

The roar of the Hawker 750 grew louder as Curtis drew nearer the plane. The fuselage door popped open, and the electronic stairs smoothly dropped down.

"I need to make a quick telephone call," said Curtis, raising his voice above the engine's noise to be heard by the government agent accompanying him. He angled his head against the elements, squinting, wiping his face with his left hand, his right gripping the phone.

Curtis had the impression that it was late in the evening, though it was only half past six. Heavy rain pounded down, the blasts of wind pushing him off balance.

Michael's telephone rang. "Curtis? Where are you?"

"In Washington."

"What are you doing in Washington?"

"I was kidnapped."

"Kidnapped! Oh, my God! By whom?"

"By the President of the United States."

"Curtis," Michael yelled into the receiver. "They got Simone. She called me. You have ninety minutes to get her out."

Curtis cupped the phone under his chin and put his left hand over the speaker. "Listen carefully. Go through Danny's papers, logs, documents, anything of Danny's I got from Schaffhausen. Rip it apart.

"The President is convinced we have the codes and the bank account number."

"I am coming with you!"

"No you are not. We are hours away from a financial meltdown. These are the President's words. We can't afford the time. I need you to figure out the codes! I will get Simone. The papers, Michael, please! His advice was not to look for something hidden, but rather to look for something that's there, but we are not supposed to see. Danny most likely had hidden the codes within Dante's *Divine Com-*

edy, just like the letter-number key combination to the safety deposit box at Schaffhausen."

"We looked through all of his papers, Curtis. We examined every inch of every document, every log, every gold certificate, every disk and every newspaper cutout. There is nothing there!"

"Listen to me, Michael. Somewhere in that box, there is something that we missed, somehow, I don't know how, that will lead us to Scaroni's account and to the trillions of dollars the government needs to save the world from economic collapse."

"Okay."

"How is Cristian?"

"I called the hospital as soon as I got back, less than twenty minutes ago, but couldn't get through. Should I—"

"No, Michael, first and foremost Danny's papers. Michael," he looked at his watch, "we have about five and a half hours."

"How are you going to get Simone back?" The line went dead.

***

The flight to La Guardia and trip in a government vehicle had been oddly disturbing. First Curtis studied the layout of the Church, then he retraced his thoughts, stopping and peering again, at the more critical items of everything that had taken place over the past few weeks. He was painfully aware just how little progress he made in that time. It was as if a part of his mind were refusing to function; no matter how he tried moving his thoughts around, the key ideas blocked.

The black sedan with government license plates pulled up some six blocks from the building where the rendezvous with Simone's kidnappers was to take place. He glanced at his watch. Ten minutes left. He squeezed the automatic under his belt. He was within two blocks of an abandoned, but still imposing, two story Presbyterian wooden church, a dilapidated sanctuary built more than three centuries ago, fallen into disuse when Curtis was barely old enough to tell his first lie. This was where the trap was laid. Curtis knew they planned only to capture and force him to give up the codes. But he also knew they would underestimate him, underestimate how willing he was to risk his life to get Simone out of there. They would not realize he now knew what was at stake.

A couple walked by, laughing and groping each other. The young man was holding some item of hers in his hand, waving it like a captured flag.

The abandoned church was in front of him, dense foliage blocking the view of the stained glass on the second floor. He crossed the street and went rapidly up the solid wood staircase and pushed the door open. It creaked. They knew he was now inside.

A heavy door down at the other end of the passageway opened and then closed with a hardly perceptible creaking sound. The footsteps were muffled, but distinct, deliberate and cautious. A trap was being set up. They would never let Simone go alive, that much he knew. Think. He knew this place. The hallway veered slightly to the left before reaching a transverse arch, which led into a spacious interior.

How many were inside? Still crouching, Curtis peered into the darkness.

Silence now. No sound at all, no movement. Curtis crawled along the wall, foot by foot. A creak. Where? Who? He took out the automatic.

A shadow! It moved. A figure a black raincoat, the lapels pulled up, wide pockets recessed for powerful weapons, sprinted across the far end of the hallway. In his left hand was a long-barreled gun, swallowed by a silencer.

Veins on Curtis' neck swelled, his jaw muscles pulsating.

One, two, three! He pushed himself off the wall, keeping his head low, darted across the open space, covering it in what seemed like a millisecond. A blinding flash of light accompanied the explosion of gunfire. Curtis squeezed the trigger, aiming at the assassin at the other end of the hallway.

The Ranger crawled behind a pillar, craning his neck around him. The architecture was Doric style, characterized by a row of fluted columns having no base and a triglyph block on the top. The floor was a Florentine mosaic, made by inlaying fine, delicate, cultured stones into a white marble surface. He heard a dull whistling sound again, the whooshing sound of a fast-moving projectile hitting the the square slab beneath the base of the column, missing him by centimeters.

Adrenaline coursed through his veins. His mouth went dry, his heart began to pump wildly, and his stomach knotted. Self-consciousness evaporated, giving way to deeply laid circuits of training and instinct. There was another burst of gunfire, three in all, lethal, sudden, hitting the marble shaft less than a meter away from him. The rounds came from the same direction, but the sound felt heavier. Another gunman. How far? How many of them? The killers worked methodically, taking their time and slowly cutting down his angles of escape.

He checked his magazine. Six bullets left. His only direct escape route was to make a run for it through an open gallery and up through an arch leading to the side entrance. It was an invitation and a trap. Tempting and suicidal. He would be cut down instantaneously. He heard faint footsteps. Catlike. Someone was moving down the stairs, which meant that someone else was covering him from an elevated ramp. Standard configuration at Special Ops. Each operative had a visual connection with at least two others. There are three of them, he concluded. Curtis realized that the man moving down the stairs was a decoy. If he tried to take him out he would be cut down in the crossfire. Crossfire! That's it. The decisive bullet would come from the wing.

Curtis tried to visualize every detail of the upper floor. The main staircase merged into a double-return stair, having one wide flight from the main floor to an intermediate landing, and two side flights from that landing to the floor above, both supported by a heavy marble balustrade. The hallway on the upper floor was long and wide, leading to a wing balcony that extended along the sidewalls and blended with a covered mezzanine at each side of the hallway. Curtis was sure that the third shooter was there. Waiting for him to come out?

Another burst of fire ricocheted off the column's base. The bullets weren't meant to hit him, just to flush him out. Special Ops training, that was obvious. The sound of steps was getting louder, as if beckoning for him to show himself. Judging by the sound of approaching footsteps, the first gunman was less than 15 meters away from reaching the bottom of the stairwell. To get a good shot at him, Curtis would have to come out from behind the column, leaving himself in the open. Out of the question. He would be cut down by the third gunman covering the decoy. Don't think, act.

On instinct, Curtis suddenly stood up, maintaining his position behind the pillar, and aimed at an empty space in a wing balcony.

Someone moved. The shooter was reacting to Curtis's movement, aiming at the spot where Curtis should have been. The burst of fire hit the Florentine tiles, sending pieces into the air. Curtis aimed and fired. Instantly, he heard a short guttural cry. One shot, one dead: truly unexpected within the swirling winds of confusion.

Five bullets, two gunmen. Curtis inched closer towards the open space, slouching against the column drum. The second gunman would have to reposition himself to have an angle on Curtis now. That meant that the decoy would have to stop moving. Another crack as the decoy squeezed off a bullet confirmed his suspicion. They are buying time. Curtis heard faint panic screams and moaning to his right.

Timing was all. It would be another several minutes at least before help could arrive. Could Curtis make it to the side entrance? And if he did, how could he be sure it wasn't a trap? Yet, there was no time to plan. He had no choice. Suddenly he heard the sound of someone running toward him. Now! Curtis lunged forward, rolled over into the open and fired low, hitting the decoy in the knee.

The killer fell face first and slid a few steps towards Curtis. Without breaking stride, Curtis rolled over again, aiming at the decoy's head. He squeezed the trigger, blowing it apart, a horrible mass of blood and white tissue. A rapid succession of fire from the upper floor missed Curtis by centimeters. Bullets spattered into the wall to his right. He rolled once again and now found himself underneath the second-floor balcony.

Three shots, one gunman to go. Curtis stood still, his breath suspended, and listened. He felt the weight of the gun in his hand – Ruger .44, a Redhawk – ideal at close range. Time was on his side. He could wait it out. Surely people outside had heard the gunshots and called for help. The reinforcements would be here at any moment.

Then he heard Simone. A weak groan, somewhere above and behind him. She was strapped to a column, hands in front of her on a raised platform, stained glass windows directly behind her. God, no! To cover her, Curtis would have to step back into the open gallery space, and expose himself to the gunman on the upper floor.

Something stirred in him. He had been there before. 2001, on the outskirts of Jalalabad. His patrol unit was caught in enemy crossfire, with the Taliban having the advantage of elevation. Two of his patrol had died, he himself was wounded. He felt sick to his stomach. It was a numbing sensation, eerie and uncanny. Curtis had to reach her and cover her; otherwise, she would be dead. Three bullets. He would have to make them count.

Suddenly, he heard a faint scratch. Metal had scraped against something. Not something, marble. Marble balustrade. Another second and the shooter would squeeze the trigger. She was right in front of the killer. Surely, he was aiming at her head.

Curtis swung to his right, crouching, exposing himself as he rolled and rolled again. The muffled cracks came in staccato repetition. Florentine tiles exploded all around him. He dove to his right again, away from the column. The killer would necessarily be in front of him. Aim and shoot. Curtis sprang to his feet, his left hand steadying his right wrist, the gun centered, aimed at where he thought the gunman was standing. He fired three shots. He was out of ammunition.

A scream, then a gasp came from the upstairs balcony with the killer crashing head first to the floor. Curtis stood motionless, waiting, listening and watching. Silence. Still facing the balcony, he took one step backwards.

Curtis whipped his head up, grimacing with pain and looked over to his right at Simone, gagged and bound to the pillar. She was staring at him in relief. She was safe.

CHAPTER 53

S imone – ." She lowered herself to the pavement, trembling like a leaf. She stared at Curtis, disbelief, horror and confusion coming together in her eyes.

"Go on," she whispered in a hollow tone, hoping he could hear her, the words floating in the air. "Go on, help Michael."

"We can't do it without you, Simone." She heard him through mists of pain. Curtis was pulling her up. Holding her in his arms. Her throat was so hot, her stomach so cold. Fire and ice. He was asking her a question. She could not answer him. He was carrying her. Now running. Get to Cristian's house. Pressed against his immense chest, she let herself drift with the currents of her mind. Michael, Michael, Michael.

He carried her past a wide stone staircase in the center of the foyer and mounted into the old rickety lift. The elevator performed its usual one-man show, groaning, jerking unsteadily when it passed the second, slowed down on the third, bumping its way past the fourth, accelerating hopefully on the fifth before coming to a grudging stop on the P floor, wobbling and heaving a sigh of relief as it disgorged its furrow-browed occupant.

"Simone!" Michael leapt forward as she came through the door, and hugged her. "Are you all right?" She returned his embrace and sat down at the kitchen table.

"I am fine." Michael opened his mouth to say something but then closed it again.

"What is it?" she asked

"They got Cristian!"

"Oh, Christ! When! How!"

A numbing pain spread through Curtis. "I don't know. Two men dressed in suits took out the two guards, got in the room and kidnapped him."

Curtis grabbed the phone that Michael held out for him. He dialed an unlisted number, his hand trembling. "Yes, I'll hold."

"Any progress in the Schaffhausen affair?" Curtis asked as he waited for the White House to answer. Curtis looked over at Michael.

Michael shook his head. "Nothing. I have gone through his newspaper articles and Danny's gold certificates. And—"

"Mr. President? It's Curtis Fitzgerald …. Yes, sir, thank you, sir… I am back and we are working on it … I know sir. We are very aware of it. Mr. President, this may not be the right time to mention it, sir, but Cristian Belucci has been kidnapped at gunpoint from Mount Sinai Medical Centre. Thank you sir, I will."

"Well?"

"The government will put out an all points bulletin. The police and the FBI will sweep through the streets, federal agencies will work with their undercover people down in the gutter. If he is still alive, they will find him." He paused, then walked over to the television set and turned it on. "They may find him, hopefully in better shape than O'Donnell."

Simone hobbled out of the room, returning with a pad and a pencil in one hand, Danny's notebook in the other.

It was eight minutes past ten on the wristwatch hanging from the hook of the table lamp.

"I think I may have figured it out." Simone pulled out Danny's worn out diary and pointed to a text written in a margin on page seventeen:

> Midway upon the journey of our life
> I found myself within a forest dark,
> For the straightforward pathway had been lost.
> Then I moved on, and you behind me followed.

"What?" Curtis asked. He slipped off his coat and listlessly dropped it on the couch in front of him.

"The text is wrong."

"What do you mean?"

"*The Inferno*, Canto I. The last line should read:

> Then *he* moved on, and *I* behind *him* followed.

"Which appears several stanzas later in the text."

"Why would Danny add this line to Dante's opening?" asked Michael.

"Dante allows his characters' words to take over the poem more and more as he progresses through it by giving them, rather than the narrator, the first or last word of a canto," explained Simone.

"Except in this case, Danny has written himself into the story."

"That ad-lib invention wasn't just a doodle," she added. Michael nodded.

"Look for something that's there, something we are not supposed to see," repeated Curtis. "The President's press conference is scheduled for midnight."

"That's an hour and fifty one minutes from now." Michael said. "The first three lines are the opening sequence of Canto I." Simone continued, her voice shaking slightly.

"But the last line—"

"Which has been jumbled."

"Exactly, comes much later in the text." She pointed to Danny's last line: Then I moved on, and you behind me followed.

"All right. We are looking for a thirty-two number combination," said Curtis nervously glancing at his watch. "Would you agree the text is a standard method for encrypting sensitive information?"

"Absolutely," replied Michael.

"We'll need a cypher to unlock it."

"What are the options?" asked Simone.

"First of all, modern or ancient?" asked Curtis.

"Based on Danny's dexterity with Kabbalah and enneagram, I'd say old." Michael looked at the two of them.

"There are reflectional ciphers, such as a mysterious Gnostic one known as Abraxas that is known as substitutions. No, this won't work," he added quickly.

"Why not?"

"All groups of numbers resulting from the translation of names into their numerical equivalents have a basis in one of the first ten numbers. The digits are added together, which gives us a number or the number, but not the cryptographically-strong pseudo random number strings of a thirty-two number combination.

"In plain English, the World Bank has just announced that the global economy is hours away from wholesale collapse. The Asian Development Bank reported that more than $150 trillion in invested wealth vanished into thin air over the past three months. And like Damocles' sword, the hundreds of trillions in derivatives and bad debts are still hanging over the world banking industry.

"If the World Bank emergency meeting this morning, International Monetary Fund emergency session this afternoon, and our own government's high level Presidential committee meeting prove anything, it's that if you're waiting for officialdom to save you, you'll be waiting until Kingdom Come. Your ONLY hope is to take control of your own destiny ... to engineer your own bailout. Understand what I am saying: You are on your own. Your government has abandoned you."

"Danny's Schaffhausen bank codes, when transcribed, were simple." Curtis began, "A six digit number and a phrase. This won't do. Too cumbersome. Next. We have one hour and thirty five minutes left."

"There are the famous Peterborough tablets in Ontario, Canada. The writings have been identified as a form of Scandinavian runes or, actually, pre-runic characters called Tifinagh used by the Tuaregs that dated to 800 B.C."

"What does it have to do with Dante?"

"The tablets heavily relied on depiction of a leopard, a lion and a wolf at different stages of their existence."

"The same animals who blocked Dante's attempt to escape when he found himself lost in a forest," added Simone.

"Exactly."

"No, it won't do. Input data has to relate to 32 hexadecimal characters encoded through 4 bits of data using a key algorithm. It doesn't work with images. Michael, we need text ciphers."

The time grew short, the doodles on the page ... long. They were digging, prodding, probing, reworking and rejiggling the math, forcing their minds to function, painfully aware of their precarious state of captivity in the zoo of numbers.

"Wait! Wait!" Simone yelled.

"What is it?" asked Curtis anxiously.

"That's what Danny meant by 'Then I moved on, and you behind me followed.'"

"What?" asked Curtis, tension registering on his face.

"He is inviting me to follow him into Canto I. It was sort of a friendly competition between us, to see who knew Dante better. We both excelled at the regular Dante trivia, so Danny and I kept inventing games and we would challenge each other to a competition. Danny had made up this game to see who could recite the lines of Canto I in an alphabetical order. To help him remember, he would sing the ABC as he went through the text. For example, the first line with the first letter "A" appears in line 4, "B" in line 8 and so on."

> *"Today, in a historic Taxpayer Revolt millions of Americans from coast to coast have taken to the streets, making their voices heard. Nearly everywhere you look, you see faces of angry taxpayers demanding that Washington stop bankrupting America ... stop throwing our money at millionaire CEOs who destroyed their own companies. For tens of millions, the party is over, their lifelong dreams of a life in a land of the free shattered, dreams destroyed, their families left penniless and destitute. Today, they are taking to the streets; their actions may yet give millions of Americans a ray of hope for a better future."*

The three of them stared at the television screen. Curtis looked at his watch. "We have forty-five minutes before the President speaks. I'll take A to I, you take J to R," he said looking at Michael.

"No, there isn't any J in Canto I," replied Simone.

"Then how the hell are we going to do the alphabet," said Michael.

"Take a breath, baby. Only the letters that are there. And only the first time each letter appears in the text," she clarified.

"Get the book."

"Thirty eight minutes." added Simone warily staring at her watch. Simone opened Dante's Comedy to Canto I and Michael scanned the first few lines.

Midway upon the journey of our life
I found myself within a forest dark,
For the straightforward pathway had been lost.

Ah me! how hard a thing it is to say
What was this forest savage, rough, and stern,
Which in the very thought renews the fear.

So bitter is it, death is little more;
But of the good to treat, which there I found,
Speak will I of the other things I saw there.

I cannot well repeat how there I entered,
So full was I of slumber at the moment
In which I had abandoned the true way.

But after I had reached a mountain's foot,
At that point where the valley terminated,
Which had with consternation pierced my heart,

Michael picked up the pen and started writing. Line 1, first letter: M=1. Line 2, first letter: I=2. Third line: F=3. Fourth line: A=4.

What if they were wrong? What if Simone had simply made a mistake and unwittingly sent them down the rabbit's hole ... Curtis reeled himself in, shut down that line of thought.

The phone rang. "Curtis?"

"I think we almost have it, Mr. President."

"I will call you in the next ten minutes. It will be the longest ten minutes of my life, Curtis."

"Sir?"

"Cristian Belucci is still missing. We are doing everything humanly possible to find him, believe me."

"I believe you." Nothing else needed to be said. There simply was no time. He hung up.

It was astonishing how quickly they were running out of time – and the President of the United States would be making his appearance in front of the entire world in a little over half an hour. His words would change history.

Curtis' eyes came into focus just as Michael was writing down the entire combination in alphabetical order.

"48102725831220213582167191817557. Count! How many?" asked Michael, holding his breath.

"Thirty two!" exclaimed Simone.

"The number! Cryptographically strong pseudo-random number strings of a thirty two number combination!"

"Call the President."

***

It happened with the force of a mercury-filled bullet on impact. A figure in black exploded through the large double doors. A tall, well built, man sporting a healthy tan slammed his right shoulder into Michael at full force, propelling him across the room.

"Truly remarkable! The three of you have done a truly remarkable job." He pointed his gun, a Heckler & Koch P7 mounted with a silencer, at Curtis. The assassin reached out, grabbed Simone by the forearm and violently pulled her to him, lashing his left arm around her neck, the automatic pressed against her temple.

"You!" She gasped, her breath suspended.

"You know what they say. If you don't succeed at first—"

To Simone, the killer's voice and a French accent came back like a far away radio station picked up by chance.

"You must be Curtis. I have heard a lot of wonderful things about your special talents. The pleasure of this encounter is truly mine." With his gun trained on Simone's right temple, he unbuttoned his black coat with his left hand. "My name is Pierre. Please sit down."

"I don't know how you got here, I don't know who you are and I don't know what you want," exclaimed Curtis, slowly recovering from the shock.

"The number, of course."

"So you can destroy the world?"

The Frenchman smiled. "You have to disbelieve the declared story, in order to arrive at a simple truth."

Curtis shook his head. "Unfortunately, we don't know it. Like a fool, I thought we could solve it. What we have is only partially accurate. Danny's riddle has proved to be too difficult."

The assassin studied the Ranger's face, then sighed and shook his head. "Really? I have overestimated you. I was told you were a man of many resources, perhaps even my equal, but you are just like those third-rate-book hacks." He released Simone, pushing her with considerable force toward Curtis.

The telephone rang and Curtis lunged for it just as a bullet exploded within inches of his hand. Curtis froze.

"Tell the President, you need another couple of minutes." It rang a second, then a third time. "Two minutes! Do it! Pick up the phone!"

Tentatively, Curtis put his hand on the receiver. "Yes?"

"Do you have the number?" The President's voice was gruff and devoid of all emotion.

"We need another couple of minutes, Mr. President."

"We found Cristian Belucci."

He knew, he just knew. "I don't know if I want to hear this, Mr. President."

"We have a definite identification of his body. May God have Mercy on his soul."

Curtis moved away from the desk, away from the putrid smell that suddenly had filled his nostrils and his lungs. "I don't pray," he whispered, his steely resolve skin deep. Then, even quieter, he repeated it again, "I don't believe. God is the only safe thing to be." He shook his head and closed his eyes almost involuntarily, the darkness comforting for a moment. "What was the cause of death?"

"Poisoning. Chemical toxicity of unknown etiology."

"Are you absolutely sure it is him?"

"We are comparing DNA samples of the deceased against Belucci's records. Help us find the number and stop this madness."

"We need another couple of minutes, sir." He hung up.

"Cristian?" asked Simone haltingly, memories stirred. Michael blinked, tears rolling down his face.

"The number, Mr. Fitzgerald. I remind you that the gun is in my hand, not yours." There was a click; the hammer snapped into firing position.

"What if I refuse?"

There was a brief something in his eyes. "Then, I will kill you, along with your friends."

"Then, you will die a poor man."

The Frenchman smiled again and then shrugged. "I have never been a poor man."

Curtis tried to hear the hesitation in the apparently authoritative pronouncement. There was none. He really didn't need the money. Then, why did he want the number? "Who are you working for?"

"For me." Standing in the frame of double doors was someone the three of them were intimately familiar with.

Curtis bolted forward in the chair, stunned, his body tense, his eyes wide, his body temperature on fire. "Cristian." he said, barely audible.

"What about the hospital, the shooting?" Michael stammered, an expression of shock and betrayal on his face.

"The Octopus had begun to watch me too closely, I feared they would figure out my plan before I was ready for them to. It was a necessary yet acceptable risk when the world's fate and fortune hangs in the balance," replied Cristian, glancing over at the Frenchman. "Pierre is an expert marksman. He knew how to make it look bad, but miss the vital organs. Please believe me, I never had any intention of getting the three of you involved. At this moment we are enemies, and neither would pretend otherwise, but this would not have happened had your brother not stolen the combinations." His eyes were level, penetrating. "Your brother's death was an unnecessary and wasted death, but he would not give up the number. What was I to do?"

"You ... killed my brother!" snapped Simone, her voice guttural, her emotions reeling, her eyes boring into him, unable to tear her gaze from the sight of a man whom she profoundly admired and whose loss she mourned only moments ago.

"What made you think that by killing Danny you would uncover the number?" Curtis asked, his eyes on the French assassin's weapon.

"We had profiled you, Simone. Enneagram, personality type."

"It was inevitable," said the World Banker, adding derisively, "But we knew you couldn't connect the dots all by yourself." His gaze was level, his smile disdainful. "We knew you would call your old flame,

Michael, and he would come running." His smile faded. He paused with a hint of a smirk.

"If I hadn't recovered the documents from Schaffhausen—" Curtis said.

"Please don't underestimate the level of planning and calculation that has gone into this operation," interrupted Cristian Belucci. " We had recovered Mr. Casolaro's documents long before you appeared on the scene." He paused. "Unfortunately for you, Simone, Danny's riddle was too good for us. We simply could not figure it out."

"You pulled me into this?" Curtis asked matter-of-factly, his voice neutral. "You were my friend."

"Pulled you in!" Cristian blurted out incredulously. "You are giving me more credit than I deserve. How was I to know Michael was going to ask you for help? Chance pulled you in, Curtis. Occasionally, one must admit, mere coincidence plays a part in human affairs."

The banker paused and sighed wistfully. "You have done a fabulous job. It was a difficult course, full of obstacles and real-life dangers. Few could have navigated it."

"Still, for the plan to work, we had to come to you for help," added Michael.

"Naturally!" Belucci said brightly. "When you called Curtis from New York, providence intervened with its fumbling subhuman inefficiency. Once Curtis became involved in the Casolaro case, I realized I could kill two birds with one stone."

"You disgusting man!" she screamed.

"Why do you need the number, Cristian?" asked Michael. "You are already one of the world's wealthiest men."

"I don't want the money … you still don't get it!" he exclaimed with irritation in his voice. "I need—"

"To keep it away from the President in order to precipitate the destruction of the world economy," added Michael, finally clueing in to all the pieces of the puzzle.

"Exactly," replied the banker.

"You think by destroying the world, you can win? Do you think you can assign a probability meter to a cataclysmic event like this?" the Ranger asked.

"In the world of high-risk finance and banking, Curtis, we do that all the time. What matters is not what happens but what might happen, the multiple chances, the darkness confronted but not embraced. New World Order out of chaos!"

For a moment, his air of equipoise slipped, but only for a moment. "Twenty-five hundred years ago it might have been said that man understood himself as well as any other part of his world. Today he is the thing he understands least. Neither biological nor cultural evolution is any guarantee that we are inevitably moving toward a better world."

"And you think you are benevolently offering us a better world?" cried Simone.

"We can defeat democracy exclusively through unarmed conflict because the privileged understand the workings of the human mind."

"You have set the world up for destruction." Said Michael.

"We have set the world up for redemption!"

Slowly, Curtis stood up. "The President will be calling any moment now. What will you do when the government uncovers the truth about whoever your double really is." He watched his two adversaries carefully.

Belucci shook his head. "I don't think so."

"Really? Then you don't know enough about forensics."

"Oh?"

"Fingerprints, dental records."

"We whitewashed them: pulled out his teeth, burned his fingerprints."

"Your DNA—"

"Cristian Belucci's DNA does not exist. I win, albeit through a seemingly perverse double bluff."

The phone rang just as Curtis took half a step in the direction of Pierre.

"Don't do it, Curtis." The banker's tone was devoid of all emotion. "Not even you will stand a chance against this man. Pick up the phone. Tell the President you don't have the number yet." The banker blinked, his cat-like grey eyes peering through the Army Ranger. "Pick up the phone!"

"Yes?" The grandfather clock struck midnight.

"We need more time, Mr. President."

The President paused, and then inhaled, "I'll call back."

Without the slightest warning, Simone lunged at Belucci, hurling her small body at the banker, her cat-like claws drawing blood from the face of the man she now loathed more than sin itself. Gunshots exploded from the killer's weapon, one … two bullets hitting Simone in the ribcage. She buckled but would not let go. She clawed at his eyes.

Now! Curtis uncoiled his body, like a panther zigzagging diagonally forward across the room towards the Frenchman, his hands, two battering rams, outstretched, looking for their mark. A single gunshot exploded just as his mammoth right forearm came in contact with the Frenchman's head. The man buckled but did not fall. Curtis felt a hot stabbing jolt of pain in his left shoulder blade as the shot pushed him back, then an eruption of blood that drenched his shirt. The Frenchman steadied himself. God, is this it? Curtis heard the clatter of something metallic on the floor to his left.

The Frenchman looked in the direction of the sound just as a heavy vase in Michael's hands came crashing into the side of his head. The killer staggered backwards, his legs unsteady, but did not let go of the weapon. Forgetting the searing pain, Curtis lunged at him, spiraled his arm downward, grabbing hold of the man's wrist, crashing his good shoulder into his body, yanking again as Pierre reeled sideways off balance, snapping his hand back, breaking his wrist. The weapon was in his hands. He fired one shot. The killer's head exploded. The man was dead. He then turned to Belucci.

Simone slumped to the floor, the last vestige of strength deserted her, just as a single gunshot exploded into the banker's stomach. "Michael." She whispered.

"Simone!" Michael felt like his soul was shattered into a thousand pieces. He began to scream and jabber and only gradually words formed.

The phone rang. Curtis lurched for it.

"Do you have the code?" asked the President of the United States, his voice trembling.

Curtis found the paper and rattled it off.

There was a short silence. "Thank God," said the President.

"Forget Belucci's corpse. It wasn't him."

"What?"

"He was here. He and a French assassin called Pierre. It was him all along, pulling the strings from behind the curtain."

"Cristian Belucci!" The President paused. "I am sending Delta Force for you."

Curtis looking at Michael as he held the limp body of his lover, caressing her face, kissing her lips.

"Simone Casolaro is badly hurt, Mr. President."

"Help is on the way. Paramedics will be there in less than four minutes. The Emergency Medical Service helicopter will be waiting in a clearing two hundred yards from the house."

Tears rolled down Curtis' face. Tears of joy and tears of sorrow.

"The history of man is a history of pain. The world will never be able to repay you for what the three of you have done for—"

Curtis cut him off. "You have something left to do, Mr. President. The entire world is waiting for your leadership, holding its breath." Curtis paused. "Good luck, Sir."

> *"Well, Jimbo, this is quite a story. A story with a Hollywood ending."*
>
> *"That's right, J.C. Who said happy endings are for fairy tales? Tonight, in front of the greatest audience in the history of the world, the President of the United States staked his claim to immortality by pulling the world back from the brink of Armageddon. The world can collectively breath a sigh of relief."*
>
> *"You said it, Jimbo. In Boston, Philadelphia, New York, Chicago, Seattle, Houston, San Francisco, Miami and countless other cities and towns across this great nation, people jumped for joy as the President gave U.S. armed forces the order to stand down.*
>
> *'With dark clouds gathering all around us,' said the President, 'I look into the future, and see reasons for hope and far greater financial security. The cascade of national insolvencies has been halted and reversed.'*
>
> *"The President ended his speech by saying, 'To this, and to my children and yours, I pledge my fortune, my honor, my life.'"*

"What a day, J.C. Too bad he can't ran again."

"If I was Congress, I would make him President for life. In fact, the Queen of England called him 'her Knight in Shining Armor.'"

"In other news, Former Secretary of the Treasury, David Harriman III was arrested by federal agents tonight on charges of murder, attempted murder, collusion and restraint of trade along with Henry Stilton, associate director of the CIA, James F. Taylor Vice chairman of Goldman Sachs and senior State Department official Robert Lovett. Details are sketchy, but this promises to turn into a media circus unseen since O.J. Simpson's murder trial.

"Finally, earlier today, Akira Shimada, a man who once belonged to a ruthless unit of the Japanese Imperial Army, has died. He came into prominence only days ago, when Shimada's testimony in front of the stunned world revealed some of the deepest secrets and abuses of power from World War Two.

"You are watching nightly news at FTNBC-TV.

"Good night everyone."

CHAPTER 54

2 weeks later ...

Simone and Michael found themselves at the shady end of an elongated bar. A soft shaft of light penetrated the lowered Venetian blinds, forming two golden ladders on the floor. She raised her hand and spread her fingers, enjoying the back-and-forth playfulness of shade and light shuttling over her transparent fingers.

"What would I do without you, Michael?" she said softly.

"Do you love me?" he replied, angling his face.

Simone looked down at her hand as she leaned slightly backwards in her chair.

Michael looked at Simone in the dim light. Her eyes were tired, dark circles under them. Yet, to him, she remained as enchanting and as invulnerable as she had always been.

She smiled, a tender Simone smile Michael knew so well. London, Florence, Moscow. Happiness. Love. He shrugged his shoulders. Somewhere within him, there was something that was wondering at the curious force that had swept him away and boldly thrust him into her strange, unpredictable, and wonderful world. He understood ... it would take time. Normality was not to be found in a matter of days or weeks. Eventually, it would come.

Curtis watched from the bar, remembering another café at Abu Simbal. It was only a few years ago; another lifetime really. He carried their drinks to the table and sat down.

"Curtis?" and then without waiting for his reply, "Can you stay a few more days?" Simone pleaded.

His mind wandered. A bay, sun-broken cloud, a small sailing ship – swift, romantic.

"I can't." Curtis said. "I really can't."

Michael knew that his friend had his own demons to slay by the way Curtis' eyes instinctively found his and then dismissed them, preferring some other object to fix on.

"Where are you going to go?" Simone asked.

"I don't know," he replied, meaning it. She leaned back, looking into his face.

"Is it really over, Curtis?"

"I don't know anymore. I don't know anything anymore." Curtis sat still, afraid to move. " We'll talk." He finished.

"Thank you, thank you," she repeated, holding him tightly to her chest.

"It's been a hell of a couple of weeks."

"Curtis, do you want me to walk you to—?" began Michael.

"No, I'll be fine. Catch an Express to Philadelphia. Haven't been home for … a long time."

Curtis thought about all that was bad out there. A world with more things wrong than right. The world that was only minutes away from opening up beneath them and sucking the entire planet into the blackness beneath. A society where the demands of those who have money take precedence over the needs of the great majority of people who don't. But there was a connection between man and the planet. Mankind must fulfill its own destiny, with its own unique life path, thus guaranteeing that the evolutionary process – life itself – is protected.

Curtis' jaw tightened, causing a sucking ache at the base of the chest.

"It's history, Michael."

"It's history."

Simone held her glass and smiled. "To you, Curtis." Michael held up his.

Curtis lifted his own cold glass. "To beauty, truth, and all those who have died defending them."

"Hear, Hear!"

The Ranger put his glass to his lips and tipped the bottom to the sky.